NOSTALGIA

A CIVIL WAR NOVEL

SUSANNAH WILLEY

For more information, or to book an event, contact:
susannahwilley@gmail.com
https://utterloonacy.com

Book design by: K. J. Harrowick
Cover design by: K. J. Harrowick

ISBN - Digital: 979-8-9882220-5-7
ISBN - Paperback: 979-8-9882220-4-0
ISBN - Hardcover: 979-8-9882220-4-0

LCCN - Library of Congress Control Number: 2025923672

DEDICATION

To my ancestors, and guardians
of family history everywhere.

And to R.C., the Harry to my Sally.

Nostalgia

They called it "nostalgia," an extreme form of homesickness that evolved into depression and often ended in suicide or lifelong disability.

In Jim's day, people dismissed these symptoms as "malingering," a cowardly excuse for avoiding combat. Today we recognize this condition as "Post Traumatic Stress Disorder," or PTSD, the result of extreme trauma both on and off the battlefield.

CONTENT WARNING

This is a work of fiction. While the story and characters are a product of the author's imagination, the book contains graphic descriptions of war injuries, amputations, and other medical procedures common during the Civil War, as well as depictions of suicide. These themes may be triggering for some readers. The author has approached these topics with care and respect, aiming to shed light on complex human experiences. However, individual reactions may vary, and reader discretion is advised. If you or someone you know is affected by similar issues, please seek support from a trusted professional or helpline.

A NOTE ABOUT MEDICINE IN THE CIVIL WAR

You might, dear reader, question the veracity of the medical treatment described in *Nostalgia*. But in the mid-nineteenth century, medicine looked nothing like it does today.

Few of the treatments and medicines that we have today were available during the Civil War. Scientists had not yet established the germ theory of disease, and nobody had heard of sterile technique and antisepsis. Wound infections were common, and the only known way to treat them was with medicines that were either ineffective or toxic. Two-thirds of all drugs were botanicals. Quinine and opium/heroin were the drugs of choice. You may have heard that anesthesia was absent for surgical patients. That is incorrect; either chloroform or ether were used.

Sanitation was poor, camps were overcrowded, organized hospitals were virtually nonexistent. Diseases were thought to be carried in the foul air; bacteria hadn't yet been identified. Antibiotics did not yet exist. Much of the medicine and treatment used were homeopathic or natural medicines. In addition, few medical personnel had experience with battle wounds and conditions; Triage practices were chaotic and uncoordinated at best.

In the ensuing years, medical treatment vastly improved, much of it due to lessons learned in the Civil War. Please bear these facts in mind as you read Jim's story.

"When we are consumed by the fear of losing, we stop playing to win and start playing not to lose."

—Anthony Robert in *TonysBologna: The Wisdom of Yoda.* 6 December 2024

CHAPTER I

September 13, 1862

Harper's Ferry, West Virginia

The heavy rain had stopped, but the air was intolerably hot and steamy as Dr. Jim Banyon steadied what was once a functioning leg.

"It'll be okay. I promise," Jim lied. Shattered by an enemy bullet, the man's tibia and fibula stuck out like splintered branches, the flesh twisted like a wrung-out dishcloth. The surrounding skin was a bloody, shredded fringe. There was nothing to do but amputate.

The young soldier, who probably lied about his age when he enlisted, lay sprawled across the weathered barn door set on wobbly sawhorses, under a canvas canopy that provided little protection from the elements.

"Ready?" Dr. Larssen, the head surgeon, absent-mindedly stroked his graying beard. His hair, the color of freshly cut straw, fell in his face as he bent over the patient. He was a tall, slender man.

Pale blue eyes confirmed his Scandinavian roots and suggested an innocence he'd lost long ago.

Jim re-tightened the tourniquet above the wound and nodded. The ruined limb spasmed as he pulled his scalpel across and around it, cutting through skin and muscle. The patient moaned, immobilized by a makeshift system of belts and straps. An ether-soaked rag covered his mouth. He was not fully unconscious, but Jim hoped the sedative would at least dull the man's wits—and his pain.

Saw teeth rasped against bones as Larssen completed the cut just above the knee. Jim clenched the patient's foot, ready to catch the leg when it fell.

Minutes later, Jim held the unsalvageable remnant of the patient's leg and dropped it on the muddy ground. He winced at the sound it made, like the thunk of a heavy stone tossed in a pond, but much more ominous: The patient would likely die, and there would be nothing the medical staff could do regardless of their skill or attention.

Jim removed the restraining straps. "It's over, soldier. You'll be fine." He didn't believe his words, but the boy needed reassurance and hope more than he needed the truth.

On days like this, time was measured in severed limbs. When there was a lull in fighting, Jim treated the rampant illnesses; poor hygiene and lack of sanitation meant that dysentery and typhoid fever were always present. Either way, the days were long, with more injuries and disease than the regiment's three medical officers could handle. Jim longed for the days when his only medical duty involved conducting a few hours of sick call, determining which soldiers would be given light duty for the day, and which ones simply needed a little motivation. After a day like today, he wished for one of those long, boring afternoons.

Perspiration soaked Jim's uniform. Beads of sweat accentuated his brown, ear-length curls, glistened on his cheekbones, and dripped from his goatee. Blood from a hundred wounded soldiers stained the apron that protected his uniform. Mud covered his boots and pant legs.

When the last remnants of daylight faded, the team worked by lantern light. By then, the pile of limbs grew past Jim's knees. Some patients lost only a foot, a crushed hand, a couple of fingers or toes, but the more severe injuries required the removal of the entire limb.

And to what end? Jim wondered. *All that extra pain and they'll likely die anyway.*

True, some survived the amputation itself, but sometimes Jim wondered why he and the other doctors bothered. It wouldn't be the loss of the leg that would kill the amputees; it would be the ensuing inflammation and gangrene, and sometimes it wasn't even that: some soldiers simply didn't want to live as cripples.

"Damned Minié balls!" Jim spat, cursing the man who invented the weapon. It was a Confederate favorite; the thing the Rebs liked best about it was the damage it inflicted on impact: the Minié flattened, sometimes splintering. Bones shattered, tissue shredded, and too often the only way a surgeon could save the body was to take the limb.

Dr. Larssen wiped the surgical saw across his bib apron. "You've got the closure?"

"All set." Jim focused his attention on the patient.

"I'll start the next one," Larssen said, gesturing to yet another wounded soldier. "Join me when you're finished here."

Jim lifted a flap of skin, folded it over the patient's open wound, and sutured it to cover the exposed flesh, leaving enough slack for drainage and healing. Evidence of white pus emanating from the wound in the next day or two would be a sure sign of healthy healing.

He finished the stitches, wrapped the stump, and raised his arm. "Bearers, over here."

Two stretcher-bearers rushed over and transferred the soldier to the hospital tent. Two more set the next casualty on the blood and tissue-stained table where Lieutenant Erskine, the regiment's medical steward, would prepare him for surgery.

It was nearly 10 p.m. when the last surgery was complete. Erskine washed the surgical instruments in a nearby bucket of water and set them in place for tomorrow. He and Jim wiped down the "operating table," rinsed out the bloody rags and hung them over its edges, and proceeded to the hospital tent where the sick and wounded waited for their attention. Currently, the tent held thirty-five men. Some of them might live until morning.

By the time they'd finished, Jim's legs felt like they couldn't carry him one more step. He dropped into a chair by the makeshift desk. Erskine plopped down on the other chair, and they consulted their notes before examining their patients.

Erskine propped his long legs on the desk and pulled a flask of whiskey from his coat. He took a swig and held it out, grinning. "Nightcap?"

Tall and lanky, Tom Erskine was a good six inches taller than Jim and looked more like seventeen than twenty-two. His nose was broad, his lips full, his face clean-shaven. He kept his dark brown hair close-cropped, which only emphasized his oversized ears. His eyes attracted people's attention at first glance: one iris was deep brown, the other azure blue. It was an inherited trait that, according to family lore, was the doom of many an ancestor declared a witch and burned at the stake. But Tom's sincere smile gained the trust of even the most frightened patient.

Jim reached for the flask. What he really wanted was a comfortable bed and a soft pillow. His head ached, his eyes felt puffy, his eyelids drooped. He struggled to read his notes, fighting to stay awake. His brain fogged with fatigue, and when he finally managed to concentrate, he struggled to process what he'd read. He cursed under his breath at the smallest moan from a restless patient. Couldn't they let him be for just one minute?

Jim rubbed his tired eyes and tried to concentrate.

How many amputations have I performed today? It was too much to think about.

Enough to open a second-hand store, his inner voice quipped.

His sardonic sense of humor, at least, was still intact.

He took a long pull of whiskey, wiped his mouth on his sleeve, and handed it back to Erskine. They sat in silence for a few moments, then Jim stood, giving his partner a stack of notes.

"Private Dudley's dysentery hasn't improved." Jim gestured toward the soldier lying on a heavily soiled cot. "Quinine and opium," he advised. The first would ease Dudley's fever; the second would ease his pain.

"Will do," Erskine said, studying Jim's notes.

"And see if you can get him up and clean his bed linens," Jim added. "They stink like a harlot's bedroom on payday."

"What about Private Nichols?" Erskine pointed to a young man across the room. "Think he's faking?"

Jim consulted his notes. The boy was seventeen

and probably lied about his age to enlist.

"I know, I know!" Nichols pulled at his tattered uniform. "Chores are late, and the hay needs mowing." His hair was blond and shaggy; too young for a beard, his teenage chin was covered with acne. He stared at an invisible someone, flailing his hands. Although he had no visible physical injuries, Jim was hesitant to release him.

He watched Nichols for a few minutes, re-read his notes, and shrugged. "Not sure. I'll keep him a couple more days if the big bugs will let me," he said.

"Betcha the brass love that attitude," Erskine said. "I can just imagine Captain Anthony's reaction." Erskine puffed out his chest and took on a snobbish tone. "That boy's a malingerer! I demand you get him out of that bed and back to duty this instant!"

"Yes, sir, Captain Pegleg!" Jim laughed and saluted, using the bastardized name given to Captain Peleg Anthony by his men.

He took another swig from the flask, pointed toward the vial of powder sitting on the desk, and gestured toward Private Nichols. "Maybe try a little opium on him, too."

Erskine nodded, scooped up the patients' notes, and stood.

"Private Dudley, how's it going?" He put on his most reassuring smile and went to work.

That night, Jim squirmed on his cot, unable to sleep, and thankful for a tent of his own. The unrelenting heat and humidity hadn't eased when the sun set, and his mind raced, replaying the past eighteen hours of work: the wounds, the surgeries, the growing pile of useless limbs. Amputated legs had become a sight as common to him as dead branches downed by wind and rain. He should be immune to the images by now, but they haunted his dreams.

It wasn't at all what Jim expected when he joined Lincoln's Army. He'd imagined treating broken bones and bandaging wounds, maybe applying a few stitches when necessary. He was sure there would be plenty of time to study the conditions he'd seen in the veterans at his private practice. Maybe he'd even find the root of the alcoholism that plagued so many veterans like his Uncle Isaac. He would save lives and make a name for himself because of it. What better way to establish his expertise than by saving the lives of loyal soldiers? His reputation as a war surgeon was guaranteed. He'd return home a hero.

But the devastating wounds, the rampant disease, the deaths from malnutrition and starvation were so much more than he'd bargained for.

CHAPTER 2

May, 1848

Ira, New York

Bessie's long black tail swished uncomfortably close to Jim's face as he adjusted the plow behind her. A twelve-year-old Morgan, Bessie had been around longer than Jim, and was his favorite horse. Her chestnut-colored body glistened with sweat as Jim guided her across the fallow field.

A low rumble echoed in the distance. Jim scraped his hand over his sweaty face and pushed back the brown curls that refused to stay out of his face.

A flash of lightning and the ensuing rumble of thunder pulled him out of his gloom. He glanced at the sky and saw the dark clouds on the horizon creeping closer and closer.

I'd better get a move on, he thought, *or I'll get no plowing done at all.*

Surely his older brothers had plowed the fields when they were younger, but it was hard for Jim to imagine it. Even the youngest of the three was seven years older than Jim, and already successful in his career. Jim was a late-life baby who would always be catching up.

"I bet they were too important to spend their days behind a horse's ass even back then," he mumbled. Bessie pricked her ears, shaking her long mane as if Jim's comment offended her.

He was tired of feeling measured by his siblings' success.

"Heman's got the farm, Richardson's a college bigwig, Charlie's got the feed mill," he complained. Even his sister, Matilda, had married a well-known local preacher.

"How in the Sam Hill can I top that?" Since his Grandmother Beckwith died, Bessie was the only one who bothered to listen.

The new life stirring in the fields, forests, and trees made him restless. He wanted a new life, too. One far away from the drudgery of the farm and the disapproving faces of his family.

"It's just not fair that everyone expects I'll be as successful as they are." Jim angrily flicked Bessie's reins. The horse jumped, turning her head as if to ask what his problem was. Jim returned the glare.

For God's sake, he mused, *they've had ages to establish themselves.* And what path could he choose that nobody had already claimed? His father wanted him to follow in his footsteps, to one day take over his medical practice. He thought he'd like a medical career. But his father was well-respected across the county. How could he ever compete with that?

He wished Grandma Beckwith were still alive. She understood what it was like to be the youngest, how it felt to be undervalued. A no-nonsense, stubbornly independent woman, she'd crossed the iced-over St. Lawrence River alone to marry his grandfather. She didn't mind reminding her son and grandchildren that she could damn-well take care of herself.

He was just a kid when he told Grandma Beckwith his fears. Tears dripped from his cheeks as he shared his worry that he couldn't be like the rest of the family.

"You needn't give two thoughts to your brothers," she told him as she put a steaming cup of cocoa in front of him. Jim took a warm oatmeal cookie from the tray she held and sniffed back his tears.

"They worked hard to get where they are, but that doesn't mean there won't be a place for you." She patted his shoulder and offered him her handkerchief.

Jim wiped his eyes. "I know," he said. "But it just feels like there's nothing left for me."

Granny Beckwith was eighty-eight years old when she died. Her white hair was thin and wispy; her skin hung loose on her arms, a tissue-thin membrane that accentuated the ropy veins prominent among her wrinkles.

But her mind was still sharp, even if her body wasn't. In those last days, she was bedridden, but she reached out a trembling hand as Jim entered her bedroom. Jim tiptoed to her bed, leaning in as she gestured for him to come closer.

"Your time is coming," she whispered in a tremulous voice. "You're just as good as anyone else, maybe better. Don't you ever forget that."

Her death left a deep emptiness Jim couldn't fill. He so badly wanted to believe she was right about him, but there were days when his siblings' success made him want to quit before he even got started.

"Why even bother?" he said. The horse whinnied.

"Was that a yea or a nay?"

Bessie only snorted.

Dusk settled across the cornfield as Jim unhitched Bessie and led her toward the barn. The family homestead, settled by Jim's grandfather after the Revolutionary War, was a small village in itself. Aside from several houses, there was a smokehouse, toolsheds, and several barns. Jim's grandparents occupied the bottom floor of the main house. Jim and his parents lived upstairs. His brothers, uncles, and cousins lived in various houses surrounded by fields of wheat, rye, and tobacco.

"Goddamn son-of-a-bitch!" Uncle Isaac's voice carried across the field. Jim dropped Bessie's reins and ducked behind a nearby shed as Isaac staggered towards Jim's cousin, weakly swinging a heavy switch in his trembling hand. His face contorted in rage. His scraggly brown hair hung in clumps around his shoulders; his long beard desperately needed a trim.

Now what? Jim wondered. Uncle Isaac's tirades were as constant as the rainfall, and, as usual, Jim's cousin, Napoleon, was the target. Napoleon Bonaparte Drown, named in honor of the famous French general, was Jim's closest friend. He was a skinny kid, tall for his age, with dirty blond hair that was long and tangled, and a face that would be handsome if he ever smiled. His deep blue eyes held a mixture of anger and fear. Jim and Napoleon were born in the same year, only a month apart, and both had just celebrated their eleventh birthday. Being so much younger than the rest of the family had made them close, like two Davids fighting an extra-large Goliath. They did almost everything together, and the grown-ups seemed to be relieved the boys had each other to rely on.

Jim couldn't remember a time when Uncle Isaac had been sober. His father assured him that Isaac was once a kind, hard-working man, but Jim never knew that Uncle Issac. To him, he was nothing more than the neighborhood drunk and the laughingstock of the town.

Uncle Isaac's curses slurred into incoherent growls as he swung his switch at everything and nothing. His baggy overalls hung from his shoulders, threatening to fall.

Good, thought Jim. *He'll pass out any minute now.*

Isaac stumbled to the ground; the switch fell from his hand into a puddle. "Dinner time!" a voice sing-songed from the back door.

"Let's get you cleaned up, dear." Leta, Napoleon's mother, helped Isaac up from the ground. Her voice was calm and reassuring. "Hurry now; your dinner's getting cold."

"It's the kid's fault," he mumbled.

"I know, dear," she said, putting his arm around her shoulder. As she led her husband into the house, she raised an apologetic eyebrow toward Napoleon and tipped her head toward the main house. *Go to Jim's house,* her eyes pleaded. *It's safer there.*

Jim ran to Napoleon and helped him to his feet. A purple bruise blossomed on his cousin's forearm. His cheek bled.

"I gotta go help Ma." Napoleon turned toward his house.

"No, you won't." Jim grabbed Napoleon's arm. "Your Ma has it under control. You need to get out of his sight for a little bit." He gestured to Napoleon's face, gently touched the bruise on his arm. "Are you okay?"

"I'll live." Napoleon wiped his face, staring at the bloody smudge on his hand. "Thanks to Ma. She always knows how to get him off me."

"Come on up to the house." Jim took Napoleon's arm and led him toward the homestead. "Mother can tend to that cut while we give your pa time to calm down."

Twenty minutes later, Mrs. Banyon had washed the blood and dirt from Napoleon's cheek, given him a clean shirt, and set a plate of fresh bread and jam in front of him.

"Are you certain you're okay?" Jim's mother, Deborah, smoothed Napoleon's hair. "I'm sure the doctor would take a look at you."

Napoleon shook his head. "Ma says he doesn't mean it, that it's just the liquor that makes him nasty. She swears he wasn't the same after he came back from the Mexican War."

Deborah nodded. "War does strange things to soldiers. Ever since he came home, he's been having awful nightmares. Used to be the smallest noise spooked him under the bed. I think drinking was the only way he could make it stop."

Napoleon shook his head. "I don't think the

man ever had a heart."

"He did once. The liquor changed him." She put a hand on Napoleon's shoulder. "I'm sorry it's so hard for you."

Napoleon gingerly touched his cheek. The anger in his eyes had dissipated, replaced by steely determination. "I don't know about war, but if this is what liquor does to a man, I will never touch a drop."

CHAPTER 3

1850

Ira, NY

Napoleon was thirteen when his father died, and it was his fault. He'd imagined his father's death, prayed to God to make it so.

I might as well have held a knife at his throat.

He'd dreamed of all the ways his father could die. Perhaps he'd go to bed one night, drunk as a skunk, and not wake up the next morning. He could fall off his horse in a drunken stupor, hit his head on a rock, and die. Or—Napoleon liked this one best—his father might raise his belt to whip him, grab his heart, and fall dead on the ground.

Would God damn him for his blasphemous prayers? Surely He'd understand. Surely He'd save Napoleon from his abusive father.

Alcohol had overtaken Isaac's life and his body. Jaundice in his liver yellowed his skin. Tremors that made it difficult for him to walk plagued his limbs. His nightmares had become more frequent and spilled over into days filled with paranoia. It took little to enrage him, but he was so weakened by the many years of drinking, he had little strength, and his rages fell on deaf ears. He spent most days in his chair on the front porch, mumbling at the air.

Truth be told, he no longer had the strength to beat his son.

On the morning Isaac died, he sat on the porch, drunk before noon and mumbling as usual. Napoleon, returning from morning chores, was coming in from the barn when he heard his mother's voice. He peeked around the corner of the house.

"Can't you go even one day without liquor?" Leta shook her head in disgust. "If it weren't for the vegetable garden and the livestock, we'd have nothing to eat. You spend every penny you can scrape up on God-forsaken whiskey. Don't you care about your family?" Leta straightened, her hands on her hips.

"You tell him, Ma," Napoleon whispered under his breath. He hoped she'd kick him out. Send his sorry self down the road for good. No matter how many times his mother hid his father's whiskey, or poured it into the creek, the man always managed to get more. Jim raised his face upward. *Please, God.*

Isaac turned his head with effort. His eyes were glassy and unfocused as he spoke to his wife. "Don'sh care a whi—." His words slurred, impossible to understand. He drew in a breath as if he were prepared to say more, but instead, he started gagging.

"That's great, Pa," Napoleon mumbled. "Puke all over your wife. That'll show her who's the boss." He almost hoped his father heard him.

But instead of vomit, blood spurted from Isaac's mouth, splattering against Leta's apron and over her shoes. He choked and gagged, trying to stand. Isaac fell to the porch, the river of blood still gushing from his mouth.

"Go get your uncle!" Leta screamed. She tore off her apron and shoved it against Isaac's mouth. "Hurry!"

Napoleon raced to the main house. His mind raced faster, filled with images of blood endlessly spewing from his father's mouth.

Was he dead? The thought evoked a feeling of relief, for which Napoleon immediately felt shame. *What kind of boy would wish his own father dead?*

The front door slammed as he burst into his uncle's waiting room and tore through to the examining room. His startled uncle looked up from his patient, his stethoscope still against his ear. "Napoleon!" Impatience bordering on anger flashed across his face.

"It's Pa!" Napoleon struggled to speak as he gasped for air. "He's bleeding all over the place! Hurry!" He took off before his uncle could answer, racing out the front door and down the steps toward home.

"Isaac!" His mother's pleas punctured the air long before he saw her.

"Hang on, Isaac." Leta choked out the words between her sobs. "Allen's on his way."

When his house came into sight, Napoleon knew the truth. In the distance, his mother huddled over his father's motionless body. Blood covered the porch and dripped down the steps. His father was dead.

Napoleon stopped, his breath coming in gasps. He looked behind him to be sure his uncle wasn't far behind before he collapsed. Doubled over, his legs gave way, and he fell to the ground. He didn't know if his sobs came from grief or gratitude, but the torment was over.

"Take your mother up to the house," Allen's

voice was calm and professional as he moved to shield Isaac's body. He set his medical bag on the porch step and knelt in front of him.

"His esophagus tore open, along with the surrounding veins." Napoleon's Uncle Allen shook his head and laid his hand on Napoleon's shoulder. "There's nothing you could have done to stop it."

Napoleon's father was dead at the age of forty, half of his life controlled by alcoholism. No one could have predicted he would bleed to death—maybe it had nothing at all to do with his drinking. From this day on, Napoleon would not worry about how and when he might die. Sometimes death came for you in unusual ways—he wouldn't wait around to see how it came to him. Living his life day-by-day was his vow now. Marriage and children were not for him. He would never subject anyone to the torment he and his mother suffered. He would never touch a drop of liquor. From now on, life was for living.

CHAPTER 4

July 1859
Ira, New York

"Can you believe it?" Jim proudly held out his newly earned medical license like a kid showing off his schoolwork. "This will be the first addition to my new office."

"Doctor James Dana Banyon." His wife, Maggie, smiled and kissed his cheek as she set a plate of warm cinnamon rolls on the kitchen table. The smell of crisping bacon wafted through the air; fresh eggs sizzled in the iron skillet. The percolator burped with brewing coffee. Her brown eyes sparkled with pride. "A new career, a new wife, and a new baby on the way."

Jim stroked Maggie's long, dark curls and returned the kiss. The scent of lavender on her skin reminded him of how much he had missed her. "The two years away from you seemed like forever."

Two years that could have been one, he grumbled to himself. The second year of medical school was a repetition of the first, but that's what the state of New York required — a waste of time to Jim's mind.

He'd graduated from Albany Medical College with honors, achieved excellent marks on his medical treatise and high praise from the doctors who'd judged his oral examination.

Not a feed store or a farm handed to me by my father. Not some high-falutin' position out west, or a prestigious marriage. A medical degree—and I did it myself.

Jim relished the thought of all that lay before him. Money. Recognition. Success in his own right, a life with the woman he loved, a child on the way. He sighed contentedly and picked at a cinnamon roll. At last, his life was nearly complete.

He might be only twenty-two years old, but he had a far wider knowledge of medicine than his father, Allen, would ever have. He'd seen procedures his father could never have imagined, learned the details of treatments and medicines his father had likely never heard of. Father believed poultices and opium could cure any malady; Jim knew better.

His chest clutched; a fleeting sense of panic. After all these years of striving to be someone, here he was on the threshold of success. But could he take that first step?

What if I fail? The worry nagged at Jim. *What if I'm not good enough?*

Jim shook away the thought, silencing it with reminders of his accomplishments. And once he'd built a successful practice? Nothing could stop him.

He put his arms around Maggie and pulled her onto his lap. As he caressed her growing abdomen, he felt a small thump.

"Wiggling already! That's a sign of a healthy baby for certain." Jim smiled as he imagined holding his newborn child. "Now all I need is a medical practice."

Maggie laid her hands over his. "We'll stay here, won't we?"

Jim thought for a moment. "I suppose we could. But I doubt there are enough patients here to support it. Everyone sees my father when they're sick."

"We could move into town." Maggie stood and returned to the stove, picked up her spatula, and carefully turned the eggs. She poked at the bacon, testing its crispness. "There must be someone there who will sell their practice."

Jim shook his head. "I've found none yet. At least none that have the potential I'm looking for."

"What about Syracuse or Auburn? They're bigger—you could even work at the hospital."

"Maybe." Jim stroked his newly grown goatee. "But that would take you away from home," he patted Maggie's belly. "I know you want our child to be close to his grandparents."

He hated being so indecisive with Maggie. But he'd considered all the possibilities, and each one had risks—risks he didn't want to take.

"What if I stay here for a while and work with Father?" Jim spoke the words as if they had just come to him. "I can teach him what I learned at medical college. I'm sure he'd appreciate the extra knowledge."

"Will that make you happy?" Maggie asked. "Will it make enough money?"

"It won't be a king's ransom." Jim shuffled his feet under the kitchen table. "But it will suffice for now. I will happily consider accepting the lower salary if it means allowing you to stay near your family." Jim put his arm around Maggie's waist.

"It will be a boon to Father as well," he continued. "I can modernize his practice. It's enough for now.

A practice of my own and a larger salary can wait a little longer," Jim said, kissing her on the forehead. "I'll go talk to Father tomorrow."

That wasn't exactly the truth: Jim had already had this conversation with his father. For every suggestion his father made, Jim had a reason it wouldn't work. But Father finally offered a solution.

"Why don't you join my practice until you find something more permanent?" he asked.

Jim understood that his father always wanted him to run the family practice. But that wasn't what Jim wanted. He wanted to get out of hick country and go where the money and prestige were. He was determined to work his way up in the medical community and become an esteemed surgeon or a medical school professor.

But what if I'm a failure? What if, after all his braggadocio, he ended up stuck where he swore he would never be? What if he really couldn't be successful on his own?

Maybe a year or two with his father wasn't a bad idea. "I'd be honored to work with you." Jim swallowed the lie. At least he could support Maggie and the baby.

Nostalgia

Jim closed the leather-bound ledger, where he kept his daily patient notes. Setting it aside, he picked up its companion, his personal journal. It was a practice he'd started in medical school. A way of emptying his thoughts onto paper while they were fresh in his mind.

He opened the ledger to the first blank page, dipped his pen in the inkwell, and wrote:

I have worked hard to prove my worth amongst my highly successful father and siblings. My medical degree is the culmination of that work, and I intend to make a name for myself within the Banyon family and in the medical community. This distinction is something I have earned and deserve. One might consider this braggadocio although my belief is that I will become what I impart: successful, intelligent, accomplished.

My deepest fear is that I walk the razor's edge between notoriety and abject failure. I conceal this fear with outward confidence. Sometimes I try to deceive even myself.

Although I have had numerous opportunities to open a practice of my own, I will work with my father for the time being. I feel it is my duty to educate him in the newest medical techniques, as his apprenticeship with the local, rural doctor was limited. To his credit, he has the bedside manner I lack. I expect he will impart that knowledge as we work together.

CHAPTER 5

December 1859
Ira, New York

Jim stepped into the waiting area, where the morning's patients waited. High-backed wooden chairs lined the walls. A small table held a few well-worn issues of *Harper's Weekly* for patients to read as they waited. In the corner, the cast-iron stove crackled with the familiar smell of wood smoke. A recently arrived patient stood by its side, rubbing his hands to absorb the warmth.

In a chair by the office door, a young mother soothed a fussy child who sat on her lap. The little boy couldn't be over two. Sweat matted his blond hair, his cheeks flushed, his blue eyes glassy.

Just a childhood fever, thought Jim. Although it would require close attention in case the symptoms worsened, sulfate of quinine should suffice.

Across the room sat Henry Jackson, his grimy overalls splattered with blood and a bloodied rag wrapped around his forearm. Jim approached

Henry and cautiously loosened the bandage. The cut was not deep, but it would take a few stitches to close the wound. Cuts, both superficial and serious, were common among the farm families. From harvesting crops to butchering livestock, sharp implements were always close by.

"Keep the bandage tight," Jim told Henry. "We'll get to you soon."

Jim motioned to the man beside him. "You're next," he said, walking toward the examining room. A local farmer, Ezra Whitney, shuffled uncomfortably behind him.

"Been bound up a while," Ezra said as he eased onto the examining table. He loosened the straps of his overalls and pulled up his shirt. "Belly feels like it's about to explode."

"Lie down and I'll have a look." Jim palpated Ezra's abdomen, noting its rigidity. "It does feel like you're backed up some." As he continued his examination, he felt a hard mass, too large to be fecal matter.

"I'll be right back." Jim's words held no emotion as he walked out of the room. He found his father in his office, making notes about his most recent patient.

"Can you come take a look at Ezra?" Jim stood nervously in front of the desk.

Allen looked up from his notes. "What's his complaint?"

"Severe constipation. But it appears there is a large mass in his abdominal cavity."

"What's your diagnosis?"

Jim tensed, reluctant to voice his thoughts. "I'd rather hear your opinion first."

His father nodded and followed Jim to the examining room.

"How's the family, Ezra?" he said as he entered the room, reaching to shake Ezra's hand.

"All good." Ezra's discomfort was in his voice. "Feels like I got a goddamn stone caught in my belly."

Allen examined Ezra's abdomen. His fingers curled slightly as he felt the mass inside.

"Give my best to Ellie." He nodded to Ezra, and he motioned to Jim to follow him.

Jim closed the door as he entered the office. "What do you think?"

"You already know—it's most likely cancer. That's a diagnosis you shouldn't need me for."

Jim blushed and stammered. "I—I just wanted

you to confirm it."

"It's a darn shame," Allen sighed. "I've known Ezra all my life. Knew his parents and grandparents, too. The man's too young to die."

"I saw cancer often at medical school." Jim recovered his composure. "I assisted in two cases and witnessed countless others." He raised an eyebrow. "You know even surgery can't help him. He has a year at best."

"Do you think I don't know that?" Allen glared at him. "Are you going to be the one to tell him?"

Jim nodded. "I will." His palms were sweaty as he returned to the examining room. Explaining medical diagnoses to his patients in layman's terms was something he'd never get used to.

I know the medicine, damn it. I can diagnose and treat any situation with both eyes closed. Why can't I just treat a man and be done with it? Truth was, he simply didn't have the rapport with patients that his father had. He saw the illness, not the man.

Ezra tugged on his overalls and hitched the bib as Jim returned. "What's the verdict, Doc?"

Jim's expression was grave as he addressed his patient. "I have determined that you have a large tumor in your abdomen that is probably cancer.

The only treatment I can offer is surgery to remove as much of the tumor as I can, but that likely won't help much."

Jim shook his head, reminding himself to put his hand on Ezra's shoulder as a sign of sympathy. "Surgery would only prolong your life for a short time, and that's only if I can remove the tumor. Otherwise, the only thing we can do is make you as comfortable as possible and give you medicine to help with the pain."

He looked away, unwilling to face the dying man. "I suggest you make your peace with God."

"You sure I just ain't bound up?" Ezra asked.

Jim turned to look at his patient; Ezra's blank stare made him flinch.

"There's gotta be a tonic or something that'll get me going again," Ezra pleaded. "What about an enema?"

Jim mentally shrugged in frustration. Why did these people come to see him if they wouldn't believe him? He stifled his impatience, trying to imagine words his father might use. "I'm sorry. It's too late for any of that."

Ezra blinked back tears and stared at the floor.

"Will you tell Ellie?" he whispered. "I don't

think I can."

"I'm sure Father will gladly do that for you." Jim turned and left the examining room. He shook his head as he walked toward the anteroom for the next patient, frustrated with the backwardness of these people. The man had waited too long. *They all do, trying every bit of folk medicine they can until it's too late.*

CHAPTER 6

April 1860

Ira, New York

"I didn't go to medical school to practice folk medicine." Jim paced the office in frustration. "My family deserves to have a decent home; I deserve to make a decent salary."

A large wooden desk dominated the office Jim shared with his father—an image of ordered chaos. Medical journals and notebooks filled one corner; a pile of correspondence waited to be answered. Bright light filtered in from the open windows. A large grandfather clock patiently tick-tocked from across the room and chimed the hour.

"Medicine is the wrong profession for making money." Jim's father drummed his fingers on the desk, struggling to control his impatience.

"For you, maybe. But I went to medical college. I graduated with honors! Despite that, here I am, with no acceptable prospects in sight." Jim sighed heavily. "I won't be some backwoods doctor like you who gets paid in chickens and cornmeal!"

Glass jars and bottles filled with tinctures, powders, and compounds rattled as his fist slammed against the table. The cast-iron mortar and pestle inched towards the edge of its shelf.

Allen's eyes darkened. He gritted his teeth, his fists clenched under his desk. "If you don't enjoy working here, why do you stay?"

"You know why." Jim was getting tired of this argument. "Any decent job is miles away. We'd have to move, and Maggie wants to stay near her family."

Jim's father shook his head. "That's not the whole truth. Of course, Maggie would like little Jessie to be near her grandparents, but I know she'd move with you if you asked her to."

Jim scrubbed his forehead. "I can't take Maggie away from home."

"Then open your own practice here." Allen stood and went to the glass cabinet that housed an array of instruments and tools. He absently rearranged scalpels, forceps, and bone saws, inspecting the wooden tube they used to listen to patients' hearts and stomachs. It was a technique he used often when he needed to find calm and perspective.

"With what patients? Nobody here wants to

listen to me." Jim's voice rose in frustration. He fiddled with the scales and weights they used when compounding medicines and angrily swiped at the bundles of dried willow bark and foxglove that hung from the shelves. "They all want this hocus-pocus medicine you give them."

"It seems like you have an excuse for everything."

The tone in Allen's voice was tense; his jaw tightened. Jim noticed the change; he needed to let it go before his dad became angry.

He stopped abruptly and dropped his head, a small acquiescence. "They're not excuses, Father." His voice was barely a whisper. "They're the truth."

"Son," Allen's voice softened as he put a hand on Jim's shoulder and looked him in the eye. "You're always one excuse away from being a successful physician. It's not your brothers who are stopping you. It's not me. It's not Maggie or the baby. The only one stopping you is you.

"You might hide it better than you once did, but you're the same scared little boy you've always been." He struggled to keep his voice calm and gentle. "You act all brave and arrogant on the outside, but on the inside, you're terrified of failing.

You see your older brothers, look at them, and think you can never measure up. So you come up with excuses to make you feel better."

Jim jerked away from Allen; their fragile truce was broken. "What would you know about success? Before I joined your practice, you were just another country doctor." He shook his finger at Allen. "I came aboard to help you learn modern medicine—the medicine I learned at a legitimate medical college, not as an apprentice who gets his education from folklore and family tradition. You don't know me if you think I'm afraid of failing."

"Maybe I know you better than you know yourself." Allen replied tersely.

That was the last straw. Jim turned, stormed across the office and opened the door that led to the living area of the house, slamming it behind him as hard as he could. In the background, the mortar and pestle clanged as it fell from its shelf to the floor. His father cursed.

He ignored the concerned look on Maggie and his mother's faces as he clomped into the kitchen and out the back door. He clenched his fists but kept quiet until he was behind the barn, out of sight and earshot.

"Who the hell does he think he is?" Jim growled under his breath, then shouted to the cows grazing nearby, who raised their heads for a moment before they returned to their grassy snack. "I am not a coward!"

Another disagreement today. It seems Father is intent on pushing me out of the practice. Does he resent my superior knowledge, or is he embarrassed by my indecision and cold exterior? I could go out on my own, but I fear there is not enough room for two medical practices here. I would as soon stay put as I would to expend the cost of establishing a separate office only to have an empty waiting room.

CHAPTER 7

December 1860

Victory, NY

Jim loved everything about his new office, especially the fact that it was his own. When a medical practice in the nearby town of Victory became available, Jim bought it. It was a proud moment when he attached the freshly made sign under the brass knocker on the front door: *Dr. James D. Banyon, Physician and Surgeon.* He was glad he'd changed his mind about leaving Father's practice.

Best move I ever made, he thought. *I'll show everyone what real medicine is.*

Or you'll be a bigger laughingstock than your drunken uncle, a second voice responded—one that sounded disturbingly like his father's.

Six months had passed since their big argument. The tension was still thick between Jim and his father even though they worked side-by-side every day until Jim bought his own practice. Jim never asked his father's opinion, and his father never volunteered one. Of course, both Maggie and his mother noticed the chill.

Although it was not his mother's way to interfere, Maggie didn't hesitate to bring it up.

"What's going on between you and Father Banyon?" she asked as she delivered Jim's tea one evening.

"Is Jessie all tucked in for the night?" Jim sipped his tea, ignoring Maggie's question.

"Yes, she is, and sound asleep," she answered. "Now tell me what's the problem with Father Banyon."

Jim sat quietly and sipped his tea, pretending to watch the snow drifting down outside.

"We don't agree on medical issues." He set down his tea and turned to Maggie. "He believes in the old ways, and I don't. It's as simple as that. My only choice was to buy a practice of my own."

"Don't you think it's about time you fixed that?" she said. "He's your father, not a fraud."

Jim wasn't so sure.

Now he stood at the window overlooking the town's main street. Darkness had already settled, and many establishments would soon close for the day. Only a few horse-drawn carriages remained as their owners finished their business.

The post office and schoolhouse were already dark. Fire and sparks still flew from the blacksmith's forge. The regular patrons flowed into the next-door tavern. Dim lamplight glowed from the modest homes scattered along the street; a faint light shone from the spire of the white, wood-clad church as its bell tolled the hour.

Jim glanced at his watch. It was getting close to dinnertime, and he still had a few notes to review. He returned to his desk and the leather-bound ledger where he kept his patient records, and picked up his pen, determined to finish.

The patient's name was Edwin Johnson. Ed, a veteran of the War of 1812, had come in that morning complaining of a severe stomachache and bloody vomiting. Next to Ed's name, Jim wrote, *bleeding ulcer?*

As Jim examined Mr. Johnson, he moved his stethoscope from Ed's belly to his chest. The wooden instrument, in use for nearly thirty-five years now, had been modified from a long wooden tube to a shape better adapted to clearly hear a heartbeat. At one end, a small, quarter-sized disc flared out from the tube; at the other end was a much larger disc that Jim placed against Ed's chest. Jim leaned over and put his ear on the smaller disc, covered his other ear and focused on the lub-dub of Ed's heart.

Well above the normal rate. Jim frowned as he mentally counted—almost 180 beats per minute. That was concerning.

"I'm not sleeping much either," Ed had said, pointing to the dark circles under his eyes. "My mind just won't let go."

Jim dipped his pen into the inkpot on his desk and added *insomnia* to his notes. He leaned back in his chair. It seemed as if he were seeing a pattern emerge. Ulcers, racing heart, insomnia, and extreme nervousness were common complaints of his patients who were war veterans. He knew for certain that many veterans drank too much alcohol—Uncle Isaac was a prime example. Many a worried veteran's wife reported their husband's sudden mood swings, and the nightmares that sent them under the bed.

Was there something about war that wrecked one's body besides the obvious gunshot wounds? Did the images of the depravity and ugliness of war linger in their minds? Seeing friends shot down in front of you? Wouldn't the memories and reactions fade over time?

His stomach growled, reminding him that his workday was done. He closed his ledger, capped the inkwell, and set his pen aside.

That evening he shared his thoughts with Maggie.

"I think you might be on to something," she said. "You should ask your father what he's observed. Maybe he's seen the same symptoms."

Jim raised an eyebrow. "You're determined that I settle my disagreement with Father, aren't you?"

Maggie smiled. "You know how I feel," she said. "And I am nothing if not a determined woman."

The next morning, Jim and Maggie entered the sanctuary of the Presbyterian Church a few minutes before the service started. Congregants stood in the aisles or in front of their seats, chatting with their neighbors. The women wore their best dresses and bonnets, most in muted colors. The men wore their best suits. Both wore heavy wool coats against the chill December air.

Parishioners filled the dark wooden pews. With slightly curved backs for modest comfort, each pew included small wooden holders that contained Bibles and hymnals. Towering stained-glass windows depicting biblical symbols and scenes filled the walls along the outside of the sanctuary; eight lined each side. The one next to his father's pew showed a lamb and wheat sheaves, donated by Jim's grandfather, one of the church founders. Jim and Maggie shuffled into a pew behind his parents. His mother turned and smiled; his father acknowledged them with a curt nod and returned his attention to his Bible.

The minister's sermon was about family, about forgiveness. Jim thought once again about the argument with his father. It might be a good time to reconcile.

When will I stop feeling like a child around him? Jim glanced at Maggie sitting next to him with Jessie on her lap. She reached over, squeezed his hand, and returned her attention to the sermon.

When the service concluded, the congregation spilled out of the sanctuary, shook the minister's hand, and lingered briefly on the snow-sprinkled front lawn. People clustered in small groups, buzzing with conversation and activity. Handshakes and hugs spread through the crowd. Tired children fussed, admonished by their frustrated mothers. Horses neighed and wagons creaked as their families boarded them for the drive home.

Jim found Maggie holding a sleeping Jessie on her shoulder and took her arm. Her eyes were questioning as she looked up at him, and he nodded as he led her to their waiting carriage.

Across the snow-covered road, Jim's father helped boost Mother into the buggy. Jim took a deep breath and walked over to him, extending a hand.

"Do you have time for a chat today?" he asked.

"I do." His father ignored Jim's hand, climbed into the buggy and picked up the reins. "We'll talk after dinner." The horses moved forward as Father flicked the reins and headed for home.

CHAPTER 8

Jim loosened his belt as he finished the last delicious bite of Maggie's apple pie. He popped what remained of the slab of cheddar cheese beside it into his mouth and wiped his face with a linen napkin.

"Ready for a chat?" His father stood and headed for the study. Jim followed.

"Take a seat, son." Allen gestured, poured two glasses of brandy and set them on the table. He reached into the humidor for two cigars, lit one, and held out the other.

Jim accepted the cigar with a nod, removed a match from its box on the table, struck it against the sandpapered side, and lit his cigar. He watched the smoke rise from the cigar tip and leaned back against the sofa.

The conversation started with small talk. The newly elected president, Abraham Lincoln, was the topic. South Carolina responded by holding a secession convention in Columbia in mid-December, voting to secede from the Union immediately. People expected that more southern states would follow South Carolina's lead.

"It's more than the slavery issue that has them so upset," Jim noted. "They don't like that a man they disapprove of can tell them what to do."

"Seems to me they're getting a little too big for their britches," Allen said. "Old Honest Abe needs to take them down a notch or two."

Jim studied his glass of brandy and took a small sip. "Do you suppose it will come to a war?"

"I can't see how it won't."

The two sat quietly for a moment, contemplating their brandy and cigars.

"I wanted—" Jim started.

Allen put up his hand.

"Before we go any further," he said, inhaling deeply on the cigar, "there's an apology due."

Jim held the cigar loosely. "From whom?"

Allen scowled. "You know from whom."

Jim resisted the urge to squirm. He set his cigar on the table.

"I suppose that means I'm the one who must apologize." The words caught in his throat, and he forced himself to continue. "I'm sorry I called your medicine hocus-pocus. I was disrespectful, and for that I apologize."

"And you're doing fine on your own, just as I said you would?"

"Yes, Father, I'm doing fine on my own."

Allen chewed on his cigar, removed it from his mouth, and contemplated.

"Then I guess we're good," he said and extended his hand. "Apology accepted. Now, what was it you wanted to talk about?"

"I was wondering if you've noticed an unusual number of suicides and alcohol problems in war veterans?" Jim asked.

Allen thought for a moment. "It seems they're more prevalent," he said. "For all they've witnessed, can you blame them for drinking too much?" He sucked on his cigar, exhaling smoke, and removed a bit of tobacco from his tongue. "Why do you ask?"

"You're right," Jim agreed. "They have plenty of reason to drink themselves into a stupor, although I'm uncertain why they would commit suicide so many years after combat.

"But I've been seeing common health issues in war veterans as well. A lot of bleeding ulcers and heart palpitations. Insomnia too. It seems as if those ailments are more common in former soldiers than the average man."

"That is interesting." Father set down his cigar and gazed out the window. "I can't say that I've noticed," he said at last, "but I'll start paying closer attention."

"I'm going to keep track," Jim said. "Maybe I can find more evidence of the physical side effects. It would be interesting to see if combat causes long-term physical damage."

This could be my big chance, Jim thought. If I can discover and prove a connection, it could bring me the reputation I deserve. Heck, they might even name the condition after me. "Banyon's Syndrome"—I like the sound of that.

I have made an interesting discovery amongst my patients who are war veterans: to a man, they display unusual symptoms: a galloping heartbeat, digestive issues which generally manifest in bleeding ulcers, and an unusually high rate of

insomnia and occurrence of night terrors. Many also have a tendency to over-consume alcohol, thus making reliable employment difficult. Could this be a clue to Isaac's struggle?

The natural conclusion is that these disabilities relate to their military experience, but as an educated scientist, I am reluctant to diagnose that without further study. My intent is to follow this small group and attempt to discover any relevant trends. I hope to add more patients to my study in order to gather adequate data to support or rebut my theory.

CHAPTER 9

January 1861

Ira, NY

"Not bad." Napoleon smiled at his image in the mirror. He smoothed back his once dirty blond hair, now darkened to a chocolate brown that made his deep blue eyes seem even bluer, like a heavenly artist had added the perfect touch of color. It was a striking combination, accentuated by a neatly trimmed mustache dipping past the corners of his mouth. His ruddy face was flawless, the scars left by his father's abuse hidden under his clothing.

He rubbed his chin and tipped his head, imagining a dapper-looking beard. *Perhaps a goatee—or maybe muttonchops*, he thought.

Men's voices floated up from the dry goods store below, interrupting his thoughts. The reflection of his dreary lodgings startled him; in his man-about-town charade, he lived in a palace.

"Not bad," he said again, refocusing on his image in the mirror. "Not bad at all." He stepped back to take stock of his clothing.

The black frock coat he wore was made of the softest wool. With a fitted waist and wide lapels, its hem fell just above the knee. Underneath his frock coat, he wore a silk waistcoat with silver buttons cascading down the front. Tan, wide-legged trousers showed off his slender frame as they tapered toward the ankles; a pair of black leather boots, polished to a shine, peeked out from under the trousers' hem. Where most men kept such an ensemble for formal occasions, this was Napoleon's regular evening attire.

In the ten years since his father died, Napoleon kept his vow to live for the day. He never touched a drop of liquor, but that didn't dampen his devil-may-care reputation. Dressed to the nines, he'd swagger down the street on any given evening, carrying his pearl-handled walking stick and knowing he was the envy of every poor married sap in town.

Let them be chained to their women and children, he told himself. *Let them drink themselves into a stupor for all I care—that's not for me.*

He held no regular employment; he made money escorting single ladies to various social entertainments. His gambling habit quickly consumed his meager earnings, leaving him barely enough to pay for food and lodging.

He smiled at the thought of strolling through town, perhaps with a lovely woman on his arm, attracting everyone's attention. His image smiled back and winked.

Of course, the reactions weren't always positive. Last night it had been the neighborhood spinsters, a duo of shriveled old women no man would want, who tsked as he passed them near the Presbyterian church.

"Sacrilegious," one loudly whispered to the other.

"May the Lord comfort his poor mother," the other said.

Napoleon snubbed his nose and kept walking.

A week ago, it was Jim who took him to task.

"You can't live like this forever, you know." Jim wagged his finger at Napoleon one night when he'd stopped by Jim's office on his way out for the evening.

"Why not?" Napoleon asked. "I'm not hurting anybody."

"You're hurting yourself. You're abusing your body and gambling your life away."

"Who made you my father?" Napoleon snarled back.

"God knows you need one, living in that dump you call home. Aren't you ever going to settle down?" Jim asked. "Marrying Maggie was the best thing I ever did."

"Good for you," Napoleon snapped, "but I don't see a bright future in marriage and parenthood. Look where it got my mother."

"You're not your father."

"You're damned right I'm not!" Napoleon's eyes narrowed. "If I wanted melodrama, Jim, I'd talk to those old spinster biddies. You're supposed to be my friend."

"I am your friend," Jim said. "That's why I'm telling you." Jim leaned back and sighed. "Look, Napoleon. Your mother needs you. She's all alone in a house full of awful memories, while you live in a musty flat you can barely pay for. Why don't you move home and save some money?"

"I'll be god-damned if I step inside that house ever again!" Napoleon rapped his cane against Jim's desk for emphasis. "Your father sees to her well enough," he said. "She doesn't need me." He'd started pacing back and forth, feeling the crush of anxiety building in his chest. Just the thought of his childhood home evoked terror in the boy who still cowered inside him.

"I'm sure Father would help you and your mother find a more suitable place."

"Oh, that would be just dandy. Am I to entertain my female friends there as well?"

"Nap—"

"You keep your complaints to yourself, cousin, and quit trying to fix me." Napoleon turned and stormed out of Jim's office.

Maybe Jim was right, Napoleon thought as he preened at the mirror.

"Nah," his image responded, "You're just right."

"Let's go charm the ladies." Napoleon adjusted his top hat, tilting it at a jaunty angle, and sauntered out the door, ready for an evening of poker and women.

CHAPTER 10

April 1861
Victory, NY

The front door of Jim's medical practice slammed against the wall as Napoleon burst in. Waiting patients gasped, startled by the noise. Awakened babies wailed. Napoleon acknowledged none of it, barging into Jim's office without a knock.

Jim looked up from his ledger as Napoleon burst into the room, holding a newspaper in a death grip, and waving it violently before he held it out to Jim. "Have you seen the morning headline?"

Jim cursed under his breath at the splotch of ink that bloomed on the ledger. *Why does he always have to be so dramatic?* Ignoring his cousin, Jim reached for his ink blotter, soaked up the splattered ink, and returned the blotter to its spot on the desk. He gave Napoleon a pointed, annoyed glare and set the ledger aside.

"What on earth is so important that you need to barge in unannounced and scare the wits out of my patients?" Jim was more than annoyed. Napoleon thought everything was about him, and Jim was getting tired of it.

Napoleon's fortunes had changed in the past few months. A fight at a social event last summer resulted in more than a few injuries and a lot of destruction, and Napoleon was in the thick of it. It was the end of his career as an escort. His source of income gone, he'd had to move in with his mother. Still refusing to enter his father's house, he spent most of his time in the barn. Far from the dapper, devil-may-care man he'd once been, he wore worn and disheveled clothes, and he left his long hair uncombed.

"Just look at this!" Napoleon shook the newspaper at Jim.

Jim took the paper from his cousin, smoothed out the wrinkles, and read the bold headline sprawled across the front page.

THE WAR HAS COMMENCED!

Napoleon paced, stirring up a smell of rank body odor behind him. "I knew this would happen!" he shouted. "Didn't I tell you the damned Confederates would make trouble?"

"So you did," Jim said. He handed back the paper, struggling to control the spike of fear he felt in his chest. *I'll be damned if I let him think he caught me by surprise.*

The inevitable had finally happened. A handful of southern states seceded from the Union, forming the Confederate States of America—they didn't believe Lincoln's promise not to interfere with their practice of slavery.

In early 1861, more states joined the Confederacy, and by February, the Confederacy named Jefferson Davis as its provisional president. Most Americans, including Davis, hoped that the two nations could peacefully coexist without further conflict. Jim's father had proclaimed his doubts.

"You can't trust a damn thing those southerners do," he'd said. "I wouldn't put it past them to put a bounty on Lincoln's head or something just as foolhardy."

Last week, the Confederates opened fire on Fort Sumter in South Carolina, after Lincoln tried to provide supplies to the Union soldiers who held the fort. Lincoln saw it as a mission of mercy; Davis saw it as an act of war.

"Didn't I tell you?" Napoleon repeated, his eyes

blazing.

"I'm guessing you'll enlist."

"You bet I am!" Napoleon shook his fist again and paced. "There's a regiment being formed up in Watertown right now." Napoleon held out a large placard.

VOLUNTEERS WANTED!
AN ATTACK UPON WASHINGTON
ANTICIPATED!!
THE COUNTRY TO THE RESCUE!
A REGIMENT FOR SERVICE
UNDER THE FLAG OF THE UNITED STATES
IS BEING FORMED IN JEFFERSON COUNTY
NOW IS THE TIME TO BE ENROLLED!
Patriotism and love of Country alike demand
a ready response from every man capable of
bearing arms in this trying hour, to sustain not
merely the existence of the Government, but to
vindicate the honor of that Flag so ruthlessly
torn by traitor hands from the walls of Sumter.
RECRUITING RENDEZVOUS
Are open in the village of WATERTOWN, and at
all the principal villages in the County for the
formation of Companies, or parts of Companies.

**Officers to be immediately elected by those
enrolled
WATERTOWN, APRIL 20, 1862
WM. C. BROWNE, Col. Comd'g 35th Regiment**

Jim skeptically read the placard. *Napoleon? Enlisting? I'll believe it when I see it.*

Located over eighty miles north of Cato, in Jefferson County, Watertown was a fair hike away, and Napoleon had no way to get there. "You don't want to think about it a bit?" he asked.

"What's there to think about? I'm defending my country!" Napoleon stopped. He raised an eyebrow as if expecting his cousin to jump up in a burst of patriotism. Jim did not jump.

"You aren't going?" Napoleon took a step back in disgust. "It's your patriotic duty!"

Jim scrubbed his face and composed his thoughts, searching for a reply Napoleon would accept.

"There's a bounty as well," Napoleon added. "That might not mean much to you, but it's a godsend for me."

There it is. Money, not patriotism.

"Enlisting may be fine for you. You're single

with no one to worry about. But I have Maggie and Jess to look out for. I can't just abandon them."

"What better way to look out for your family than to join the fight and get rid of the damned Confederacy?" Napoleon paced faster. His boots banged against the hardwood floor. "She's got your family and hers right here, doesn't she? They can look out for her while you're gone."

Jim sighed. It was just like Napoleon to rush to such a decision. To Napoleon, life was all about taking risks and savoring victories. Jim preferred to consider the route ahead before starting a journey.

Except when Father pushes me out the door.

No, having Maggie by his side was more important for now. Nor was he inclined to leave her and Jessie just to prove his loyalty to his country. There would be other ways for him to serve. As he read the details of the attack on Fort Sumter, an idea began to form. Something he couldn't quite name—it was no more than a niggling at the back of his mind that might move him out of the rut he felt stuck in.

"Well?" Napoleon stopped pacing and stood at Jim's desk, palms hard against its surface, his face flushed and sweating despite the chill spring air.

Jim sat quietly. Inside, he was fuming. He'd had enough of people telling him what to do—especially Napoleon, who couldn't commit to a cup of coffee long enough to finish it.

"I'll stay with my family," he said. "There may come a time when I decide to enlist, but until then I'll support the Union from home."

Napoleon slapped his hands against the table, rattling Jim's empty coffee cup and unsettling his fountain pen. "I always knew you were the coward of the bunch." He tore the newspaper in two, threw it on the floor, and stormed out. The front door banged, and his footsteps clomped angrily down the porch steps. Jim could hear him muttering all the way to his horse.

"What's got into Napoleon this time?" Maggie stood in the doorway holding a sleeping Jessie. "It's a good thing he didn't wake the baby, or I'd have his hide!"

Jim couldn't help smiling at the image of Maggie chasing after Napoleon with a cast-iron skillet or the fireplace poker. *That* would be a sight! But Napoleon's reason for stopping by this morning sobered his thoughts.

"It's not good, Maggie," he said. A shiver raced

through him as he considered what might come next. He looked at his wife grimly. "The South has declared war."

Maggie's eyes widened; her face paled. "Will you go?" she asked timidly.

Jim took her in his arms. "Let's not worry about that for the time being."

Will I go? He asked himself.

He didn't have the answer.

Cousin Napoleon dropped by this morning to announce his intention to enlist in the Union Army. He is dismayed that I will not answer the call beside him. Father agrees with Napoleon, contending that it is not only my duty but also my chance to make a name for myself, as he insists I constantly complain of. Am I making excuses? Avoiding risks? I want to stand for my country, but at what cost? Will I achieve notoriety or shame?

CHAPTER 11

October 1861
Falls Church, VA

Dear Jim,

It feels like I've been sold a bill of goods when it comes to fighting for my country. The minute we arrived in Virginia, they put us to work building abattis, defensive structures built of trees with their branches still intact, laced with barbed wire, and pointed toward the enemy. One particular line is several miles long and about four hundred feet wide. After we finished the abattis, we had to build lunettes—small fortifications made of earth and stockade. If I'd wanted a job digging and cutting trees, I'd have put in with the lumberjacks instead of the U.S. Army.

Now we're assigned to picket duty near Falls Church. We do nothing but drill and picket, day in and day out, but at least it's soldiers' work. The only thing it's got me so far is a tin full of tobacco I got from a Reb picket across the ditch, in exchange for a bag of coffee. (Seems like we can be the best of friends when the exchange of tobacco and coffee is involved.)

Needless to say, army life is nothing but hard work and boredom. It would be nice to see a battle or two, and maybe even kill some Rebs, before my enlistment is up.

Give my love to Maggie and Jessie,
Napoleon

Jim sat at his desk and re-read Napoleon's latest letter. Hearing from his cousin was always a highlight of his day. The two of them had settled their differences before Napoleon reported for duty. They embraced, patted each other on the back, and promised not to argue like that again.

In the years since Uncle Isaac's death, life had been a struggle for both Napoleon and his mother. Leta drifted through the days like a rowboat in dense fog, doing what she had to and little more.

Napoleon quit school and hired on as a hand for Jim's brother, Heman, who ran the farm. He moved into the small barn beside their house and stayed warm sleeping next to their small flock of sheep. His mother served him his meals there, behind the barn when the weather was pleasant, inside the barn when it wasn't. He came and went through the barn's back door, doing everything he could to avoid seeing the site of his father's death.

His friendship with Jim kept him sane. They spent hours hunting for deer and partridge, fishing for brook trout in the stream behind the house. They sat side-by-side as the geese honked their way north or south, no talking needed as long as they had each other to lean on.

And then Jim announced his intention to attend medical school in Albany.

Napoleon's deeply tanned face paled to a winter white. His eyes glistened with tears as he struggled to speak. "Y-you're leaving?" His voice was a whimper. "Why would you do that?"

"You know I've always wanted to be a doctor," Jim said. "I want to learn the newest techniques, the newest medicine. I can't do that by staying here."

Napoleon stared at the horizon. "I hate it here," he said. "I hate working for Heman. I hate cutting hay and mucking stalls and milking cows. And now you're abandoning me."

"You don't have to stay." Jim put a hand on his cousin's shoulder. "You could work the railroad, or hire on at some factory in the city. There are lots of things you can do besides farming."

"But you won't be with me." A tear slid down Napoleon's face. He quickly wiped it away, embarrassed.

For a moment, Jim reconsidered his decision. Napoleon needed him.

But will I resent him if I give up medical school for his sake? Maybe what Napoleon really needed was to stand on his own.

"You know I can't always be with you. We'll set out on our own adventures and write each other all the time. Besides, I'll only be gone a year or so."

On the day Jim left for Albany, he and Napoleon embraced. "I'll be back soon. I promise."

Since his cousin's enlistment, Jim followed the war news faithfully, alert for mention of the New York 35th Volunteers, Napoleon's regiment.

The battle at Bull Run in July shocked everyone; the fact that the Rebels were still fighting in October brought the reality of the war closer. But Jim hesitated to enlist and expose himself to enemy fire or risk imprisonment in an enemy jail. He'd learned so much in medical school, but little of that knowledge would help him treat the injuries of war. Besides, the study he was conducting on the physical effects of battle on veterans was important. A survey among his medical peers had gathered a significant amount of data that seemed to agree with what he'd learned from his own patients.

The subject of enlistment was a source of frequent debate with his father, especially after Maggie's brother Frank joined up.

"I don't like speaking of war in front of the women," Allen remarked as they sat in the study one Sunday after dinner. "Have you read the latest news?"

"I've been trying to avoid it," he said. "The fighting seems so far away from us that it doesn't much matter." He gazed out the window, imagining his girls. His life was full; he was content. Why would he leave that behind to go to war?

Allen stiffened in his chair and scowled. "Your brother-in-law didn't hesitate to enlist."

That old argument. Jim was tired of being

compared with men whose lives were nothing like his own. Frank was like every other single man with no obligations. They had no idea of the responsibilities of fatherhood.

"You might want to consider paying more attention to what's going on in our country, son," Allen continued. "The Rebs are making a lot of noise, and it doesn't look like they're going away anytime soon."

"I imagine it will be some time yet before the county gets up a regiment." Jim contemplated his cigar. "Let's hope the Union puts them back in their place well before that."

Allen blew a long stream of cigar smoke into the room. "You seem to enjoy citing the county's lack of a volunteer regiment. That won't last forever, you know. What are your intentions when they form one?"

Jim shifted uncomfortably in his chair. He didn't want to think about war. He didn't want to consider leaving his family to risk his life in battle. Every time he thought about it, the old insecurities came up. What if he couldn't live up to the task of treating wounded soldiers? What if, God forbid, he was injured—or killed? He might sound like an annoying echo to his father, but voicing his hope that the war would end soon was the only way he could contain his anxiety.

Jim resisted the urge to argue. It *was* important for him to fight for the Union cause. He *did* intend to enlist... when the time came. But it was a complicated decision. He had to think of his wife and child, his successful and thriving practice. Once he decided, there would be no turning back. The finality of that statement tightened in his stomach.

What if...?

He shook his head. No, he wouldn't think about that until he had to.

"I promise to enlist when the time comes," he finally said, "and I will honor that promise. But in the meantime, my attention will stay with my practice and my family."

CHAPTER 12

November 1861
Victory, NY

"I suppose we'll be losing you to the war soon." In the months since the attack on Fort Sumter, more than one of Jim's patients had expressed that opinion. A raised eyebrow, a pause, and an anticipated pledge from Jim to sign up usually followed the remark.

Is this what the neighborhood thinks of me now? Jim had seen the sideways glances from people at church, heard his name in conversations about the Confederacy and the duty of loyal American men to defend democracy.

How many local men like Ed Johnson have volunteered to fight in the years since the Revolution? What makes me think I'm any different?

He had to talk to Maggie. She and Jessie were what counted most. Maggie wasn't prone to hysteria like so many women he knew, and she always knew what was best.

After dinner that evening, Jim and Maggie sat side by side in the parlor in front of a crackling fire. Maggie was the first to break the silence.

"I heard today the Appleby boy was killed at Cheat Mountain in Virginia," she said. "I'm planning to take a casserole to the family tomorrow, and help with the children at the funeral."

Jim nodded. "Please send my condolences to them." Maybe this wasn't a good time to bring up enlisting.

Maggie put her hand on Jim's. "Something's bothering you." She raised an eyebrow in concern.

Jim hesitated, but Maggie knew him too well to buy any excuse he could come up with.

"Father is nagging me again about enlisting."

Maggie stiffened, pulled her hand away and nervously laid it in her lap. "Why would you leave Jessie and me?" she said. "We need you here."

"Maggie—"

Maggie lifted her hand. "I know. You have to go eventually. Your father expects it from you, and I know you want to defend our country. But—" she inched closer and stroked Jim's arm. "I wish you would stay until our new child is born."

Jim tilted his head. *What did she say?*

His look of confusion blossomed into a brilliant grin. "You're expecting again?" He took her in his arms. "When?"

"Come spring." Maggie smiled and looked up at him. "I hope you can be here when our new child arrives."

"Of course I'll be here, my love." Jim wiped tears from his eyes and gently kissed her forehead, envisioning his newborn son—please, God, let it be a son—sleeping in Maggie's arms. All thoughts of enlistment melted away as he embraced his wife.

As winter progressed, the war took a turn in the Union's favor. After the battle at Bull Run, the skirmishes between North and South were minor. What had looked like Confederate strength in September now looked like a flash in the pan, and by the beginning of the new year, it seemed the Rebs were running out of steam.

Jim stoked the fireplace in the early evening darkness of midwinter. He sat in his chair and picked up the newspaper. This week saw the Union score a major victory at Fort Henry in Tennessee. In the end, it had been heavy naval gunfire and even heavier rain that had caused Confederate General Tilghman's surrender. It was an important victory for the North, opening the Tennessee River to Union traffic.

"Good news about the war?" Maggie set a steaming cup of tea in front of him.

"Seems like it." Jim looked up at Maggie and set the newspaper on the table. "How's our little one doing?" he asked, gently touching Maggie's swollen belly.

"Squirming like a hooked worm," she said, easing herself onto her chair.

"He's a strong one already." Jim patted Maggie's belly and gently kissed her cheek. "It won't be much longer before he's here."

"Maybe by then the Rebs will have surrendered," Maggie said. "Let's hope so."

"We'll pray for God's grace," Jim said, patting Maggie's hand. Maybe the Union win at Fort Henry was an omen for more victories to come. The last thing he wanted to do now was leaving his growing family and go to war.

The war rages on. Although the Union seems to be close to victory, I wonder if the time is approaching that I must enlist. There is much pressure from the community for every able-bodied man to serve his country. Unfortunately, my body is able, even if my spirit isn't.

I remain hopeful I can tarry here until our new child is born come spring. The midwife will handle the delivery, and I will be here for Maggie. Until then, I will pray for Maggie's health and the safe delivery of what I hope will be a son. Nothing could give me more joy.

CHAPTER 13

January, 1862
Taylor's Tavern, Virginia
"Davenport!" Napoleon's ears perked up at the familiar name.

"Here, sir!" a young man answered, one of a newly arrived batch of recruits. The lack of insignia on his arm announced his status as a private. He was a short man, with a scrawny body and a face accentuated by eyes the color of bluebells and hair the color of day-old straw. A scraggly beard covered most of his face; what remained bare revealed the carefree glow of youth.

Until recently, Taylor's Tavern had been just another wayside inn, overlooking the town of Falls Church. Three months ago, the Union Army commandeered it for their winter camp and re-named it "Fort Taylor." The newly arrived recruits were an attempt to beef up their numbers before the spring campaign.

A large, two-story wood-clad building, the

tavern was freshly whitewashed, its pristine exterior almost gleaming against the brown and muddied ground. Higher-ranking officers occupied the upper floor. A white picket fence enclosed the side and rear of the building; a narrow veranda graced the front. Off limits to the enlisted men, the tavern was the dominion of the officers, who sat at hand-hewn wooden tables in the warmth of the inn's oversized fireplace.

Outside, the rut-covered ground froze solid. Enlisted men loitered in groups; their breath steamed the air as they tried to warm their frigid hands.

Napoleon relaxed against a nearby tree, wrapped in his greatcoat against the cold. He waited for the soldier to look his way and caught his attention. "Your last name's Davenport?" he asked, beckoning the man to come closer. "I went to school with a Ray Davenport back home in Ira. Are you any relation?"

"Might be." Davenport lifted his hat and scratched his head. "I've got cousins who live down by Syracuse." He squatted next to Napoleon and clasped his hand in a firm handshake. "Name's Reuben. Private Reuben Davenport."

"Napoleon Drown." Napoleon stood, wiping dust and fallen leaves from his trousers. "Where're you from?"

"Forestport Station, out by Utica." Reuben instinctively tipped his head toward home, even though it was hundreds of miles away.

"Can't say as I've heard of it," said Napoleon, "but I imagine you haven't heard of Ira, either."

Reuben smiled sheepishly. "Not precisely, but I might have heard mention of it."

"C'mon in and set a spell." Napoleon beckoned to a nearby tent.

Reuben glanced nervously at his commander who was just then dismissing his troops. He nodded and followed Napoleon.

The small tent, protected with branches and packed with mud around the outside for extra warmth, stank of wood smoke and body odor. Dirty straw covered the frozen ground, making it only slightly more comfortable to sit on.

Although food was scarce this time of year, Napoleon pulled out two pieces of hardtack and motioned for Reuben to sit.

"Only got one mug," he said as he poured a cup of warm coffee and held it out. "You're gonna need coffee to wash down that hardtack, and I'm happy to share."

Reuben accepted the mug, took a small sip, and handed it back to Napoleon.

"What'd you do before you joined up?" Napoleon asked.

"Worked the railroad out in Boonville since I was thirteen." Reuben said. "My Pa's a farmer, but I didn't want nothin' to do with that."

Napoleon imagined Heman's farm and smiled. "I know how you feel."

"You got family back home?" Reuben wrestled with the hardtack, so hard it was impossible to bite into.

Napoleon smiled and held out the coffee. "Soak it in coffee a bit," he said. "Elsewise you'll never be able to eat it." He leaned back, pulling his greatcoat tighter. "It's just Ma and me now. Pa died when I was thirteen."

Reuben mushed the sodden hardtack in his mouth and swallowed. "Sorry to hear that."

"Don't be," Napoleon said. "He was a hard man."

"I've got five sisters—all older than me with families of their own. When I told my ma I was joining up, it dang near killed her. She's sure I'm gonna walk in front of a Reb's rifle or something. Pa doesn't seem to care one way or another."

"I don't think you're in any danger for now," Napoleon snorted. "In fact, you might as well get ready to be bored as a rooster without a henhouse. First, they had us cutting down trees like a bunch of beavers. Now all we do is picket duty—picket and patrol, picket and patrol, every damned day, and the Rebs are on the other side of the line doing the same thing."

Reuben nodded and picked stubborn bits of hardtack from his teeth. "I could've had that kind of boredom at home."

"Chicken-livered Rebs don't like fighting in the cold," Napoleon spat into the corner, "so you might as well get used to it."

"Fall in!" a gruff voice shouted from outside.

"That's my captain," Reuben said. He jumped up, brushed the straw from his uniform, and offered a hand to Napoleon. "Good to meet you."

"You too," Napoleon said. "You need anything, just holler."

Bad weather and unruly soldiers filled the months at Taylor's Tavern. With nothing but watered-down whiskey and gambling to entertain the idle soldiers, the men were restless for action. March brought orders, sending them to Fairfax Seminary to prepare for an advance on the Confederate troops at Centreville. The march was long and exhausting; water was in short supply, and the early spring sun burned their winter-whitened skin. In the end, all they got from their marching was the dysentery that gave the camp its name: "Camp Misery."

In April, the destination was Fredericksburg, where they established camp at "Dead Horse Camp," named for the Confederates' equine burial ground there. With every move, the troops anticipated the long-awaited skirmish with the enemy. With every move, all they got was more picket duty.

It was late May before they were called to support the Harris Light cavalry, still relegated to the sidelines. Reuben and Napoleon had become fast friends, and both of them agreed they hated picket duty worse than they hated farming.

CHAPTER 14

February 1862
Victory, NY

The northeast winds howled across the open fields as a midwinter storm blasted through the county. Jim sat in his empty office watching the snow pile up against the windowsill. The heavy snowfall made it impossible to see the buildings across the narrow street. It was late afternoon; the snow-laden skies grew darker by the minute.

The mantel clock chimed the hour. Four o'clock. Maggie would have gotten dinner started by now. Or maybe she'd taken a quick nap with Jessie. Seven months into her pregnancy, Jim supposed the baby might be slowing her down. *Maybe we'll have a boy this time.*

He glanced at the clock, then at the dwindling pile of patient notes he was working on.

I can finish the rest in the morning, he thought. *I'll go see what my girls are up to.*

The heavy downfall and howling winds slowed

Jim's progress as the horses plodded through the snow towards home. It was nearly five by the time he arrived.

Maggie will be worried, he thought. She'd probably have supper on the table, and maybe she'd be a little annoyed that it was getting cold.

Jim guided the horses into the barn and jumped from the wagon seat. He patted the nearest horse's rump. "Be right back," he said, and closed the barn's double doors behind him.

The house was quiet when he entered. The fire had burned low, and the air was chilly.

"Hello?"

Jim heard no reply. Where was Maggie? He should hear her bustling around in the kitchen. He should smell the tempting aroma of whatever she was cooking for dinner.

And where was Jessie? She always ran to greet him when he got home.

Jim's heart jumped into his throat. He threw his coat onto the chair and hurried to the kitchen.

No Maggie.

"Papa!" Jessie screeched and jumped into his arms.

Jim knelt down and smoothed Jessie's unruly

curls. "Where's Mama?"

"Nap time." Jessie pointed toward the stairs.

This late? Something's wrong; Maggie didn't like to nap when she was alone with Jessie, who, at nearly three years old, could easily climb out of her crib.

Jim lifted Jessie into his arms and started toward her bedroom. "Be a good girl and stay here while I check on Mama," he said, depositing her in the crib.

Jessie nodded and dutifully lay down. "Nap time."

"Maggie?" Jim hurried up the stairs. His heart pounded from the shot of adrenaline that flooded his system.

"Jim?" Maggie's voice was weak, barely above a whisper, as Jim entered their bedroom. The room was dark, with the heavy curtains drawn against the wind and cold.

"What's wrong?" Jim knelt by the bed.

Sweat drenched Maggie's hair. Her face was pale and worried. "I think the baby's coming. My pains keep getting closer, and I can't stop them." She burst out crying and stretched her arms towards Jim. "It's too early, Jim."

Jim listened as the wind howled. There was no time to summon the midwife, no time to get Jessie's mother for comfort.

"Don't worry, darling." Jim hugged her, willing his strength from his body to hers. He moved his hands to her belly; a strong contraction pushed against them as he felt for the baby's position. It had already dropped low in Maggie's uterus. Too soon or not, this baby was going to come today.

"I can't say I've delivered many babies," he whispered in Maggie's ear, "but I certainly know how." He kissed her sweaty brow. "We'll do this together."

Twelve hours later, Jim held his son in one hand; the baby couldn't have weighed more than a couple of pounds. One struggling breath was all the baby took, and then his chest was still. Jim turned his head and placed it close to the baby's heart. He heard nothing.

Tears came to his eyes as he swaddled the baby and held him to his chest.

"Jim?" Maggie spoke weakly, her eyes filled with worry.

Jim shook his head and laid the tiny baby in Maggie's arms. She trembled as she lifted her son to her chest and gently kissed his head.

Overwhelmed by hormones and exhaustion, Maggie burst into tears.

"I'm sorry," she sobbed. "I couldn't stop it."

Jim squeezed Maggie's shoulder. "It's not your fault." He reached out to take the lifeless body.

Maggie pulled the baby to her side. "Don't take him yet," she said. "Please let me hold him a little longer."

Jim put his arm around Maggie. His finger gently brushed the baby's yellowed cheek. His eyes welled with unshed tears. He wouldn't cry. He'd be strong for both of them.

"He was perfect," he said. "But he came too soon."

Maggie's eyes went wide. "Where's Jessie?"

"Asleep in her crib." Jim patted Maggie's arm. "I've been keeping an eye on her."

A few moments later. Jim lifted his head from

Maggie's shoulder. "I should take care of him," he said, reaching for the baby.

"There's a new blanket in the bassinet." She looked at Jim, her eyes swollen and red. "Wrap him tightly," she said, kissing the baby's head.

"Try to sleep, darling," Jim said. "I'll take care of our son." He swaddled the lifeless child, a tiny tadpole in a sea of wool.

Sunlight sparkled against the pristine snow, the sky a backdrop of deep blue. Mother Nature finished her rampage, and she'd left behind a serene winter landscape. Jim moved the bassinet into a spare room, laid the swaddled baby on its soft mattress, and returned to Maggie. He peeked into the bedroom and saw that she was sleeping.

I won't bother her now. He checked her breathing and her heart rate, lifted the blanket to be sure the bleeding was under control. As he turned to leave, Maggie's eyes fluttered open.

"Where's the baby?" She frantically scanned the bedroom.

Jim leaned in and gently touched her cheek. "He's safe in his bassinet for now. I'll take care of him soon."

Maggie stared at him.

Does she not understand?

Realization flooded her eyes; her face wrinkled in grief.

"Yes," she whispered.

"Can you let me clean you and the bed?"

Maggie shook her head. "Would you go get my mother? She can clean up and care for me."

Jim held her close for a moment, then kissed her forehead. "I'll take Jessie to my parents and bring your mother. Will you be okay alone?"

Maggie nodded. "Hurry back."

Jessie had scrambled out of her crib when Jim got back downstairs. "Baby?" she asked. Jim shook his head.

"Let's go to Grandpa's house," he said as he bundled her in her coat and hat.

The horses plodded through the thick snow cover towards Maggie's childhood home. As hard as Jim tried to urge them to a faster pace, the normally quick trip took over an hour. By the time he returned with Maggie's mother, the skies had once again turned overcast, and light snow was falling.

After checking on Maggie, he waded through thigh-high snowdrifts to the barn, where the horses still waited to be unhitched and stabled. He worked without thinking as he removed their harnesses, guided them into their stalls and gave them hay and oats.

He rooted around in the barn until he found enough bits of lumber to make a coffin. The snow was much too deep, the ground too frozen to bury their son now; that would have to wait until spring.

The saw gnawed through the boards as Jim cut them to the proper length. The hammer thumped with Jim's grief as it drove the nails deep into the wood. Jim's thoughts wandered.

What if I weren't here? He shivered at the thought. Maggie could have died.

Jim carried the finished coffin to his office. He lifted his son's body from the bassinet—*Jacob*, he reminded himself; *we were going to name him Jacob*—and laid him inside the tiny tomb. He tenderly kissed Jacob one last time and covered his face with a light cloth.

Back at the barn, he nailed down the lid and set his son's coffin on a high shelf to protect it from scavengers. The cold would preserve the body until spring, when the ground was soft enough to dig a grave.

CHAPTER 15

March 1862

Jim woke to a bright full moon shining through the bedroom window.

What was that noise? He listened carefully, only half-awake, and realized it was Maggie's voice he heard. *Must be checking on Jessie.* He adjusted his pillow and tried to sleep.

The next time he woke, the mantel clock was chiming. *How long have I been asleep?* It could have been hours or only minutes, but once again he heard Maggie's voice.

Jim dragged himself out of bed and stumbled into the hallway. In the days since the delivery of their unborn son, Jim had moved into the spare bedroom, hoping to give Maggie the time and space to heal. She was often lethargic, staying in bed for long periods, the bedroom darkened by the heavy drapes. Last night, her mother had returned home despite Maggie's pleas for her to stay.

"It's time," her mother said. "You need to get

back to living."

As he entered the hallway, Jim heard Maggie's voice. He checked her bedroom—the bed was empty. When she spoke again, he followed her voice to Jessie's room, where she stood over a sleeping Jessie, sobbing.

"Maggie?"

Maggie looked up, her eyes swollen, her cheeks red. She stared vacantly at Jim and started to tremble.

"I—I keep having nightmares. I dream I've delivered a dead baby only to discover it's Jessie." She exploded into tears, and Jim took her in his arms.

"Dear God," she said. "I can't lose her too!"

"We won't lose our Jessie," Jim reassured her. "It was just a bad dream."

"I'm so sorry, Jim."

"You have nothing to be sorry for."

"It's my fault we lost our son," she hiccoughed. "And now you've moved out of my bed, so you must blame me too."

"That's not true, my love. I wanted you to have time to heal without having to worry about me."

Maggie silently let him hold her, but soon she

started to tremble and burst into tears. "We haven't even buried him!" she sobbed. "What kind of mother am I?"

Jim held her close, rubbing her back. "You know we can't bury him until the ground thaws."

Maggie nodded. "I can't stand the thought of him in his little coffin in the barn," she sniffled.

"Soon," Jim soothed. "We can bury him soon." He guided her back to bed and tucked the covers around her. "I love you, darling," he whispered.

In the morning he found her standing at the kitchen window, staring at the barn. He was shocked to realize how pale and gaunt she looked. *She's lost too much weight. She's not likely to let me examine her, but perhaps she'll allow Father to take a look.*

"Maggie." He stepped behind her and wrapped his arms around her. She didn't respond.

After a few moments, she spoke. "What if we can't have another baby?" she kept her gaze straight ahead.

"I don't see why not," Jim said. But a niggling doubt whispered in his head. *Will it be too dangerous to have another child? Could I lose her too?*

"But we can try again, can't we?"

"It's up to you, sweetheart," Jim said, shaking away the doubts. "We'll wait a few months."

"Jim," Maggie turned to look at him, her eyes pleading, "do you still want me?"

Jim silently took her hand and led her to the parlor sofa. He gently guided her to sit and sat down beside her. "Darling Maggie," he said. "What would Jessie and I do without you? I will always want you. I will always love you. No matter what comes."

In the weeks to come, it was Jessie who filled the awkward space between them. Too young to understand loss, she filled the house with laughter, smothered her parents in kisses, and gave them peace when it was hard to find.

April 1862

Maggie and Jim buried their son in the cemetery on his parents' farm. It was a crisp, sunny morning filled with birdsong and the smell of spring.

Together, they tucked the tiny coffin into the ground and sprinkled bits of fresh soil over the rough wood. Together, they knelt and said a prayer. Jim filled the grave with dirt. Maggie placed a small marker at the grave's head:

Jacob Andrew Banyon, beloved son
b. February 12, 1862
d. February 12, 1862

They embraced, wept for the loss of their child, and placed him in God's loving hands.

CHAPTER 16

May 1862

Jim stood at the window in his anteroom and watched his last patient of the day walking toward home. The afternoon rain had slowed to a drizzle. Little rivers of mud carved into the dirt road as they tumbled down the hill. The sky was gray; a dark mist clung close to the ground, perhaps an omen of the months to come. Although it was not yet evening, the heavy skies made it seem like dusk.

The small bell above the outer door jingled. "Do you have time for an old friend?"

Jim jumped as he recognized the voice and turned to see Dr. Jacob Larssen, his former teacher. A professor from Albany Medical College, he was a valued mentor to Jim. Jim could count on him to explain the more complicated medical procedures, and he was always willing to let Jim help treat patients when other professors were reluctant to allow students to do anything but observe.

"Dr. Larssen! It's good to see you!" Jim crossed

the room and extended his hand. "Do have a seat, Doctor." He motioned to the chair opposite his.

"Can I get you something to drink? How about a cinnamon roll?" He reached for the small plate on his desk. "Maggie baked them just this morning."

"Coffee, please." Dr. Larssen took off his wet overcoat.

"Let me get that." Jim took Larssen's overcoat and hung it on a nearby hook as Dr. Larssen reached for a cinnamon roll and settled into the overstuffed chair.

"To what do I owe this visit?" Jim asked, wiping the crumbs from his mustache.

Larssen swallowed a bite of his cinnamon roll and chased it with a sip of coffee. He set down his cup and paused for a moment.

"I've been thinking about our time together at Albany Medical," he said. "Do you remember the first time you cut into a living body?"

"I do." Despite the years since his first surgery, the experience was still fresh in his mind.

Medical students filled the hospital amphitheater. Muted whispers drifted to the operating table, notebook pages rustled, pens lifted. The room was lit by gaslight; several enormous globes extended from the wall to provide sufficient light.

The patient reclined in a surgical chair, his head restrained by leather straps. He had come into the teaching hospital, a skinny boy in rags. A baseball-sized tumor deformed his cheek.

Jim remembered Dr. Larssen as he talked to his patient.

"You know we can't be sure you'll survive the surgery. There could be an infection. The tumor could be cancerous."

"I know," said the young man. "But I'm tired of it getting in the way when I eat. I'm tired of being the butt of jokes and ridicule.

"I get to stay here afterwards, right?"

Larssen nodded. He knew that escaping the poor ward, along with a warm bed and good meals, was enough to motivate the young man. Having a regular face was a bonus.

Dr. Larssen turned to Jim. "Ready, Doctor Banyon?"

Jim took a deep breath and nodded. He readjusted the chloroform-soaked cloth over the patient's nose and mouth, and picked up the curved scalpel from the table.

The sharp odor of iron rose from the boy's cheek as Jim cut. Blood flowed as he sliced along the base of the tumor; that was to be expected from the relatively thin skin and many surface blood vessels of the face. He knew he was being graded by his professors. His heart pounded faster.

At last the tumor came free. Jim held the mass in his hand, a hard, repulsive lump of flesh and veins. Laying the mass in the nearby basin, Jim returned to his patient and carefully closed the wound. The next few days would be the most precarious until the risk of infection had passed.

"You know they're going to raise a regiment in the county any day now?" Dr. Larssen's voice startled Jim.

"I heard that," Jim said, hoping he hadn't missed any of Dr. Larssen's words. "Rumors say sometime this summer."

"Looks like July." Larssen swallowed more coffee and continued. "I'd like you to sign up as my assistant surgeon. Are you interested?"

Jim felt a moment of resentment—first Napoleon and his father and now his respected mentor. *Was everybody determined to put him in harm's way?*

"I—I—" Jim stammered.

Larssen raised a hand. "I know you have a young family to think about. But the army needs experienced surgeons, and they are a scarce commodity."

Jim swallowed hard. *Of course, he's right.* He wanted to do his part. And he'd promised father he'd enlist when the time came.

Well, the time has come.

It was undeniable that the army needed him more than family for now.

"I'd be honored," Jim said, stifling the thumping

in his chest. Given the recent fifty-dollar enlistment incentive from New York, the one-hundred-dollar bounty offered by the Federal government, and the lucrative monthly salary he'd earn as a surgeon, he could hardly turn down the offer.

And if I have to go to war, at least I'll be in the company of a man I trust and respect.

"Before you go," Jim said, "let me tell you about the study I'm conducting." Jim outlined his findings regarding the effects of combat on war veterans, and his hope that he might discover a way to treat them.

"I might be able to continue the work in the field. Would you approve of that?"

Dr. Larssen thought for a minute, then nodded. "You know that's going to annoy the big bugs, don't you? But if you can get it past them and can find the extra time, I'll give it my okay." He stood, stretched, and patted his belly. "Give Maggie my thanks for the delicious cinnamon rolls." He reached for the last roll on the plate. "I'll put this one out of its misery."

Jim escorted his guest to the door and extended his hand. "I'll see you in a month or two," he said.

Dr. Larssen shook Jim's hand, put on his

still-damp coat, and turned up the collar before he stepped out. As he walked toward his waiting carriage, he turned to Jim. "I can think of no one better to work with."

Jim watched Larssen's carriage until it was out of sight, then returned to his desk. His mind raced with mixed emotions. He'd just agreed to enlist.

Whatever possessed me?

Jim pondered the advantages: there would be plenty of opportunities to learn new techniques, like better wound care, and triaging numerous injuries. Anything will be more enlightening than tending to stubborn patients who refuse to change.

He considered the negatives of enlisting: *I don't want to leave my girls.* His stomach clenched. *What if something happened to either of them?* The memory of Maggie's miscarriage panicked him. His heart jumped to his throat, pounding out in alarm. *How can I leave Maggie and Jessie in such a vulnerable position?*

But the truth was, the Rebs were running all over the Union Army. In the past month alone, the South had won battle after battle, both large and small. Most of the action was in Virginia, where General Stonewall Jackson repeatedly forced the retreat of the Union Army.

Jim chewed on a cigar stub and considered his options. Not that there were any options left: he'd made the commitment, and he would honor it. Maggie and Jessie would stay with her parents while he was away. They would be fine.

Jim forced himself to relax. Jessie would thrive with all the attention. He would ensure that his patients were taken care of; they might have farther to travel, but his father could take them on for the time being. That was the easy part.

Now all I have to do is tell Maggie.

After Maggie put Jessie to bed, she joined Jim in the living room. The rain had stopped, and the skies cleared. Jim opened a window; a warm breeze blew in with the curtains. Although they didn't need the extra warmth, the fireplace was burning low; just enough to keep it going. Jim sat with his pipe, reading the newspaper as Maggie settled down with her knitting.

"I saw an old friend today." Jim looked up from his paper. "One of my former professors, Dr. Larssen, stopped by."

"I'll bet that was a surprise." Maggie laid the knitting needles in her lap and looked at Jim. "What did he have to say?"

Pretending he didn't hear her, Jim returned to the news, but it couldn't keep his attention—he knew he'd have to tell Maggie what Dr. Larssen had proposed. *Might as well get it over with.* He set the paper on the side table and took a deep breath.

"Dr. Larssen wants me to enlist and serve as his assistant surgeon," he said. "What do you think?"

Maggie's eyes reflected the fear Jim knew she wouldn't vocalize. Neither of them spoke.

"Tell me what—" Jim was the first to break the silence.

"I think—" Maggie said at the same time.

"Go ahead," Jim said. "I won't go if you oppose it."

Maggie picked up her knitting and wrinkled her brow, wrapping the yarn around a finger. She started to knit, added a few stitches to the dress she was making for Jessie, then spoke.

"I'm wondering," she began slowly, her voice

soft and measured. "Wouldn't the battlefield be the perfect place to continue your veterans study?"

Jim couldn't believe what he heard. He knew how much Maggie supported his study—but this? This was more understanding than a man could ask for. He stood, crossed the room to where Maggie sat, and leaned down to kiss her.

"You," he said, settling on the arm of Maggie's chair, "are more than I deserve."

Maggie smiled and returned the kiss. But her heart was filled with fear.

CHAPTER 17

July 1862

Auburn, NY

The line at County Hall extended out the door and into the street. The day was typically hot; the men standing in line to enlist pulled at damp collars and wiped sweat from their faces. A banner strung above the high-pillared structure proclaimed *111th New York Volunteers Enlistment Today.*

Family members surrounded some men, while others stood conspicuously alone, nervously scanning the crowd as if they hoped someone would show up for them, too. Conversations flew back and forth as young men, eager to fight, waited for their turn to sign up.

Once inside, the noise was louder. Voices echoed across the high-ceilinged room. Papers shuffled, chairs scraped the polished floor. Long wooden tables lined the perimeter, each with the name of a town to guide men to the proper location. Enlistment posters like the one Napoleon had shown Jim hung on the walls, promoting the Union cause. A curtain hung in one corner with a sign that said, "Physical examinations." There, doctors cursorily examined recruits to check their fitness for service. The air was tense with urgency, electrified with patriotism, as the men reported to their respective tables.

Jim stooped over the deeply polished table labeled "Town of Victory", dipped a pen in the inkwell, and added his name to the list. He scribbled his signature—more of a flourish than a name—set down the pen and stepped aside for the next man.

There, he thought. *I'm doing what none of my brothers could: I'm an officer in the Union Army, an assistant surgeon pursuing a study that could change the world, and no one can take that from me.*

But what if—? He struck the thought of failure from his mind. He'd already achieved more than his brothers could have even imagined.

And he would not fail.

Jim loosened his coat to cool off. It had been an unusually hot and dry spring. Farmers cut and baled hay in late June, and they had plenty of time to let it dry before they moved it to the barn loft.

Many a barn has burned to the ground from hay stored before it's properly dried, Jim thought. *But that's Heman's problem, not mine.*

Across the room, he recognized several friends and neighbors. He set the pen on the table and went to join them.

The conversation was about money—or rather, the lack of it.

"I'm sure it was no accident. No one mentioned that the bounty they promised us won't be paid until after we've served our three years," grumbled Charlie Harrington, a scruffy-looking fellow who looked too old to enlist. "They couldn't even tell me when we'd draw our first pay."

"At least you got your uniforms for free," Jim said, patting his wallet. "Officers pay for their own, not to mention the seventy dollars I shelled out for uniform accouterments and a saddle. You guys may have to wait to get your money, but I've already spent half of mine."

He hadn't been a soldier for ten minutes and already the shine was wearing off.

"Look at this fella here," one of his friends gestured to a man in an Army captain's uniform who had just walked in. Scanning the crowd like a hungry hawk, he pushed past the waiting recruits and strutted to the head of the line, leaving behind the smell of sweat-soaked wool.

"Captain Peleg Anthony," he loudly announced as he commandeered the pen from a soldier's hand.

His skin was ruddy, his pox-scarred chin narrow and sharp. A thin mustache drooped at the corners of his mouth. He had a broad, crooked nose and eyes that were the brown of a mud puddle stirred up in a storm.

Decked out in his dress uniform, Anthony looked as if he was preparing for a parade rather than a battle. He wore a black Hardee hat, turned up on one side and secured with an embroidered eagle. His double-breasted dark blue coat, cinched tightly at the waist, fell mid-thigh, and had a dark blue velvet collar and cuffs with gold epaulets on the shoulders. His light blue trousers, piped in dark blue, matched his coat; his boots were polished to a blinding shine.

"Would you look at them chicken guts," said the old private, referring to the gold braid on Anthony's uniform. "Guess we can rest easy now that Captain Pegleg has arrived." He mimicked a limp, walking in a small and wobbly circle around his friends.

The group of locals snickered among themselves.

Anthony scowled at the pen, held it daintily in his hand as if to avoid getting ink on his pristine uniform, and signed his name, never once lowering his nose that stayed firmly in the air. When he finished, he returned the pen to the table as if it might carry germs. He briskly saluted, turned, and spotted the locals.

"What are you looking at, Privates?" He sneered. "Never seen an educated man before?"

He wrinkled his face and turned his attention to Jim's shoulder straps.

"Doctor, eh?" he shook his head. "If this is what passes for medical expertise in these boondocks, I pity the lot of you." Anthony made an about-face and strode out the door with his nose held high and his eyes full of scorn.

The old private worked up a wad of phlegm and spat into a corner. "I pity the men who get stuck with him in charge."

Peleg knew the rubes' laughter was for him, but he ignored their crude behavior. He strode out of the County Hall, his polished boots sparkling from the reflected sunlight.

What did they know about names? They sure as hell should know the name Peleg. It was straight from the Bible.

And unto Eber were born two sons: the name of one was Peleg; for in his days was the earth divided;

Plenty of men had carried the name of Peleg since then, including the Pequod's co-owner in Melville's *Moby Dick*.

People had drilled this into Peleg since he was a young child—the honor of his name and the burden he carried to live up to it. Military service was a given, and Peleg's commission in the United States Army would allow him to fight his war from the safe confines of an officer's tent. Even inclement weather would sidestep a man of his privilege.

It couldn't get much easier. His service would

earn him all the accolades he deserved, and cement his status in elite circles, without ever having to mingle with the ignorant common soldier.

At the end of the day, the new enlistees were called to order, lined up, and marched—if their uneven shuffle could be called marching—to the barracks at Camp Cayuga in Auburn, where they would spend the next month learning to look and act like an organized military unit.

The organizers grouped the men by town, assigned them a company letter, and provided them with uniforms and equipment. Unlike the officers, the enlisted men paid nothing for their gear and food. Also, unlike the officers, their clothing was plain and ill-fitting, their equipment bare bones, and their rations meager.

Each soldier received a navy-blue wool blouse with four gold buttons down the front and a turned-down collar. Worn for fatigue duty, it was known as a "sack coat." They also received a shorter "frock" jacket of the same color, with seven buttons and a standing collar, and sky-blue pants. Their shoes were brown, ankle-high, and laced with four eyelets.

Infantry headgear was a dark blue forage cap. A "kepi" was its common name, and a brass infantry horn, the 111th regimental number, and the company letter decorated the crown.

Each man received a haversack for carrying rations—hardtack, salt pork, sugar, coffee, and salt—and cooking gear, and a knapsack to carry their clothing and personal items, as well as a bedroll, canteen, and other equipment.

The one thing they didn't get was a gun.

Today I signed the muster roll. I am officially a member of Uncle Sam's Army. Maggie is so supportive; I thank God for her. The appearance of one Captain Peleg Anthony, a bit of a dandy who fancies himself an officer, marred the day. I pray I will not have to cross swords with this man; it will not end well.

CHAPTER 18

Late July 1862

Orange Court House, VA

"Another goddamn support mission!" Napoleon spat a wad of tobacco juice that sizzled as it hit the rails of the Orange-Alexandria Railroad. Once again, they found themselves assigned to support the Harris Light Brigade on a reconnaissance mission. Sporadic gunfire erupted from the town, followed by an eerie silence and more gunfire. "Fight or don't fight," Napoleon growled. "Make up your goddamn minds!"

Reuben laughed and shook his head. "Seems to me like the big bugs are as chicken-livered as the Rebs." He removed his kepi hat, wiped the sweat from his face, and chased away the gnats and mosquitoes that endlessly plagued him.

Since early summer, the 35th had seen a steady escalation in its role. Although they still hadn't seen combat other than maneuvers and minor skirmishes, they gained experience. Food was scarce. Gambling and drunkenness plagued the encampments. Many a disillusioned soldier deserted, but for most of the army, their thirst for battle continued to grow, and by the end of July they were a herd of wild stallions eager for release.

All of that changed in early August.

They were moving south this time, from Culpeper back toward Orange Court House. The day was oppressively hot as the blazing sun fought off threatening, moisture-laden clouds. Heat waves shimmered off the road ahead. Their heavy wool uniforms chafed, soaked with sweat from the inside out. Word had it that the Confederate Army, headed by General Stonewall Jackson, was moving north. General Pope's Army of Virginia had orders to stop them.

The men rose before dawn, prepared for action. Something like euphoria spread through the troops: at last they would do what they signed up for. Now they stood shoulder to shoulder, a river of blue awaiting orders.

From the distance, they sighted Jackson's troops. Napoleon's heart jumped to his throat. A momentary panic seized him. Instinct took over, telling him to run. *Run!*

Napoleon pushed it aside and focused. He glanced to his left, looking for Reuben. He was nowhere to be seen. For the briefest of minutes, silence held sway.

The orders came sharp and fast. "Advance! Hold! Fire!"

Napoleon fired. The butt of his rifle kicked against his shoulder. A gray uniform fell in front of him. He dropped behind a fence rail, reloaded, fired again, this time a miss. Artillery thundered from the Confederate lines. A soldier next to him grabbed his belly and fell without a sound, his eyes turned toward the heavens. Fate was indiscriminate, not caring for which cause a man fought.

There was no time to think. No time to plan. Napoleon was a mindless animal, doing what he was taught to do with no thought of anything other than that very minute.

Around him, chaos reigned. Men screamed. In pain, panic, confusion, rage. Adrenaline fueled their forward motion. Smoke filled the air. Napoleon choked, stumbled, and regained his footing.

The fighting continued for what felt like hours, a blur of gray and blue, of black powder and blood. As the day wore on, momentum shifted, and the

Union line faltered.

"Fall back!" The order to retreat was unexpected and welcome. Napoleon, barely registering the command, turned toward the rear and ran, stopping only to half-carry a wounded boy who had no business being within a hundred miles of battle.

He looked back just once, long enough to see the triumphant Rebs impaling his fallen comrades, looting their bloodied bodies. His face went pale, his heart ready to explode out of his chest. He steadied the boy beside him and ran like hell.

"Napoleon!" It was Reuben's voice he heard through the smoke and haze, his friend finally emerging through the thick fog, looking as befuddled as Napoleon felt. He stared at Napoleon and then hugged him fiercely. "You're alive!"

Napoleon acknowledged him, looking around to realize he had made it back to Culpeper with no memory of how he got there. The boy he carried slumped like a rag doll against his side; Napoleon wondered how long he'd been dead.

Hours later, Napoleon lay next to Reuben, straining to see the stars through the lingering smoke. Images of shattered bodies, of exploding ordnance and saber-wielding Confederates, shook him to his core. In a few brief hours, everything had changed.

He was no longer the devil-may-care man about town. No longer a raw recruit, eager to prove himself. Today he had seen the elephant, watched his friends fall dead around him, seen the enemy close up. Too close. He mentally counted the months since he'd enlisted, almost half-way through his commitment. Sixteen months of marching and maneuvering, and one day of the brutal reality of war. His job now was to stay alive and protect as many of his fellow soldiers as possible. He wondered how many more days he could manage to do that.

CHAPTER 19

August 21, 1862

Auburn, New York

The mid-August heat was stifling; the clouds that shrouded the sun fairly dripped with humidity. Jim and the one thousand men of the 111th stood in formation in front of the Western Exchange Hotel for the formal inspection and swearing-in. Dust stirred up from the movements of observers and soldiers, tinged the air a dun-brown hue and settled on uniforms and clothing. A faint odor of manure and gunpowder lingered in the air. Wagons rattled, horses whinnied, babies wailed, conversations hummed.

It looked like every person from the two-county area turned out to bid farewell to their husbands and sons as they marched to war. Thousands of spectators lined the streets. The women wore dresses of lightweight cotton or linen, with high necklines and full skirts. Ribbons and lace adorned their outfits; they wore broad-brimmed hats or carried parasols to protect their fair skin from the heat. Some men wore linen suits, complete with waistcoats, long pants, cravats, and hats. Veterans wore their military uniforms, proudly displaying their service. Others wore simple work clothes.

The mood was both somber and excited, a bittersweet farewell to loved ones doing their patriotic duty to defend the Union cause.

Well-wishers leaned precariously from the hotel windows for a better view of the ceremony. Citizens lined the cobblestone street in a sea of miniature waving flags. Reporters and photographers roamed the entire block, documenting the historical event. Here and there, tearful women rushed up to their departing soldiers for a final hug goodbye. Children clung to their father's coat-tails as the regiment prepared for its march to Baltimore, where it would join the Army of the Potomac.

The temporary bandstand, decorated in red, white, and blue bunting, stood ready for the esteemed guests scheduled to speak. The village band gathered on one side, briefly tuning their instruments as the crowd awaited the start of the ceremony and parade. Children laughed and raced through the crowd; dogs barked.

Vendors called out their wares. "Cold lemonade! Fresh pies and sausages!"

Jim's family took their seats near the front of the bleachers set up for spectators. He felt smug satisfaction seeing his brothers and sister and their families. Who was successful now?

Maggie and Jessie sat in front of Jim's parents. There were tears from Maggie and his mother when they'd said their farewells. His father's face was rigid, as if he were fighting to control his emotions, too. Jessie, still too little to understand that her father was going away, held a small flag, waving it madly and wiggling on her bottom as the town band played.

The 111th recruited soldiers from Cayuga and Wayne Counties. Ten companies, each with one hundred men and led by a captain, made up the regiment under the command of Colonel Jessie Segoine. At the age of fifty-eight, and a cabinet-maker for over forty years, he might have seemed an unlikely candidate for military command. But he had been a part of the Army, as well as local and state militias, since he was eighteen. Deep-set dark eyes reflected the wisdom earned by a man his age. His gray-white receding hair fell to his ears and curled up at the ends. A neatly trimmed mustache and beard surrounded his full lips.

Standing toward the front of the line, Jim recognized many of the assembled soldiers—neighbors like Joshua Baldwin from the farm down the road, as well as his school friends, Carl Lunkenheimer and Pete Waterman.

Dr. Larssen stood to Jim's left. With the rank of colonel, he led the medical staff. To Jim's right was Lieutenant Dr. Tom Erskine, a recent graduate of pharmacology school. His job as the hospital steward was to administer medicine and care for patients' wounds. On days when there was no fighting, Jim would be responsible for sick call and basic wound care. During battle, he might be called to the front line to assess injuries and stabilize wounds.

Together, the three men formed the regiment's medical staff.

Three men for a thousand soldiers. Jim thought. It was better than the original single surgeon assigned to each regiment, but Jim worried it was still not nearly enough.

At precisely three o'clock, the band conductor called his musicians to attention. Strains of *The*

Battle Hymn of the Republic and *Yankee Doodle* filled the air. The regiment snapped to attention. For the third time since he'd taken his place in line, Jim adjusted his sword, smoothed his uniform and the green silk sash identifying him as a medical officer, and brushed the ever-present dust from the shoulder straps that signified his rank as Captain.

The band stopped playing when the honored dignitaries climbed the makeshift steps and took their seats on stage. As the men settled, the mayor nodded to the bandleader. The crowd went silent and removed their hats as the band played *America*. A few people sang along, their voices blending to form a moving chorus.

The governor of New York, Edmond Morgan, was the first to speak, addressing the crowd and soldiers in a long-winded speech.

Although the officers toward the front of the formation were required to stand at rigid attention, the enlisted men at the back, who could barely hear Governor Morgan, were more restless.

Later on, Jim's friend, Josh Baldwin, shared the goings-on at the end of the line.

"All this skinny private standing next to me could talk about was how much the 'Goddamned wool uniform itched like hell.' Then another yokel piped up. 'I wish the old blowhard would shut up,' he said. 'I'm sweatin' like a stallion in a mare barn.'

"I had to keep myself from bustin' out laughing," snorted Baldwin. "I mean, they aren't wrong, but, speaking for myself, I was thinking more about the days ahead and how many Rebs I could kill."

When it seemed his oration would never end, Governor Morgan wrapped up his speech with the following words.

"I recently had the honor of being in Washington to hear our esteemed president speak, along with other dignitaries from across our great country. I would like to share with you the words of the Honorable Edward Jordan, Solicitor of the Treasury, and I quote:

"'Resolved, that we, residents of the District of Columbia... deliberately and voluntarily declare that, rather than witness its overthrow, we would prosecute the present war until the towns and cities should be reduced to ashes. Our fields should be desolated, and we and all that are dear to us should have perished with our possessions. Let the Union be preserved, or the country made a desert.'

"It is inherent upon us, as citizens of the United

States of America," Morgan pointedly looked at the crowd and the soldiers, "to join in this resolution to hold the Confederate Rebels accountable for their treasonous actions."

A cheer rose from the crowd—as much in relief at the end of the governor's discourse as in his message.

The rest of the speeches were mercifully short, ending with a brief message from Colonel Segoine, who then descended the platform and called his troops to marching formation.

At the front of the line, the drums struck up a marching cadence. The fifes joined in, their shrill pitch belting out *Yankee Doodle*, and the regiment was in motion.

One thousand men, their backs rigidly straight, marched in disciplined formation. Boots clomped in unison on the cobblestone, their sound nearly overtaking the fifes and drums. Flags frantically waved, the crowd cheered. Dozens of people ran alongside the regiment as it marched toward the train station, perhaps trying to grab every moment they could before their loved ones went out of sight, perhaps never to be seen again.

The men and boys of the 111th New York

Volunteers were on their way to the train that would carry them to war. Jim wondered how many of them would return.

Elaborate ceremony in Auburn. Noted speakers, a marching band. Flag-waving and cheering from all. We marched out of town to the train station and are bound for Baltimore, Maryland, to join the Army of the Potomac.

What have I done?

CHAPTER 20

Early September, 1862
Harper's Ferry, West Virginia

Jim stood at the top of Loudoun Heights, put his hands on his back, and stretched, willing the kinks and aches out of his tired body. The climb had been strenuous but invigorating, giving him a badly needed distraction from his medical duties.

Far below, the Potomac River twisted through the mountains, its murky water muddied from the recent rain and the tumbling rapids of the Shenandoah as the two rivers joined forces on their way to the capital in Washington, D.C.. He watched the sun rise, shades of brilliant pink and orange, and wondered how many soldiers would die today. Up to now, the deaths had been from disease and exposure after the miserable trip from the North, but the Confederates would arrive with their muskets and heavy artillery soon enough.

What would the battlefield look like, strewn with bodies, both Union and Confederate? Jim tried to form an image in his mind. *What do I know about combat and battlefields?* He wondered. Both were as foreign to him as the deserts of Arabia. A twinge of doubt crowded his thoughts. *Was I right to enlist?* Once again, his thoughts went to his wife and daughter. Would they be all right without him?

What if I never make it home? Jim pushed the worry aside, packing it into his "sack of worries"; the doubts, regrets, and fears he kept buried in a corner of his mind. Perhaps one day he would take them out and reexamine them, but for the time being, he had more important things to think about.

The 111th had arrived at Harper's Ferry after a four-day journey from Auburn, but it might as well have been a lifetime. By train, cattle barge, and steamer, in relentless rain, the regiment made its way to Annapolis and the Army of the Potomac, only to be redirected to Harper's Ferry, a prime target of the Confederacy. The rain relented as they boarded the westbound train, but the weather was humid with the ever-present threat of thunderstorms.

The more concerning danger during their journey was that of hostile crowds: Southern supporters threw rocks and bottles at the train as it passed through the countryside. At stations along the way, the Union troops stayed hidden inside the railroad cars, holding their breaths, fearing an attack, until the train began moving again.

On the peninsula below, the town of Harper's Ferry appeared deserted, stuck in a hollow with only a few neglected buildings and the shell of the burned-out Armory remaining. Across the Potomac River to the north, the high cliffs of Maryland Heights towered over the town, and to the south across the Shenandoah loomed the cliffs of Loudoun Heights.

Most of the town's residents had left months ago. Other than a few stragglers and the scattered contraband slaves' camps, the only sign of life came from the Union encampment just south of town, on a high rise known as Camp Hill, once home to the town's more affluent citizens.

The former Armory Paymaster's house now served as a hospital, dominating the array of Union tents surrounding it. Medical staff from the various regiments rotated duty at the hospital and billeted in an adjacent building.

Both armies considered Harper's Ferry a key strategic location, pointing the way down the Potomac to Washington, D.C.. To the west lay

Bolivar Heights, not as high as Maryland Heights and Loudoun Heights, but, at nearly seven hundred feet, one of the tallest areas on the peninsula.

Jim breathed in the crisp, late-summer air. He intended to hold it in his lungs as long as he could; it would be the last fresh air he'd have today. He whispered a brief prayer, nodded to the rising sun, and gingerly picked his way down the steep embankment toward his temporary home.

Infantrymen gathered for morning assembly as Jim entered the Union encampment and hurried across the makeshift training ground to the hospital tents. He watched the young privates as they ran around the flat, grassy plain like a bunch of kids playing capture-the-flag.

Too young, too innocent, he thought. He shook his head. *These kids only think they're ready for combat.*

A hundred yards from the medical tents, Jim released his breath, tentatively sniffed the air and pulled his blouse over his nose. Pools of runny feces and vomit, blood and urine accumulated in ditches behind the tents before draining down the southern end of Camp Hill and into the Shenandoah River. As the day wore on, the oppressive heat would make the foul air even more disgusting.

Stinks worse than a skunk in a rainstorm, he thought.

Everyone knew it was only a matter of time before the Confederate Army arrived. Rumor was that Lee's Army of Northern Virginia had already left Frederick, Maryland, en route to Harper's Ferry. Once they arrived, there would be hell to pay, and more bodies to bury—likely at least one of those boys playing tag.

The medical tents were already overflowing with soldiers complaining of various ailments. Most of the complaints were phony, grounded in the soldiers' panicked realization that they would soon see battle. Jim would likely spend much of his day weeding out the fakers to make room for battle casualties.

"Gives a bad name to the men who are genuinely ill," he grumbled to no one but himself.

Jim thought of Napoleon. How many battles had he fought already? How many bodies had fallen on his battlefield?

I should write to him as soon as I get settled in, he thought, *but right now I have sick soldiers to attend to.* He took another deep breath, lifted the flap of the temporary hospital tent, and walked inside.

That afternoon, Jim's attention shifted to the active veterans who were a part of his study. Each showed varying degrees of what he considered war-related distress. The new recruits, like the ones who played outside, seemed oblivious to the upcoming danger—they were hungry for action. But the veterans in Jim's care already displayed signs of anxiety. They complained of increasingly violent nightmares; their hearts pounded like a galloping stampede. Indigestion was a constant companion. These symptoms were noticeably worse since they left Annapolis.

In stark contrast to the boys' naïveté, the veterans knew what was coming.

CHAPTER 21

September 8, 1862
Near Washington, D.C.
Smoke curled lazily from the remains of last night's campfire. No matter where Napoleon sat, the smoke followed him. His eyes watered, and not just from the smoldering fire. It had been a week since their battle at Bull Run, and Napoleon had hardly slept. Every time he closed his eyes, he fought the same battle. Gray uniforms falling all around. Carrying the wounded, boy after boy, and all of them dead. He splashed through ankle-deep blood, entrails, and body parts. As soon as he started to nod off—BLAM!—a head exploded in front of him, the remaining bodies still running, like banshees in the night.

A chill permeated the morning air; a reminder that fall was quickly approaching. Reuben sat next to Napoleon, wrapped in his greatcoat for warmth, staring at the faint embers. Behind them, tents dotted the barren field, white as tombstones. He cupped his hands around his mouth and blew hard against the coals. Each time he blew, the coals glowed brighter until small flames licked their way to the pile of kindling he'd laid on top of the fire.

"How long do you think we've got?" Reuben asked as he rubbed his hands for warmth.

"To rest, or to live?" Napoleon snorted. "I'm not sure which is better."

"Were we fools to enlist?"

Napoleon thought for a moment. "It seemed like the patriotic thing to do, didn't it? How could we have known?"

Reuben picked up a stray stick and stirred the fire. "I've killed rabbit, partridge, deer. But that was to feed my family." He opened his hands and stared at his palms as if they were covered in blood. "Mutilating humans with shells and cannonade makes no sense at all."

Two days ago, they'd crossed the Potomac at Long Bridge, marched through Washington, and set up camp about ten miles east. In the near distance, the Capital Dome shone brightly in the morning sun. It was supposed to be a respite, a chance to sleep without fear.

The first night, the liquor came out. Drunken

brawls followed. Pistols waved threateningly, their owners too drunk to take aim. Occasionally, the sound of gunfire pierced the air; for some reason, God saw fit to prevent them from killing one another.

For a moment, the smoke cleared. Napoleon looked out over the patchwork of freshly cut hay and split-rail fences that reminded him of home. He thought about his father.

He understood now: his father drank to drown the nightmares, but it never worked. Napoleon gambled: different addiction, same reasons. If he could just win enough money, he could—what? Buy a cure to erase the memories? A million dollars couldn't do that, but he kept trying anyway; as the pressure to pay his debts mounted, it seemed like everyone wanted a piece of him.

Desertion wasn't an option—at least not yet. But his goal had changed. He would keep fighting. Not for patriotism, not for glory. Just to stay alive and go home.

Less than ten days later, his plan would be put to the test.

CHAPTER 22

September 14, 1862

Harper's Ferry

The early-morning explosion pierced Jim's ears and jolted him awake.

Was that real or a dream? Jim struggled to clear his head.

That was close. Too close.

He scrambled for his boots.

"Jesus Christ!"

"What the hell?"

Curses flew from the tents around him.

On the previous night, Colonel Dixon S. Miles, the Union garrison's leader, had instructed several regiments to protect Bolivar Heights.

And now they're here.

The bugle's "Call to Arms" sounded across the encampment. The drums went silent; the air crackled with anticipation. Jim's heart thumped wildly as the Union commanders barked out their orders.

"Fall in!" Soldiers hurried to their positions, stood at attention, and awaited orders.

"Fix bayonets!" The men hastily fixed bayonets and shouldered their rifles.

"To the trenches!" In a surprisingly orderly fashion, the troops scrambled to the nearby trenches, hunkered down, and waited for further orders.

Jim hurried to the field hospital they'd established only yesterday in an abandoned barn. Dr. Larssen stood in the doorway and addressed the ten men of the regimental band, pressed into service as stretcher bearers.

"I want you to be ready with the ambulances." Larssen nodded toward the two- and four-horse-drawn carriages alongside the barn that would deliver casualties to the makeshift hospital. "Lieutenant Erskine, open the medical chests and lay out the surgical instruments. Make sure we have enough bandages and medicine."

Dr. Larssen turned to Jim. "Get as close as you can to the battle line and get an aid station ready."

Jim nodded, gathering up bandages, tourniquets, and a bottle of whiskey. They were all the supplies he'd need—just enough to stabilize the wounded before moving them to the field hospital.

The morning passed slowly. The men in the trenches twitched and waited for orders as occasional cannon fire echoed across the valley. One shot seemed like dozens. Young men who had only a month before walked behind a plow now cowered behind the trench walls, their eyes wide with fear, desperately seeking a way out and a path home.

By early afternoon it was too late to run as the Confederates at Loudoun Heights opened fire on Bolivar Heights and Camp Hill. An hour later, artillery fire erupted from Jackson's forces on School House Ridge. Confederate soldiers at Maryland Heights joined in shortly after: the Union forces faced a three-way attack.

Cannonballs whistled past. An occasional shell detonated in the trenches, heedless of the men's meager defenses. When the shell burst, its densely packed shrapnel flew in every direction, shredding bits of flesh and blood as it embedded itself in the crumbling dirt walls.

From his position just beyond the artillery fire, Jim heard the screams of the wounded.

"Doc!" a soldier hollered. "He's hit bad!"

A panicked wail from another. "My leg! It's gone!"

But there was nothing Jim could do until the shelling subsided.

At dusk, the Rebel fire eased, then stopped. Jim and Erskine cautiously crawled to the trenches. Bodies sprawled everywhere, most covered in blood, some missing various body parts. Erskine fell to his knees, vomiting. Jim put a steadying hand on his shoulder and forced down the bile in his own throat. The reality of war hit hard, a gut-wrenching punch that far outweighed anything Jim could have imagined.

Armed with bandages and whiskey, they searched for injured survivors, while the able-bodied soldiers swiftly organized themselves into a line of battle and prepared for a counterattack.

When the Rebel lines stayed quiet, Union soldiers relaxed and lowered their rifles, but kept a watchful eye on the Heights.

Out of nowhere came a blood-curdling war cry; the Confederate cavalry charged from the woods just beyond School House Ridge. Their horses' mouths frothed from their bits and the reins the Rebs held in a death grip, splattering bits of spittle on the riders. Dust clouded the air; bits of dirt and grass flew from the horses' hooves. They were mere yards from the Federal troops when the Union soldiers panicked, broke rank, and fired into the confusion. Men stampeded everywhere; some defended their ground, some ran for cover, some high-tailed it for home. It was impossible to distinguish Union fire from Confederate fire. Soldiers endlessly loaded and fired their guns. Bullets flew everywhere, and there was no safe place on the plains above Harper's Ferry.

As the gunfire subsided, Jim and Erskine once again rushed out to retrieve the injured. In the heap of bodies, Jim spied what remained of a familiar face: Jed Acker, a private in Company H. Sprawled face-up on the bullet-riddled ground, a gaping hole occupied the space where his left eye had been. Jim knelt beside him and touched Acker's neck.

This is silly. Jim shook his head. *Of course he's dead.* But he had to check.

His friendship with Acker went back to their early youth. They'd both attended grade school down the road from Jim's house. A one-room building, the schoolhouse was built on his father's property; Jed's family lived just over the nearby hill. Jed, who was two or three years younger than Jim, fished for hours with Napoleon and Jim in the creek behind Jed's house.

And now he was gone.

Blood pooled underneath Jed's head where the bullet had exited. Jim stood, not wanting to believe what lay before him, then crouched again, closed Acker's remaining eye, and called for the stretcher bearers. Now it was personal.

In a low building behind the burned-out shell of the Armory, Colonel Miles met with his senior officers for a council of war. Miles was not the highest-ranking officer in the room. That distinction belonged to Brigadier General Julius White, who had arrived in Harper's Ferry a few weeks prior, but he followed military protocol and put himself under Miles' command rather than challenge Miles' authority.

Yesterday, Colonel Miles' position was firm. "General Wool has ordered that we defend Harpers Ferry at all costs. I am told reinforcements are two days from here. Surely we can hold out that long."

"If we could recapture Maryland Heights, we'd have a chance of winning," suggested White.

But now, Confederate troops had the Union forces trapped in a bowl-like valley near Bolivar Heights. The Union was in a terrible situation, reflected in the tone of the officers' meeting. Confusion and near desperation filled the room.

"We need to evacuate immediately," advised one officer. "Morale among the troops is deteriorating. Our only choice is to escape and regroup."

"Not a chance in hell." Miles paced the room. At the age of fifty-seven, Miles still held a commanding presence. He was tall and slender, with a full head of gray hair and a long beard that was meticulously trimmed. His eyes burned with a fiery determination.

"Are you mad?" shouted an officer. "We're surrounded and running out of ammunition. How do you propose we defend ourselves?"

Miles calmly approached the officer. "You surrender at your own peril, sir," he growled. "As for this officer and his men," he swept his arm across the room, "our job is to hold Harper's Ferry to the last. And that I will do."

CHAPTER 23

September 15, 1862

Harper's Ferry, WV

It was well before sunrise when Ruth pushed back the tent flap and stepped onto the dew-soaked grass. She wore a stained white cotton slave dress—the only dress she owned — and carried a dingy head wrap in her hands. To the east, the sky was slowly brightening, illuminating the Potomac River as it wound its way towards Washington, D.C. She made her way to the river's edge, splashing the chill water on her face and arms. Inhaling deeply, she tied the head wrap around her black curls, filled her lungs with the brisk fall air and thanked God for her freedom.

In the distance, a rooster crowed, welcoming the day. A gunshot now and then broke the quiet of the morning. Otherwise, all was still.

She made her way to Camp Hill, just coming alive with the bustle of contrabands like her— runaway slaves who were happy to help the Union soldiers any way they could, in return for protection from the Confederates and slave-owners.

The women cooked, mended, ironed, and soothed injured and sick soldiers at the hospital. The men transported goods, built fortifications, carried the wounded, and buried the dead. Every one of them lived in fear of the Confederate Army currently camped on Maryland Heights above Harper's Ferry. Their goal was to drive out the Union, recapture Harper's Ferry and the contrabands, and sell them back into slavery.

"Mornin' Miz Goddard." Ruth nodded to the woman who met her at the hospital's front door.

Abba Goddard, a Mainer who had followed her hometown regiment to the front, smiled. "A good morning it is," she said, and beckoned Ruth inside.

Abba closed the door, leaving her smile behind. "We've had a hard night," she said. "The surgeons worked most it." She shook her head. "Too many amputations. Too many deaths. I don't know how they can abide it."

Ruth nodded. She'd seen a lot of death in her life. Babies born too soon. Children dying from overwork and undernourishment. Entire families brought down by dogs or bullets as they tried to escape. The day she said goodbye to her parents was the worst. Being too old and feeble for the strenuous travel, they stayed behind.

Her job at the hospital was easy by comparison: sit by the soldiers' bedsides, hold their hands, sing her mother's favorite hymns, pray for God's mercy. Many a boy seemed to mistake her for his mother in the last moments before death. It didn't matter—she could be anyone's mother when needed.

Throughout the day, she did other chores. Changed dressings, fed broth to feverish soldiers, hauled water, scrubbed floors, gladly doing whatever was needed. All the while, the cannonade boomed in the distance. Artillery rained down from Maryland Heights like sharks in a feeding frenzy. Neither soldier nor citizen was safe from the Confederate fury.

"Have you had word from Dennis?" Ruth jumped as Abba interrupted her thoughts.

Ruth shook her head. "Nary a thing." Her husband had left camp a few days earlier in search of a way north and a path to freedom. Living under the protection of the Union forces had been the safest option until now. But with the Confederates bearing down, it was time to run once again.

The most important thing was to protect their daughter, Denna. Named after her father, Denna was the very image of Ruth's mother. A sharp pang pierced Ruth's heart as she thought of the parents she would likely never see again.

She was hauling buckets of water when she heard Dr. Banyon calling from behind the hospital, where they performed surgeries.

"Ruth! I need you now!" he shouted. He motioned for her to come, his hands covered in blood.

Ruth rushed to his side, keeping her eyes on his face so she wouldn't have to look at the bloodied soldier who lay on the makeshift table.

"Yes, sir, Dr. Banyon," she said, out of breath from running.

He pointed to the soldier on the table. She took a deep breath and looked: his left leg was a bloody stump, a tourniquet wrapped just above his missing knee.

"I need this sewed up right away," Dr. Banyon said. "Needle and thread are over there."

Ruth gulped and shook her head. "I can't do it, sir. I'll hurt him."

Dr. Banyon put a bloody hand on her shoulder.

"You have to, Ruth, or he's going to die. Everyone else is busy with their own patient."

She quickly gathered up the needle and threaded it. "What do I do?"

Dr. Banyon had already moved on to another patient. "It's just like fixing a hole in a pair of trousers," he said. "Sew it tight and bandage it up, then loosen the rag tied around his leg and make sure the stitches hold."

Ruth hesitated. The boy on the table moaned; she pulled away.

"He won't feel it, Ruth," said Dr. Banyon. "The ether hasn't worn off yet."

As the afternoon wore on, the fighting escalated.

"We've got to set up a field hospital out on Bolivar Heights," Dr. Banyon said to Ruth as she sewed up a wound. "You're coming with us."

They worked through the night amidst the echoes of exploding cannonade and firing rifles. The cries for help, the screams of pain were nearly more than Ruth could take. When they ran out of bandages, she tore pieces of cloth from her dress to help stanch the bleeding.

It was nearly dawn when she felt Abba's hand grab her shoulder.

"Hurry, Ruth!" she said, her voice a panicked whisper. "We've got to get you and your friends out of here."

Ruth's heart jumped. "What's happened?"

"There's a rumor that the Union is about to surrender. Hurry! The Confederates will be here any minute to take back their slaves."

One word jumped into Ruth's head.

Denna!

After taking the Union soldiers as prisoners, the Confederates would target the contrabands. No one at the camp would be safe. *Denna* would not be safe.

Ruth pulled away from Abba. "I have to get Denna!"

"You can't." Abba caught Ruth's dress and pulled her back. "There's nothing but Confederates between here and the Armory. They'll take you too."

An image of Denna struggling in the arms of some Rebel soldier jumped into Ruth's mind. Her dress tore off as she pulled away from Abba; she was a lioness, intent on protecting her young.

"Denna!" she screamed frantically. "Denna!"

Dr. Banyon grabbed her by the waist; Erskine held her legs.

"Don't be a fool, Ruth," Dr. Banyon said. "We'll have to pray the good Lord protects her until we can get her back."

Ruth went limp, crying, screaming, pleading for her baby. But she knew they were right. There was nothing they could do.

CHAPTER 24

September 15, 1862

Harper's Ferry

His arms loaded down with medical supplies for the battle lines, Jim struggled to raise the tent flap. Although the sun was not up yet, he was already hard at work, treating the wounded and bracing for more, while snatching what bits of sleep he could. In time, he and the men of Company H would mourn the death of their friend, Jim Acker. But they had a score to settle first.

Inside the tent, Jim bent to set down the medical supplies just as an officer tore open the flap from outside and stormed in, nearly knocking Jim to the floor.

"Where the hell are my men?" The officer glared at Jim and pinched his narrow lips tightly closed. Jim immediately recognized the accent of privilege: Captain Peleg Anthony.

"Good morning, Captain Pegleg." He had no intention of hiding his disgust for the man.

Anthony glared at Jim, but gave no answer. As if he'd just noticed the hospital odors, he pinched his nose with his thumb and forefinger. "This place stinks like a piss-hole," he mumbled.

Anthony scanned the room like a wolf searching for its next meal.

"Who's in charge here?" He slammed his fist on a nearby table; glass vials clinked, bandages fell to the floor.

Dr. Larssen had been watching the exchange between Jim and Anthony with interest, but now he strode forward, extending his hand. "Dr. Jacob Larssen, head surgeon of the 111th New York Regiment," he said. "How can I help you?"

"You're keeping my soldiers from their duty." Anthony broadly gestured. "I want them released this minute."

Dr. Larssen scanned the room. "You have all those who are able," he said. "These men are not currently fit for duty."

"What about this man?" Anthony pointed a scrawny finger at Private Nichols, who sat upright in his bed, still mumbling to himself.

"You can see he's not fit for duty," Dr. Larssen said. "I've placed him on medical leave until he improves."

"Not fit for duty?" Anthony exploded. "There's nothing wrong with this man other than being a malingerer and a coward. I demand you release him to me immediately."

"I'm afraid you don't have that authority." Dr. Larssen kept his voice even. "The medical corps does not take orders from the military. You'll have to speak to the Surgeon General," he said. "If he has time for you."

Anthony's face was purple with rage as he turned his back on Dr. Larssen. "I'll do that," he snarled. On his way to the door, he pushed past Jim. "And you," he sneered. "I'm going to make your life hell."

It was a battle they were certain they'd win, and the men of the 111th had been up before sunrise, dressed, armed, and ready for the fight.

Along School House Ridge and west of Camp Hill, they could just make out General Jackson's massive army lined up with their artillery at the ready. On the northern shore of the Potomac, at Maryland Heights, stood more Confederate artillery, manned and ready to fire.

Across the Shenandoah, the view confirmed the dismal news: In the middle of the night, the Confederates had lined the far riverbank at the foot of Loudoun Heights with heavy artillery. Rebel soldiers stood by their cannons, torches in hand, and prepared to fire on command.

The Confederate forces surrounded thirteen thousand Union troops under the command of Colonel Dixon Miles, leaving them with no means of escape.

Heavy artillery fire exploded from the Confederate guns.

The Union troops waited for orders, but none came.

"Where the hell is Colonel Miles?" a lieutenant shouted. He fixed the bayonet onto his musket, ready to attack.

Another soldier nodded towards a nearby house. "All the big bugs are in there, trying to figure out how to save their hides."

"Jesus, there's Rebs everywhere," said a third.

"We're buzzard fodder."

Inside the house, Colonel Miles and his brigadiers held a council-of-war.

"We're out of long-range ammunition," he told his subordinates. "There's no way we can withstand another attack." There was no choice but to surrender.

At nine a.m., Miles and his brigadiers sat astride their horses while the Union army raised white flags of surrender along its lines.

"What the hell?" The Union soldiers couldn't believe what they saw.

"We can win this!" shouted another. "Miles is a goddamn coward!"

The ground shook as a Confederate shell exploded just in front of the assembled officers. Shrapnel ripped through Colonel Miles' leg as his horse fell to the ground. The brigadiers didn't move, paralyzed by shock and disbelief.

"If that isn't God Almighty showing his displeasure, I'm a goddamned Reb." The soldier spat in the dust, his fellow soldiers voicing their "amens."

The order came down from their commanders: Stack your arms and prepare to surrender.

"Are you shittin' me?"

"What the hell?"

"Goddamned Miles sold out. He's a traitor and a coward."

"I don't care if we're surrounded. Don't care if we're out of ammunition either. Death is a hell of a lot more honorable than surrender."

That evening, acting commander Brigadier General White rode out to Stonewall Jackson and formally surrendered.

CHAPTER 25

September 16, 1862

Harper's Ferry

Damp morning mist clung to the valley around Harper's Ferry as Erskine struggled into the hospital tent, manning the front end of a stretcher that carried yet another wounded soldier. Sweat drenched the armpits of his uniform blouse; dirt and blood covered his arms.

"You won't believe what Miles has done." Erskine and his partner lowered the heavy stretcher and moved its occupant to a vacant cot; his breath was ragged from the exertion.

Dim lantern light flickered against the tent walls. Erskine could taste the coppery tang of blood that hung in the humid early-morning air. Both Jim and Larssen bent over their patients; Jim sutured a fresh wound, Larssen's amputating saw rasped through broken bone.

Jim looked up from his patient and raised an eyebrow. "Fish-eyed again?" Jim asked. Miles was notorious for his constant drunken state; he'd been relieved of duty once before. Jim tied off the sutures and wound ragged strips of cloth around his patient's bloodied arm. He and Larssen had spent most of the night tending to the wounded; the only thing he cared about right now was sleep.

"Worse," Erskine muttered. "He gave us up when we were about to win."

The sound of surgical instruments at work filled the silence as Erskine's words sank in. His news was jarring, but the surgeons couldn't pause and consider the ramifications. Too many lives depended on their quick, efficient work.

"Miles is a coward," Larssen grumbled, the thunk of the leg he'd just amputated providing the exclamation mark to his opinion.

"We surrendered?" Jim's heart jumped in his chest. What exactly would that mean for the 111th? Would they go to a prison camp? What about his patients? Some of them couldn't be moved. Did Robert E. fuckin' Lee even care?

"The big shots are still discussing terms." Erskine wiped his face on his sleeve and dropped onto a cot. "But Miles won't get a say in that."

"Did they relieve him of his command?" *Son-*

of-a-bitch deserves it.

Erskine sniggered. "You might say that. They shot his horse clean out from under him and blew off Dixon's leg. He died this morning." He looked around the tent and lowered his voice. "Some guys are claiming it was his own men who killed him. Serves him right, though. The man's a damned know-it-all who knows nothing." Erskine spat at the tent flap. "His stupidity killed a bunch of men, and now we're all prisoners."

"Not to mention these fellas." Jim swept his arm across the row of amputees. "Who knows what will happen to them? Might live, might not. Crippled for whatever life they have left."

"How long do you suppose we have before the Rebs round us up?" Larssen asked.

Erskine shook his head. "Not sure. Last I saw, the Rebs were busy looting our supplies. They have our weapons, our artillery, and our food. I imagine they'll have us lined up and out of here by tomorrow."

As the morning passed, the brightening sun burned off the morning mist, and Confederate soldiers moved through the Union encampment collecting arms and prisoners. Two sentries entered the medical tent, confiscated everyone's weapons, and stood guard as the surgeons hurried to stabilize as many patients as they could before the Confederates hustled them out of Harper's Ferry.

Rumors spread that they would go back to New York, and maybe home, while the big bugs negotiated an exchange of prisoners. Could he leave his patients so he could visit his family? Jim wondered. It seemed a selfish act.

As the prisoners formed up and waited for the Confederates' next orders, the news came that Colonel Dixon S. Miles was dead.

Not one of his soldiers felt remorse for what they believed was a most cowardly act.

Jim, you're like a scared little boy... his father's words echoed in his head. He, too, had believed he was smarter. Less than a month in the Army had shown him just how wrong he was. Was he any better than Colonel Miles?

Our first foray into battle, and I have already witnessed more death and destruction than any man should bear. Too many bodies litter the battlefield, too many souls perish from disease caused by fouled water and tainted food. Amputation, a word that should rarely escape a doctor's mouth, has become a common utterance. It is often the only course for saving a man's life, although I am uncertain it is always the most desirable choice.

The result of our valiant effort at the Ferry was the surrender and capture of 13,000 Union soldiers courtesy of the coward, Colonel Dixon Miles. Where we go next is anyone's guess.

CHAPTER 26

September 16-20, 1862

Harper's Ferry to Annapolis

"There they are!" A young boy wagged his finger at the line of prisoners as they passed through town. He curved his hands around his mouth and booed.

"Cowards!" The accusation came from deep within the crowd. Jeers spread up and down the street. Jim's horse ducked its head, hit by a large glob of spit. The taunt became a chant. "Harper's Ferry Cowards! Harper's Ferry Cowards!"

The prisoners bristled under the verbal assault. No one seemed to care that it had not been their idea to surrender. The man who deserved that honor was already dead.

As an officer, Jim rode his horse, following the ambulances that carried the sick and wounded. The hundred-mile trek gave him plenty of time to reflect on his first month in the army. In one month, he'd already seen soldiers who would never be the same. The boys who marched from Auburn with fire in their eyes were already old men, their eyes jaded with visions no one should have to see.

Captain Anthony rode alongside the marching prisoners, his eyes searching for the poor fool who might fall out of line. He sat ramrod-straight on his personal and ornately decorated "war horse" that stood a good two hands higher than the rest.

"Looks like Pegleg's on his high horse again," sneered a prisoner who staggered from the long march.

Captain Anthony had ordered all ambulatory patients to march in the prisoner lines, regardless of their medical status. Although Jim vehemently protested, Private Nichols marched as well, although it was obvious the boy still did not know where he was.

"I'll get you home, soldier," Jim whispered in Nichols' ear as they set out from Harper's Ferry.

Captain Anthony was going to be a problem. Jim wished he'd kept his mouth shut at the field hospital in Harper's Ferry. But there was something about Anthony's smug, arrogant behavior that set him off.

Somebody has to stand up for the enlisted men, he mused. *It might as well be me.*

Erskine pulled up alongside Jim. "Where do you think they'll send us?" The question had yet to be answered, but speculation had run rampant since the surrender in Harper's Ferry. Usually, they gave captured soldiers parole—they "released" them if they promised not to take up arms again until the Union and Confederacy arranged a formal prisoner exchange. But where would the Confederates send them?

"Who knows?" Jim shrugged and thought of Maggie and Jessie. He still hoped that they would go back to Auburn until the armies arranged an exchange. "But wherever the enlisted men go, I'm sure the medical staff will stay in Annapolis and tend to the more seriously injured men."

And Nichols will be one of them, even if I have to go to the Surgeon General to ensure it.

Four days later, the miles-long contingent of prisoners reported to Camp Parole in Annapolis.

Later that afternoon, Jim and Erskine settled in the medical tent. Although they had moved the more seriously wounded to the city hospital, on the former grounds of the U.S. Naval Academy, the 111th's men with minor injuries or illness stayed in the tents on the grounds of Camp Parole. Jim kept a wary eye on Private Nichols, tying him to his bed so he wouldn't wander off.

"How did you get Pegleg to go along with that?" Erskine pointed to Nichols, who sat placidly on his cot, talking to himself.

"I told him Nichols might be coming down with measles," Jim smirked and winked. "I don't think Pegleg's going to get anywhere near him."

Jim scanned the small medical tent; they might as well still be at Harper's Ferry, given their surroundings. Both sat at a desk piled high with patient notes, sipping from their communal flask of whiskey.

"You think they'll send us home to Camp Cayuga?" Erskine looked hopeful.

Jim shook his head. "I heard we're going to Camp Douglas until the brass can work out an exchange." Jim repeated the rumors he'd heard when they reached Annapolis. *No trip home, no chance to see my girls.*

"Where in hell's half-acre is that?"

"Chicago."

Erskine rolled his eyes.

"Used to be a Union recruitment center. Until now it's been a POW camp for the Confederates, but I imagine they'll move all those boys out before we get there." Jim sighed.

"The enlisted men are leaving on the twenty-second. The medical team will stay here a few more days, but once we sort the sick and injured men, we'll head for Chicago, too."

That means I'll have less than three days to get help for Nichols.

"I've made some inquiries," Jim said. "There's a hospital for insane soldiers in Washington that might admit our Private Nichols."

Erskine shook his head. "I've heard about insane asylums. Are you sure you want to do that to Private Nichols?" His eyes widened. "You're not going to let them lock him up and throw away the key, are you?"

"You know I wouldn't do that," Jim said. "Nichols and I have an appointment with the director tomorrow."

The next morning, Jim sat in front of the desk of Dr. Pliny Earle, director of the Government Hospital for Insane Soldiers, having delivered Nichols to their medical staff for assessment. Atop a hill in Washington that overlooked the Potomac and Anacostia Rivers, it was the only federal mental health hospital in the United States.

Dorothea Dix founded the hospital in 1855, and its mission was to care for insane soldiers and veterans. Architects designed the buildings with mental patients in mind—they were light and airy with plenty of space, long corridors and large windows that provided a sense of calm and openness.

"I've heard excellent reports about your treatment here," Jim said. "I hope you can give Private Nichols the help he needs. He certainly isn't fit to fight in his current condition."

Dr. Earle studied Jim's written notes on Nichols.

Leaning back in his chair and putting his hands behind his head, he said, "You know that, until recently, they considered war a treatment for insanity A lot of the medical community believed fighting for their country would give insane men purpose and a common cause, thus reducing their insanity."

Jim's eyes widened. "Apparently, those doctors have never been at war."

Earle straightened and leaned forward, forearms on his desk. "A different viewpoint led to the founding of this hospital: we base our mission on the principles of moral treatment, and that people can treat insanity humanely.

"It is my opinion—and the opinion of this hospital—that insane soldiers are neither cowards nor malingerers," he continued. "Battle scars these men as deeply as it scars those with physical wounds; they truly need our help."

And I've only just begun to understand that, thought Jim. *Perhaps that knowledge is something I can apply to my study.*

Later that afternoon, Jim returned to camp without Nichols.

Captain Anthony was waiting for him.

"How dare you smuggle one of my soldiers into a mental hospital?" Anthony waved his hands, pacing back and forth. "You said he had measles!"

"He may have measles for all I know," Jim shrugged. "The hospital will determine that."

"You're a damned liar!" Anthony ranted. "You know there's nothing wrong with him—he's a malingerer, and you know it."

Jim squared his shoulders and glared at Anthony. "What I know is that this man needs help," he said. "How can you expect him to fight when he hardly recognizes his own name?"

"The man's a faker," Anthony huffed.

"Doesn't matter. He's in the hospital now, and you can't have him back."

CHAPTER 27

September 22, 1862
Camp Parole, Annapolis, Maryland

Dear Maggie,

The last letter I wrote you I directed you to write to Baltimore and instead of going there we went to Annapolis, the capital of Maryland, and we are ordered to be ready to march tomorrow and it is said we are to go to Chicago which I think is probable as there are no accommodations for us here. Some of our officers have telegraphed to Wm. H. Seward to have us sent to the barracks at Auburn. Whether it will be so or not, I can't say. I think we will go to Chicago.

Jim paused. Could it be only a month since he'd said goodbye to his family and marched off to war? It felt like a lifetime. Back then, he was confident, ready to serve, and eager to extend his study to the active military.

Had he known that the Union officers were as much an enemy as the Confederates, he might have stayed home. It seemed they all valued rank and status more highly than honor and country. At every turn, the big brass got in his way, especially Captain Anthony, who, true to his promise, had made it his mission to make Jim's life miserable.

And now they were all prisoners, thanks to the cowardly Colonel Miles.

He thought about his girls. What would they be doing now? Did they miss him as much as he missed them? When he left, Maggie still mourned the loss of their son. For that matter, he did too. He needed to hear from her, to know she was all right.

Does life go on as usual in Ira? Now that their boys were prisoners of war, had feelings changed? He imagined a more somber mood than he'd seen at the send-off ceremony.

And where would they end up as they awaited a prisoner exchange? Surely the big bugs would have the compassion to send them home to Camp Cayuga instead of a thousand miles further from home than they already were.

Jim tried not to dwell on it. Soldiers suffering from dysentery and malnourishment, and those who had suffered minor injuries, filled the field hospital. Thank goodness he'd got help for Private Nichols.

He had been up all night tending patients. He was tired, frustrated, and more homesick than he wanted to admit. The pre-dawn air was crisp, but it wouldn't be long before the sun made the hospital an oven.

... We have had a long and hard march from Harper's Ferry and going a long distance out of our way. We started on Tuesday morning, the 15th, and arrived here last night, the 21st. I am not homesick, but I want to see you and Jessie more than I can tell... I never knew before how much I was attached to my family and how much I loved you and Jessie.

"I heard the Colonel say we're definitely going to Chicago," said Erskine. Already, sweat stained his uniform.

Jim jumped at the interruption. He glared at Erskine, then reminded himself that Tom had been up all night and was probably as cranky as he was. He took a deep breath.

"Sounds about right," he said. "I can hear them now: 'Might as well send 'em west a few hundred miles.' They'll end up in cushy officers' quarters while the rest of our boys suffer."

A nearby patient woke and sprang from his cot. He looked around the tent, his eyes wide. "Where in hell am I?"

"In the bloody hospital!" Jim growled.

Erskine rolled his eyes at Jim as he strode toward the boy's cot. "What can I do for you, soldier?"

Jim went back to writing.

We are waiting for orders... How I want to hear from you and Jessie. When I get to some place to stay, I want your and Jessie's pictures, and I will send you mine as soon as I can get it taken...

"I'm back." Dr. Larssen strolled into the hospital after a brief nap. The staff rotated their three-hour sleep schedule, giving each man a chance to rest.

"Your turn, Jim." He gestured toward the empty cot set up in the far corner.

Jim threw his pen onto the table and jumped to his feet. "Why in the blue blazes can't people leave me alone?"

Larssen held up a hand. "Whoa, Jim! No need to snap my head off." He pointed to the corner. "Go sleep. We'll talk later."

Jim dropped his head. "Sorry." He scooped up his pen and paper and retreated.

As he settled on the cot, he laid the letter on top of his journal, dipped his pen in the ink bottle, and continued.

I want to see how Jessie looks. The little bird, she is such a good little girl. Tell her that her Pa loves her and thinks of her often. Good bye Maggie. I will tell you where to write when we get settled for good. Goodbye again.

Yours as ever,

J.D. Banyon

Chicago, he thought. *Why on earth would they send us to Chicago? He'd heard of the detention camp there—Camp Douglas. Was that where they were going?*

His eyes felt so heavy. He closed them, but before he went to sleep, he made one last prayer— for his girls and for his safe return home.

CHAPTER 28

September 14-18, 1862
Western Maryland

He thought seeing his father die was the worst thing he would ever witness.

He was wrong.

The nightmares wouldn't leave him, and every day of battle added to the images that haunted him. His dreams were a war museum filled with artifacts that came to life as he slept.

General Lee's crossing of the Potomac into Maryland on September 4th shattered the brief respite from battle. His goal: move the pressure from war-torn Virginia to Washington and Baltimore, and capture the Union garrison at Harper's Ferry. If his troops could loot the Maryland farms for food, if he could sway Maryland to join the Confederacy, he might yet turn the tide in favor of the South.

Ten days later, McClellan's army marched through Frederick in pursuit of Lee.

Napoleon gasped for air as he struggled to climb the steep face of South Mountain. Massive boulders, covered in a slippery film of sand and pine needles, impeded the regiment's progress; fog hung in the mountain air, blanketing the trees and blurring the landscape.

As they passed through Turner's Gap, gunshots cracked. Bullets whizzed through the air, but from where? The sound echoed through the hollows, making it hard to know their direction. Napoleon crouched behind a boulder, ready to fire. The order came to close up ranks; and the men cautiously moved forward. Load, aim, fire. Load, aim, fire. The rhythmic movements had become instinctive. The Confederates retreated.

But victory came at a price. It was the bloodiest day in American history. Their commander, General Reno, was dead; the cost in casualties was a draw.

That evening, Napoleon sat by a small campfire near Turner's Gap. He jumped at every crack from the burning branches. His hands trembled as he cleaned his musket. Someone's whiskey flask lay discarded beside him; he stared at it and wondered if drinking oneself into oblivion might be the answer after all.

Canteens, torn haversacks, and the bodies of men who would fight no longer littered the trail behind him. Stars glimmered through the smoky haze, and Napoleon wondered: How much further until they reached the summit, and would he live to see it?

On the seventeenth of September, the 35th New York Volunteers reached the banks of the Antietam, where they'd first battled Lee's Army fourteen months ago. *It's like we're marching in ever-dizzying circles*, thought Napoleon as he tightened the strap on his haversack. *Rebs chasing Johnnies. Johnnies chasing Rebs in an endless dance of death.*

Rifles in place, they marched through the cornfield, knowing the stalks offered little protection.

The Rebels opened fire; three soldiers fell dead. Men dropped to their bellies as Confederate shells screamed overhead, shredding cornstalks and leaving behind smoke and fire. Napoleon fired, reloaded, fired again. A man to his left screamed for his mother. No one could hear the lieutenant's commands.

The Confederates had taken cover in a shallow ditch known as the Sunken Road. It provided just enough cover for them to duck down and avoid enemy fire, and enough of a sight line to mow down the approaching Union forces. At midday, McClellan drew back with heavy losses.

But later that day, the Confederate advantage became a weakness when the Union maneuvered into a position that allowed direct fire into the ditch.

The Rebs emerged from their hiding place and charged. Gray raced toward Blue, screaming like banshees. Blue ran forward, muskets firing. Men fell, dead or dying. Napoleon glanced to his right, nodded at Reuben and moved forward. *Load, aim, fire. Load, aim, fire.* He knew the drill so well he didn't need to stop.

By nightfall, the fighting had subsided.

Napoleon's hands shook as he took a deep drink from his canteen. Even the water tasted of gun smoke and blood. His face was wet with sweat—or was it tears? He didn't remember crying.

From his position he could see the Sunken Road, filled with bodies both blue and gray, tangled in an awkward embrace. As darkness fell, McClellan's army lay on their arms, desperate for sleep.

The next morning, Lee's army slipped back into Virginia. Although the battle at Antietam was a Union victory, nearly 23,000 soldiers were killed, wounded, or captured, and Lee's detention of McClellan's forces had allowed the Confederate victory at Harper's Ferry.

The regiment made camp near Sharpsburg at Horseshoe Bend on the Potomac River. Here they would stay for a brief rest while they recuperated from the devastating battle. Now their battle was with contaminated water, which caused severe diarrhea and fever. They wore tattered clothing and shoes worn down to nothing.

Napoleon sat beneath a tree, his musket across his knees, alert for enemy fire, although it was rumored the Rebs had long since retreated. The stars were out again, cold and distant. He didn't feel like a hero. He felt like a survivor.

CHAPTER 29

September 29, 1862
Camp Douglas, Chicago, Illinois

Dear Jim,

It looks like you were right: we will spend our internment at Camp Douglas. The place is a nasty, muddy, sickly hole, thanks to the heavy downpour that has pounded us since our arrival. It smells like an overflowing latrine.

Let me relate what has happened with the regiment since you saw me last. As you know, on the 24th of this month, we were ordered to the harbor where we boarded a steamer, traveled up Chesapeake Bay, and arrived in Baltimore about 3 p.m. From there we were marched to the railroad station and loaded onto cattle cars still covered in dung, leaving a slippery floor and the stench of a cow barn after a long winter.

Well, Jim, our hope that we would go home was wrong, but as the railroads diverged in

Nostalgia

Harrisburg, our train turned west. I imagine even now you can hear the groans and complaints from over twelve-thousand men, wondering if we were being sent to fight the Sioux uprising in Minnesota. I almost wish that were the case.

All along the way west, crowds gathered to cheer us. Nearly every town's railway station had a platform filled with well-wishers. Even in the countryside, people lined the tracks, waving flags and cheering. I can tell you our spirits were considerably raised as we chugged through the rain to our destination.

I do hope the big bugs will not waste our precious time debating our exchange. In addition to the mud and stink, the camp itself is a disgrace. After the last Confederate prisoners left, they made sure to make the place uninhabitable, although it was no palace when they were here either. Rotted food and tattered bits of Confederate uniforms still litter the ground, rats the size of small rabbits lay dead on the field while their living brothers scamper through the filth and hide under the barracks along with a host of other critters, hoping for scraps and whatever else they can find.

Speaking of barracks, the Rebs made a fair

mess of them before they left. They broke up all the bunks and burned them, then shat and pissed all over the barracks floors. It will take days to make them livable.

By the time we arrived, the only place left was the horse stable. Eight men crammed in a fourteen-by-eight-foot stall is far from ideal, but, believe it or not, the stable is in better condition than the barracks.

The medical compound wasn't in much better shape when we arrived. The Rebs destroyed every bottle of medicine and stole every bit of our supplies. There were no dressings, no medical instruments, and of course not a drop of whiskey. Dr. McVickar and I spent most of the day cleaning up the mess and organizing what we could. Thank God our medical provisions came the next day.

Jim, I have never seen such disarray and disorganization as we have here. I can only hope that by the time you arrive, we will have everything in order and working smoothly.

Yours Sincerely,

Tom

Sergeant Thomas Erskine, medical assistant

Jim stared at his new orders. *I should never have left Harper's Ferry,* he thought. A stubborn bout of pneumonia kept Larssen hospitalized at the Ferry. Jim wished he'd insisted on staying with Larssen until his health improved. Today he received orders to report to Chicago two weeks early because of a severe typhoid outbreak at the Camp Douglas internment camp, which took him even further from his commanding officer.

Given the deplorable conditions Erskine described, it didn't surprise Jim to hear soldiers were getting sick. He was not feeling well himself.

No matter. He shrugged. *I have my orders, and there is nothing to be done until I get to Camp Douglas. Hopefully, I will have improved by that time.*

It was a long, lonely ride on the train going from Baltimore to Chicago. The train flew through the countryside, bleak and empty without the well-wishers Erskine had described. Jim remembered the train ride after their send-off in Auburn. It seemed a lifetime ago, when everyone on board, from bright-eyed boys to resolute men, was eager to defend their country. Then the mood was almost jolly; the train filled with conversation and laughter.

Was that only weeks past?

Two days later, Jim sat on his horse outside the gates of Camp Douglas. Just the short horse ride from the train station had soaked him to the bone. Raindrops dripped from his hat and down the back of his neck. He felt like he'd never get warm.

I'm frozen, feverish and wetter than a drowned rat, Jim thought, *and the next few weeks won't be any better.*

"Believe it or not, the place is in a lot better shape than it was," said Erskine as he met Jim by the front gates.

The rain had eased some, and Jim surveyed the area that would be his home until the big bugs settled their differences.

A long brick building that served as post headquarters stretched east to west and dominated the front of Garrison Square. The other three sides of the square held the officers' quarters, although many officers billeted with a local family since they were required to pay for their own room and board. The parade grounds, normally smoothed and leveled for troop drills and practice, occupied the center.

To their far right, the enlisted men's barracks

teetered precariously on stilts, providing a space for mud and mold to accumulate. Rats, moles, voles— even an occasional raccoon or possum—made their homes there.

The 90x24-foot buildings, arranged in groups of four on the western side of Camp Douglas, were weathered-gray and desperately in need of repairs. They reminded Jim of the "Irish shanties" he'd seen built along the Erie Canal at home. Broken bunks littered the barracks, a small sign of the mess the Union faced upon arrival. It could be weeks before the wood dried enough to burn.

"Our men are in the horse stables in back," said Erskine. "The rest of the barracks were already full."

Jim shook his head. "I can see why so many men are sick."

"Hospital Square's over there," Tom said, pointing at a large compound to his left. "Hospital is on your left, medical officers' quarters are on your right." Tom flicked the reins and steered his horse toward the compound.

A large man in a blood-stained bib apron stood by the hospital's front door, wiping his hands with a rag. Perhaps in his early forties, gray streaked his dark hair; dark circles rimmed his bloodshot eyes.

He extended his hand. "Dr. Gerald McVickar," he said. "Head surgeon."

"Dr. James Banyon," Jim said, smiling and returning the handshake.

"Glad you're here. We need all the help we can get." McVickar studied Jim's face. "Are you feeling alright? You look a little peaked."

"Not at my best," Jim admitted with a rueful smile. "I'm hoping it will pass."

"Let's hope so," Dr. McVickar said with a small laugh. "We need more doctors, not more patients." He opened the front door and motioned to Jim to follow him.

"We've isolated the typhoid patients in the south wing." McVickar continued as he led them inside. "That was the first place we got cleaned up and in order. I'll give you a tour later.

"Disease is our biggest enemy so far. Besides typhoid, there's the usual chronic diarrhea and dysentery, as well as cases of tuberculosis and malaria. Measles is rampant, and of course there's pneumonia. That's all housed in the north wing."

"Some doctors think foul air might be to blame," Jim said.

McVickar snickered. "Well, the air around

here definitely isn't good. But it wouldn't surprise me if dejected morale causes problems too," he continued. "When you don't see any hope in your future, it's awfully hard to care about your health."

Jim nodded. "Where are the injured men?" he asked.

"Across the square in a separate building." McVickar pointed at a building several yards away. "Trying to keep them as far as possible from the contagion. There are several wives there who've come along to be with their husbands. Some of them have been willing to help with nursing care," said McVickar, "and we're grateful to have them."

He paused, and once again studied Jim. "Is it yellow jaundice?" he asked, pointing to Jim's discolored eyes.

"I think that's likely," Jim said. "But I'd just as soon work through it if I can."

McVickar nodded. "I'll keep you busy as long as you're able. You'll let me know if it gets worse?"

"I will."

"Good enough." McVickar moved back to the front door. "I'll show you to your quarters."

It was past midnight when an exhausted and feverish Jim at last left the hospital. He lay on his cot, listening to the relentless rain as it pounded the roof of the medical quarters, and re-read his latest letter from Napoleon.

September 21, 1862
Dear Jim,

If I thought I'd seen the worst that men could do to one another, I was wrong. The past week has been the bloodiest battle yet.

We have camped near the Antietam River, and the battlefield of the past few days is in sight. The wind sends the stink of battle over the campground; scavengers tear at the remains of the dead. Retrieving the dead and wounded—what few survive—is our primary mission.

I have heard the rumor that the battle at Harper's Ferry was a disaster, and that the Rebs took over ten thousand Johnnies prisoner. Colonel

Miles was a coward, and you are lucky to be rid of him.

The weight of our losses lies heavy on my mind. Yesterday, I came across a man whose blood poured from his mouth; where his wound was I do not know. I thought of my father, his blood pouring from his body, and for a moment, I was in two places at once.

Jim, I know you see death every day like I do. I don't know how you manage. For myself, I'm not sure how much longer I can. Reuben and I have one another to cling to. God forbid something happens to him. I fear I might go insane.
Your cousin,
Napoleon

CHAPTER 30

October 2, 1862
Near Sharpsburg, MD

Reuben raced into Napoleon's tent, his face flushed with excitement. "President Lincoln is here!"

"President Lincoln? Honest Abe? *Here?*" Napoleon sat bundled in his greatcoat, shivering against the chilly morning air.

"He's meeting with General McClellan this very minute," Reuben stopped to catch his breath.

A bugle sounded across camp, signaling the order for the men to assemble. Napoleon jumped up, grabbed his musket, fixed the bayonet, and rushed outside.

The company formed up; the staff sergeant advancing down the line. "Look sharp, men! General McClellan has ordered a review for the President."

The company marched to McClellan's tent, where the General, President Lincoln, and his staff stood chatting.

As Napoleon emerged through the trees, he

could barely believe his eyes. President Abraham Lincoln, the savior of the Union, stood before him, taller, thinner, his face longer than Napoleon had imagined. But what struck him most was Lincoln's presence, his solemn face, the weariness—not of fatigue, but from the weight of responsibility.

The officers surrounding the President stood stiffly in deference to their leader. But Mr. Lincoln, despite his weary face, was relaxed; he smiled as the company approached.

Napoleon glanced at Reuben beside him. "We look like a bunch of vagabonds," he said.

Reuben smiled, pointing to where Lincoln was already shaking hands and chatting with the enlisted men. "Old Abe doesn't seem to mind a bit."

Lincoln advanced down the line of soldiers, hands clasped behind his back, like a sergeant inspecting his troops. But instead of shouting criticism, the President shook hands with each man, asked questions, and smiled.

"Where are you from, soldier?" he asked a young private.

"Watertown, New York, Sir," he said, "and proud to serve my country."

Lincoln nodded. "Watertown—isn't that near

Canada?"

"Yes, sir," the private puffed out his chest. "Best place to live in the whole danged country."

Napoleon snapped to a salute, his heart pounding as Lincoln stopped in front of him and extended his hand. "Another New Yorker?" he asked.

"Yes, sir," he said.

"Rough battle, was it?"

Napoleon saw right away that the President's concerns were genuine, not just some trumped-up show of interest for the benefit of the cameras and reports. Unable to speak, he simply nodded.

Lincoln put a hand on Napoleon's shoulder. "We're grateful you held."

Napoleon watched as Lincoln moved on, stopping for every soldier, shaking his hand, offering his thanks, and Napoleon understood what he was fighting for.

This man bore the weight of a nation, yet here he stood, in muddy shoes, his face lined with sorrow. He had faced the effects of war. Despite it all, he'd managed a smile.

As the men sat around the cookfire that night, each bragged of his encounter with Honest Abe, holding out the hand that shook the hand of the President of the United States. Napoleon was quiet. He thought of their brief conversation, the concern and the caring, and as he cleaned his musket and watched the embers fade, he felt a steady hand on his shoulder.

CHAPTER 31

October 1862

Camp Douglas, Chicago

The sound of officers returning from breakfast drifted into Hospital Square as Jim made his way down the hospital steps. The aroma of frying pork wafted across the compound from the enlisted men's cooking fires; that and hardtack would suffice for their meal.

The detainees finished repairing the damage left by the Confederate prisoners. After roll call at five a.m., the men cooked their breakfast over a small fire: as always, hardtack and coffee were on the menu, and sometimes a bit of rancid pork. They might linger around the campfire if weather permitted, but otherwise there would be long hours of nothing to do until the 11:00 inspection. A few of them might start up a game of cards; some played a new sport called baseball to while away the time. Jim often heard the chants and cheers from their makeshift ball field when he was on duty. He might have thought of joining the game if he'd had time to think at all, but usually he was too busy trying to keep their comrades alive.

The days were unusually hot for October. Not even a cool wind found its way from Lake Michigan, a mile or two to the east. By nighttime, the chill damp from the lake invaded their barracks, and Jim would be glad for his heavy wool uniform, but for now it chafed and grew damp with sweat.

He'd lost three men last night, all to typhoid. Ten men still lingered, but Jim expected they'd die by the end of the day. Regardless of which disease faced them, there was little Jim and his colleagues could do. They treated their patients with quinine and gave them morphine or whiskey for pain. For fevers, they used Fowler's solution, a diluted liquid form of arsenic, and prescribed calomel, turpentine, and castor oil to treat diarrhea and dysentery. In the end, all one could do was watch and wait, hope that the soldier would survive, and pray that the disease didn't continue to spread.

Exhausted from the long night of sitting vigil by his patients, Jim's steps were sluggish. His head sagged as he crossed the square to his barracks in search of a little sleep.

It makes a body wonder what the point of trying to keep them alive is, Jim thought. *Hippocrates said physicians should "do no harm." But I wonder how often I have violated that commandment by not letting my patients die in peace.*

Thank goodness it wasn't his day to see the soldiers presenting themselves at daily sick call. The job required him to determine whether to admit ill and injured patients to the hospital, excuse them from duty with orders to stay in quarters, or assign light duty. But this morning, his sleep-deprived brain was too addled to make decisions about the severity of their complaint. Yesterday had been a different matter, and it seemed half of the camp was trying to get out of work for the day.

"Got a roaring headache." Private Jemison was one of Jim's regulars, showing up for sick call at least once a week. "I've been running a fever all night." *Damned hospital rat,* Jim thought. The man was a classic malingerer, hell-bent on ducking duty.

Jim knew the man's symptoms would mysteriously disappear before he got back to his barracks. He sighed and played the game, placing the back of his hand on the man's forehead. "You're as cool as day-old porridge," Jim said. "Report for duty."

But there were soldiers who needed the time off. With disease so prevalent in camp, it was important for illnesses to be diagnosed and treated as soon as possible, and with some patients, it was difficult to tell if their ailments were real or fabricated.

As he approached his quarters, a voice behind him shouted. "Doctor!" Jim recognized the voice: it was Major Anthony and, as usual, he sounded unhappy.

"Who the hell gave you the authority to put my men on sick leave?" Anthony's eyes were on fire as he hurried to catch up with Jim.

I'm too tired to mess with this jerk, Jim thought. He'd been back on duty only a few days since his own recovery from yellow jaundice. Although the fever and chills had subsided, he still felt weak, and more tired than usual. He was grateful it hadn't been something worse.

Jim straightened his back and addressed his superior, in no mood for the disrespect he usually showed Anthony. "The United States Army—that's who."

"You know half those assholes are faking," Anthony snorted.

Jim took a calming breath. "I know *some* of

them are," he said. "If you want to examine them yourself, be my guest. You can decide whether they really have typhoid."

Anthony paled. He put one hand over his face and thrust the other towards Jim, palm out. "You got more cases of typhoid?" He hurried off towards the post headquarters without waiting for a response.

But it wasn't typhoid that concerned Jim the most. Since Harper's Ferry, he'd seen an unusually high number of men complaining of difficulty sleeping, irritability, and stomach distress—the same physical symptoms he'd noted in his war veteran patients at home.

At Camp Douglas, many of the same soldiers grew anxious and lethargic, lost their appetites, and had trouble focusing. Was it the dismal conditions that spurred their anxiety? Or could it be something else?

Maybe I should add these symptoms to my study, Jim thought. *There might be a correlation there.* He wondered how Private Nichols was getting along at the Insane Soldier's Hospital and made a mental note to contact Dr. Earle when he had a quiet moment.

Jim turned his thoughts to the day before. Colonel Segoine, the commander of the 111th Regiment, had arrived at Camp Douglas with great ceremony. With all the troops gathered at the parade grounds, the colonel solemnly returned the Regiment's flag.

"Under personal danger, I retrieved our colors from the hands of the Confederacy," he puffed out his chest and stood tall. "The minute the doctors declared me recovered from a serious illness, I hurried to Chicago to put the flag in your hands."

And I'm a monkey's uncle, Jim thought. Bile rose in his throat. He knew the true story of the Regiment's flag, and it wasn't Colonel Segoine who had rescued it. Jim had witnessed Colonel D'Utassy at Harper's Ferry as he gently folded the flag, hiding it in his trunk. Colonel Segoine was nowhere to be found.

What an old fool! Jim had lost what little respect he'd had for the man ever since Segoine sided with Colonel Miles as he raised the flag of surrender.

Arriving at his quarters, Jim sat on his bunk trying to release the stress of the hospital, the stench of disease and death that seemed to follow him everywhere. He was feeling pretty lonely just then, and the long hours combined with recovering from the jaundice weren't helping.

Even though he was exhausted, his mind was still busy thinking about his patients, and he knew he wouldn't be able to sleep just yet.

Oh, how he wanted to go home, to hold his girls and return to a normal life. But, he reminded himself, he'd enlisted for three years. If he resigned now, he'd lose his bounty money and his chance to learn more about battle symptoms. He would return home a failure.

I'll write home, he decided. He hadn't heard from his parents in a while; he needed to feel that connection to home. Reaching into the tattered backpack at his bunk's foot, he pulled out paper and pencil and began writing.

Dear Father,

I was very sick for some time with the yellow jaundice but am better now and mostly recovered.

This war, in my opinion, must close in a year. I consider we have our last piles of soldiers in the field and what is done this fall will have a great influence on the issue; if it continues much longer, the government is bankrupt and never can recover itself.

Dr. Larssen has arrived, and I have been sent back to my own regiment.

Camp Douglas is getting muddy and nasty as the changeable fall weather comes. I hope earnestly and trust that we will be relieved from staying here for very long...

Jim continued, inquiring about folks at home, telling his parents what he'd been doing. When he had at last relayed his news and emptied his mind of the last few days' occurrences, he folded the letter, tucked it in his knapsack, and tried to sleep.

CHAPTER 32

October 1862

Camp Douglas

The camp's officers gathered around the table at post headquarters. The room smelled of pipe smoke and fallen leaves; a heavy frost covered the windows. Today's discussion was camp morale.

Newly appointed camp commander, Brigadier General Daniel Tyler, summed up the problem. "Negotiating the exchange will take at least another month. Now that the grounds and buildings are acceptable, the parolees have little to do. With no pay and no prospect of going home, they're restless. This place is a powder keg waiting for a match."

Major Anthony, promoted on his superior's death at Harper's Ferry, represented the 111th. "I say we put them to work," he said.

"What would you have them do, Major Anthony?" Tyler raised an eyebrow as if to say, *I'm listening.*

"First," Anthony explained, "they need to learn

how to march. When these men got to Harper's Ferry, they were nothing but country farmers. They had no guns, no discipline, and no training. Now, we can't give them guns, but we can implement drills twice daily."

"Seems to me the terms of our parole say we can't perform any military duty," another officer noted. "Wouldn't that be assisting the North? We're not allowed to do that until we're exchanged."

"I disagree." Anthony scowled at the man. "We aren't training them to shoot, or even to fight. All we're doing is teaching them how to march and follow orders."

"We could assign them hospital duty," Captain Larkin suggested. "The medical team always needs help."

"We could organize some sort of recreation," said Lieutenant Ripley. "Maybe start a baseball team."

"For God's sake, they aren't children!" Anthony clenched his fists under the table. "I intend to hold drills daily for anyone who decides to behave like a soldier. The devil can take the rest."

In the end, the committee didn't give Anthony their blessing to hold drills, nor did they tell him he couldn't.

The next morning, the men received the news.

"Major Anthony has ordered morning and afternoon drills to commence immediately," the messenger announced.

Soldiers, stripped to their undershorts and lounging on cots, groaned. "We're goddamn prisoners!" one man shouted from across the room. "We ain't supposed to be drilling, and you can't make us!" The rest of the men grunted their agreement.

The messenger shook his head and returned to camp headquarters.

"Some Reb told them the terms of their parole exempted them from duty, and now they feel like they've been double-crossed," he said to Anthony's aide. "They aren't wrong."

"Yeah, you tell that to old Pegleg." The aide jerked his head toward the door to Anthony's office.

When the call sounded for the troops to assemble for drill, only the rats showed up. Major Anthony shouted for his aide. "You go tell those goddamn pussies to get their asses here, now!"

The aide saluted and headed for the prisoner barracks. Ten minutes later, he returned by himself. "They refuse to report." He shook his head.

Anthony angrily threw his papers on the floor. "I'll go get them myself," he said, stomping off. The stench that met him as he approached stopped him outside the barracks doors.

"Report for drill, damn it!" he shouted from the rutted yard, his stance rigid and ready for battle.

"I'm not breaking parole," a soldier shouted from inside. Several bunkmates agreed.

"Can't go, I got the shits," came a call from another barracks.

"I think I got typhoid."

The excuses came in bunches, a chorus of refusal.

"Don't make me come drag you out!" Anthony roars. His face flushed red; his hand drifted to his saber.

The barracks went silent.

Intensified by the hot afternoon sun, the stink was making Anthony gag. He'd be damned if he let them see him vomit. "You can all face court martial for all I care," he grumbled, swallowing the bile in his throat, and retreated to headquarters.

Day after day, the detainees at Camp Douglas spent most of their time inside, unsuccessfully hiding from the unending rain. The occasional dry day might allow some outdoor exercise, but aside from daily inspection, there was little to do. No one paid attention to Major Peleg's demand for daily drills. Not even the other officers tried to enforce it.

Their food was barely edible: the meat was rancid, the rice infested with worms. The sutler's store sold good food, but the men hadn't received their pay for months. Sickness was everywhere, adding to the stink and misery.

The days got shorter; the nights grew colder. Bored to death and mad as hell, eight thousand restless men felt like abandoned livestock. It wouldn't take much to start a stampede.

Brigadier General Tyler tried a fresh approach, giving the enlisted men day passes to town. "Maybe that will get it out of their system," he told the assembled officers. But most nights ended with the officers searching every saloon and brothel in the city for their men, and herding them back to camp, sometimes at gunpoint.

Anger turned to frustration and resentment.

"Send us to fight, let us go home, but get us out of this stinking hole of death."

It became a battle cry. A small group of men broke down a fence and took off for home. The authorities tracked them down, brought them back to the camp, and forced them to pay the expense of their retrieval. Tyler ordered them to march wearing a barrel, singling them out as the most cowardly of the Cowards. The humiliation only added to their anger.

A few nights later, the parolees overwhelmed the guards on sentry duty, bent their bayonets, and filled their musket barrels with sand or acorns. Some guards were physically attacked. The guards pushed back at Tyler, unwilling to stand guard duty at the mercy of the mobs.

Tensions built. Regiments fought one another. One afternoon outside the sutler's store, men from an Ohio regiment bickered with a group of soldiers from New York. Nobody remembered what the fighting was about until the sutler emerged from his store. "I can see why they call y'all the Harper's Ferry Cowards!" he jeered.

The powder keg exploded. Soldiers on both sides looted the store. What they couldn't carry was smashed to pieces, including the store itself. It was the start of a violent unrest that would last for weeks and ended in the burning of twelve barracks and cookhouses.

At roll call the next day, the stench of smoldering wood hung in the heavy morning air. Bushels of charred rats littered the grounds.

"That's one way of getting rid of rats," one officer joked.

"If those prisoners want meat that isn't putrid, they should eat them," said another. "That'd take care of two problems at once."

But by early November, cooler weather seemed to have brought cooler heads to Camp Douglas. Upon the formal exchange of regiments, the authorities returned the men to their Annapolis commanders.

It was nearly Thanksgiving when Erskine appeared in Jim's doorway.

"I heard we're leaving tomorrow."

Jim looked up from the patient he was tending.

"The enlisted men, but not us. We'll stay here until we clear all our patients for duty. There's about forty here now, so it might be awhile."

"Think we'll join the regiment in D.C.?" Erskine asked.

"I heard they might send us to the hospital at Fairfax Seminary," Jim said. "That'd make me a lot happier than dragging half-dead soldiers off a battleground."

"Hard to say." Erskine gestured to the patient-filled room. "I'm not sure watching them die in a hospital bed is any better."

The discontent of our exile at Camp Douglas has come to a boiling point. Conditions are disastrous: poor, often inedible food, tainted water, muddy conditions mixed with interminable heat and humidity, and the overall humiliation of being branded as the "Harper's Ferry Cowards." The enlisted men rampaged yesterday evening, setting fire to barracks and destroying the sutler's store in revenge for his pronouncement of their cowardice.

CHAPTER 33

December 1862-June 1863
Various locations around Washington, D.C.

December 10, 1862

The big bugs have finally exchanged us and sent us to Annapolis to aid in the capital's defense. I am to be posted at the hospital at Fairfax Seminary to care for the lingering sick and wounded. This assignment will afford me the time and subjects to continue my study, which now includes more recent enlistees.

If Private Nichols' deteriorating mental state made me question my diagnosis of malingering, my tenure at Fairfax has convinced me that there is more to this condition than laziness, or even cowardice. Many show signs of deep emotional trauma, and I tend to believe that these traumas are real. While this may seem a not unnatural result of watching one's comrades die in most ghastly ways, the effect appears to go deeper than a temporary sense of loss and grief. I have heard this condition referred to as "nostalgia," a deep yearning for home, but I am convinced it is much more than homesickness, especially since my conversations with Dr. Earle.

The first thing Jim noticed when he stepped off the train in Alexandria, Virginia, was the destruction from constant battle.

This is truly a desolate country; not a family in miles, Jim wrote to his father, *the abandoned houses are the very personification of loneliness. ...in my opinion, the opening of good weather will witness the most terrible carnage this continent ever saw.*

Not a spear of grain nor any sign of the usual crops was visible for miles; homes and farms stood empty, their fences destroyed, the land rutted by the wagon wheels burdened with people who fled for their lives.

There was no birdsong, no rustle of wildlife. Not a sound echoed across the barren fields. The stench of old wood smoke hung in the air. What trees had once stood were chopped down for fuel; stumps and sawdust were all that remained.

The 111th made their encampment at Camp Pomeroy, a few miles south of Alexandria, part of a large military contingent responsible for defending Washington, D.C.. Sixty-eight forts and an array of blockhouses, rifle pits, earthworks, moats, abatis, and entrenchments comprised the city's fortifications. If the Rebs attacked, they'd have their hands full.

At Pomeroy, Jim shared a 10x12 tent with two other officers. It was larger than the tents of the enlisted men, but the cold ground, the damp air, the thin straw tick, and the endless supply of lice were just the same. Their only comfort was a small wood stove.

On most mornings, he rose well before dawn with the rest of the regiment, stretching the ache from his bones. After breakfast at the officers' mess, he rode the few miles to the hospital at Fairfax Seminary, where he would stay until well after dark.

Fairfax Seminary stands on a hill with beautiful ground around it, he wrote to Maggie in late December, *with large trees in front but not a sign of cultivation except of the arts of war. The word is that we will remain here until spring at the earliest. I hope that is so.*

Since their arrival at Harper's Ferry, he'd kept track of each soldier's heart rate, digestive issues, and sleep patterns. Of the original fifty, nearly forty men remained.

Less than six months had passed since their enlistment, but already Jim saw changes. Could he attribute the physical changes to the stress of combat? Maybe. But Jim was seeing more changes that he couldn't yet account for. Nothing like Private Nichols' stupor, but more than a few men now had that haunted look in their eyes that announced they'd seen much more than they'd wanted to.

"Where in hell are my men?" Anthony's distinctive voice shook Jim from his thoughts.

Oh, great. Now I have to deal with this fool. Jim stood, straightened his jacket, and went to the foyer, where Anthony growled at a private who'd had the misfortune of drawing guard duty that morning.

"Good morning to you, Major," Jim gave a limp salute and mimicked a bow. "I am currently treating twenty-seven patients. Which ones would be yours?"

"Anyone from Company H is mine, and you know that, you arrogant son of a bitch."

Jim gestured for Anthony to follow him and returned to his desk.

"Corporal Jones has bloody dysentery," he said, referring to his notes. "Private Myers is recovering from a malarial attack." Jim mentioned a few more names and looked up. "Will that be all, Major?"

"No, soldier, that will not be all. What about Corporal Harper?"

Jim took his time, scanning one note after another. "Ah, Harper," he finally said. "I'm keeping him for observation."

"Observation of what?"

Jim consulted his ledger. "Patient shows signs of extreme stress," he read in a monotone. "Dangerously rapid heart rate. Patient has neither eaten nor slept more than a few hours since his admittance. Suspect stomach ulcer."

"In other words, another deadbeat."

"Not at all. How effective can a soldier be if he is undernourished and sleep-deprived?"

"He's no different from the rest of my men. If he isn't incapacitated by injury or illness, I want him released for duty. Today."

Jim nodded, but he had no intention of releasing Corporal Harper until he was good and ready.

CHAPTER 34

May 31, 1863
Centreville, VA

Jim sat hunched over his desk, poring over patient records. The oil lamp's dim light cast a warm glow on his weary face; lines of concentration and burden etched his forehead. Although the door was closed against the sights and sounds of the patients who filled the hospital's main room, the odors of antiseptic, blood, and dying flesh filled the air.

I should write to Maggie soon, he reminded himself. A week had passed since they had put him in charge of the Brigade Hospital in Centreville, and he eagerly wanted to share the good news.

"Jim," she called softly, her voice barely above a whisper.

He looked up. His heart nearly stopped at the familiar voice. *Am I dreaming?* His eyes widened in surprise and then softened as recognition dawned. Maggie: the most beautiful sight he'd seen in months.

"How did you—?" He jumped up, hurried around the desk and wrapped her in an enormous bear hug. The sounds of the daily hospital routine faded into the background as Jim and Maggie embraced. "I never want to let go," he said.

"I missed you so much," she whispered, her voice trembling with emotion. Beneath his shirt, she heard the steady thump of his heartbeat; it was a rhythm that had been her anchor during their separation.

"I missed you too." Jim pressed a gentle kiss to the top of her head. His lips were warm and soft; his beard tickled her nose. "Every single day."

Maggie leaned back and stared at Jim's face. "The beard looks good on you." She smiled and stroked his goatee. "You look tired. When was the last time you slept?"

Jim shrugged. "Sleep doesn't happen much around here, and it's a good thing, too. I don't want to sleep away a minute of your visit."

Maggie smiled. "It's been a long trip from home," she said. "Maybe we can spare some time for a nap."

Jim poured two cups of tea, then pulled out a chair and gestured for Maggie to sit. "How long can you stay?"

"As long as you'll have me. Jessie is with her papa and gramma," she said. "I'm sure they won't mind keeping her a little longer."

"How is my little bird?" Jim asked. "She must be growing like a weed."

"She is," Maggie said, "and chattering like a magpie."

Jim smiled at the image: a mass of blonde curls flitting around the room, jabbering all the way. "That's my Jessie."

"She asks about you every day. 'When will Daddy come home?' I tell her you are helping people. I tell her you are brave, and you will come home as soon as you can."

"What's the latest news?"

"Nothing much has changed, except that we've lost a lot of young men to a senseless war." Maggie gently blew across her tea to cool it. "I hear often from women who have lost a son or husband in the fighting. They want to know if you were with them when they died." She swallowed hard. "I don't know what to tell them." She looked into the distance, tears in her eyes.

"But the church bells are the hardest. Every day

or so, they ring for another soldier's death." The thought sent shivers down her spine. "We've all come to dread the sound."

"I think sometimes it's the women who have to be the bravest of all." He held out his arms for Maggie; she set her teacup on the desk and let Jim pull her into his lap. "I can't imagine how they endure it." He kissed her softly, leaned back, and smiled.

"Strangely enough, I was just thinking about writing you a letter." He told her about his new assignment, mentioning his temporary detachment from the 111th.

"Does that mean you won't be near the fighting anymore?" Her face brightened with hope.

"Not as much, anyway," he said. "But right now the whole Corps defends the capital. Small skirmishes represent the worst of the fighting, and, as you can see from the battlements, our defenses here are strong. That's given me a chance to continue my study."

"Have you come to any conclusions yet?" asked Maggie.

"I've seen some interesting tendencies," he said, "but nothing conclusive. Although they're not part of the study, I've treated a lot more men with similar symptoms." Jim set down his cup and continued.

"Recently I've stumbled onto some other unusual symptoms: many of the soldiers complain of recurring nightmares; some lapse into a fugue-like state as if they're still in battle. One or two so completely that I've had to commit them to an asylum."

Jim sipped his tea. "Have you heard anything from Napoleon?" He hadn't had a letter from his cousin since Antietam—he wasn't even sure Napoleon was still alive.

"I'm sure he writes his mother when he can," Maggie shrugged, "but not often enough to suit her."

Jim nodded. "Writing materials and time are two things most of us have precious little of. I'm just happy to hear he's well."

"Dr. Banyan!" An orderly burst into Jim's office, his eyes wide. "You're needed immediately!"

Maggie, embarrassed by the orderly's interruption, jumped from Jim's lap.

Jim stood, straightening his uniform. "Tell

them I will be there directly," he said. "Then come back here and show Mrs. Banyon to my quarters." He turned to Maggie as he left the room. "I'll be back as soon as I can."

Maggie smiled as the orderly opened the door to Jim's room. The room looked just as she'd expected a man on his own might keep one: the narrow bed unmade, clothes carelessly strewn about. The air was stale; she crossed the large room and opened its single window, letting the scent of hollyhocks and dust drift in. She picked a shirt off the floor, held it to her nose and inhaled deeply. *That's a scent I've missed so much.*

A chipped porcelain basin sat near the bed, with a pitcher of water and what remained of a bar of lye soap next to it. A threadbare towel hung on the wall nearby. Near the foot of the bed sat Jim's open trunk, wrinkled shirts spilling out. Underneath the window stood a simple writing desk, scattered with half-finished surgical notes, and a small, pewter gas lamp. She recognized his worn leather-bound journal, bookmarked with an empty envelope.

At the opposite end of the room, the fireplace glowed with the remaining embers of a morning fire. She took the clips from her hair, let it fall around her shoulders, and reminded herself to add a log or two lest the fire go out.

The door clicked softly; Maggie turned as Jim walked in and enveloped her in his arms. "Finally, we're alone," he said. "I need a nap."

He led her to the small bed. "I suppose we'll have to spoon a bit if we're both going to fit." Maggie lay on her side, scooting to the far edge of the bed. Jim lay on his side next to her and wrapped his arm around her slender waist.

"Did I tell you how much I missed you?" He buried his nose in her dark curls, inhaling deeply. "You smell wonderful."

They lay together quietly for a few moments. "I have to get back to my patients," he finally said.

"Is there anything I can do to help?" Maggie asked.

"Just your being here helps immensely. I'm sure the sick men would love some female attention as well."

"It would be my pleasure," Maggie said. "I'll do whatever I can to ease their suffering."

CHAPTER 35

June 1863

Brigade Hospital

All is quiet on the Potomac. Jim gazed out of the hospital ward's large window. The relative calm couldn't last much longer if the rumors were true. It wouldn't be long until they'd be on the move again and Maggie would have to return home, but for now, Jim would enjoy every moment he could with her. Jim sighed and turned his attention to his patients.

"The Lord is my light and my salvation; whom shall I fear?" Jim listened as Maggie read from the Bible.

Who should they fear? The enemy. The disease, the wounds, the images of the dead that would never leave. He was a religious man, but Jim knew there was a greater threat that maybe even God couldn't handle.

Maggie is a godsend to all of us. He reflected on the hours she spent sitting with the hospital's patients, talking with them about home, reading to them. *They are very grateful for every attention,* he had told his father, *and in no respect shall they be neglected if I can prevent it.*

"Though a host should encamp against me, my heart shall not fear: though war should rise against me, in this will I be confident." Maggie paused and gently touched the now-sleeping soldier's arm.

Jim watched as she moved gracefully across the room. He wished he could have her naïve trust in God, but he'd seen too much evidence of man's capacity for violence to have confidence about anything. For now, he'd take every minute with her and enjoy the respite from battle.

At midday they shared a small meal. Jim reviewed his notes; Maggie watched, filled with curiosity.

"What are you writing?" She asked, craning her neck to see his paper.

"I write these notes for each of my patients." He slid the paper closer so she could see it. "Just like in my office at home."

"They help you keep track of your treatments?"

"That's right." He looked up at her. "But unlike at home, I feel like I know these men more intimately. I've experienced their battles, too. I look in their eyes and share their horror."

"Does it give you nightmares like it does them?" she asked.

"It gives me frustration. Their injuries are not like at home—not illnesses or physical injuries—I know how to treat those. But the nightmares? The horrors? How do I fix their minds?"

Maggie sat silently, considering his words. How could she help ease *his* suffering?

"Jim," she said tentatively, "would you show me your world?"

Jim rubbed the back of his neck. "What do you mean?"

"I'd like to see what you see every day. Not just the hospital wards. Could we ride out into the country? Is it safe? Show it all to me."

Jim smiled. "It would be my honor."

Jim steadied the small stool as Maggie climbed into the mare's sidesaddle and adjusted her dress, a soft blue summer linen that draped gracefully down the horse's side. Her thin gloves, more for propriety than protection, complemented her outfit; she held a lightweight riding crop in her right hand, and carried a small reticule of essentials—a lace handkerchief and a tin of lemon drops.

Her dark hair was braided and pinned in a tight circlet. A wide-brimmed felt riding hat protected her face from the sun. The lightweight veil tied just above the brim trailed behind her; a sprig of lavender tucked into the band.

"Comfortable?" Jim asked.

When Maggie nodded, he mounted his horse and flicked the reins. Maggie urged her mare forward and steered it next to Jim. "Where to first?"

Jim smiled. "Follow me, Madam."

They began in Centreville, moving past the earthworks that marked what was once a Confederate camp, long since abandoned. Jim guided them through stands of oak and pine, one sprouting the bright green leaves of springtime, the other already shedding its excess needles.

"This is what they call 'Bull Run,'" he said,

pointing to a small stream, its banks overgrown with reeds and wild grasses. "'Run' is a southern term, I think, like a small stream." The water rushed over rocks and downed limbs as it made its way east to the Occoquan River and Chesapeake Bay.

"Blackburn's Ford is just down that way." He nodded to their left. "It's quiet now, but back in '61 there was a pretty fierce battle there."

"Before your time, then." Maggie said.

"Yes." Jim nodded. "But the battlefields are all the same for the most part. What were once beautiful rolling hills and farmland are now ruined by the forces of man and their desire to destroy one another."

They turned their horses west and north toward Warrenton Pike. Telegraph lines followed the wide dirt road like sentries; supply wagons, many broken beyond repair, scattered across the landscape.

"It's a beautiful place," Maggie said. "Even with the remnants of battle, I can imagine what it once was." She slowed, turning toward Jim.

"You remember it too, don't you?"

Jim stared into the distance. "What I remember are the wounded. I remember where they lay. I remember where they bled and died."

They continued in silence; by the time they reached Centreville, the horses were breathing hard, covered in sweat from the uphill climb. At the stables, Jim helped Maggie dismount.

She touched his shoulder lightly. "Thank you for showing me."

He gently kissed her cheek. "Thank you for seeing it.

"I should get back to my patients," he said. "Will you be coming with me?"

Maggie nodded. "Let me change out of my riding clothes." She subconsciously shook the dust from her skirt. "I'll meet you there presently."

Maggie sat next to a patient with a book and began reading as Erskine barged into the ward. Every person in the room jumped as the door slammed against the adjacent wall. Bottles of medicine that sat on small tables next to each bed tinkled as they bumped against one another.

He grasped a newspaper in one fist, waving it wildly; his voice was shrill and loud. "Have you heard the latest? Word is that General Lee is headed north. Some of the big bugs think he's planning a raid, maybe into Pennsylvania." The nearest patient grabbed the newspaper from Erskine's hand; a wave of anxious voices filled the room.

Maggie looked at Jim, her question in her eyes: *Shall I start packing?*

Jim shook his head. *Not yet*. It was a gesture so slight that not even Erskine noticed it.

June 25, 1863

Maggie has been visiting for a few weeks. I wish she could stay longer. However, word is that Lee's army is moving north towards Pennsylvania, and the Union must respond. I saw her to the train this morning and must prepare for the injuries and illnesses that will certainly ensue.

CHAPTER 36

July 1, 1863

Gettysburg, Pennsylvania

Napoleon heard the battle well before he saw it.

They'd been traveling for days, chasing Lee's Army north from Maryland. They pushed themselves to the limits of their endurance, marching thirty-five to forty miles a day in unpredictable weather and subsisting on hardtack and rancid pork.

Morning mist still hung in the air as the unrelenting sun bore down. Dust, campfires, and powder smoke caught in moisture-soaked air made breathing a chore. The fighting started early that day, and the battlefield was already littered with bodies.

None of this was new to Napoleon. Since he'd enlisted, he'd been a part of many battles. From Bull Run to Antietam, and most recently, Fredericksburg. In the two years since his enlistment, he'd gained the rank of corporal and joined the 80th regiment, known as the Ulster Guard, when the 35th mustered out in June.

One battleground melted into another, scattered with the dead and dying, Federals charging at Rebs, the roar of cannons and the screams of the wounded. Napoleon was a specter, driven from one battle to the next. He'd kept his vow to avoid liquor, but he better understood the demons his father was trying to erase.

The enemy fired the first shots at the Chambersburg Pike, where Confederate General Heth's corps skirmished with the cavalry of Union General Buford, while the 80th waited in reserve. Buford's objective was to Delay the Confederates to allow for the Union Army to arrive. To that end, he set up picket lines to the west and north. Their orders to attack came mid-morning.

The 80th was on the left flank as Devin's I Corps formed a line of battle along the Hagerstown Road. As the battle intensified, they retreated to the seminary at the edge of town. Late in the afternoon, the Union line collapsed, forcing a retreat to Cemetery Hill, south of Gettysburg.

Napoleon and Reuben stood sentry along the Taneytown Road that night. Below him, he could make out the shadows of the walking wounded, slowly making their way to the field hospital. Behind them were the more seriously wounded, carried on stretchers, covered with blood and as pale as death. Riderless horses wandered the battlefield, occasionally stopping to sniff at a body, perhaps searching for their owner.

Napoleon watched the never-ending line of casualties until the darkness hid them. Even then, the screams and pleas of the wounded echoed across the ridge.

As the night progressed and the fighting eased, Napoleon stared at the stars still glowing in the night sky. The Big Dipper was near the horizon in the northwestern sky, the Little Dipper slightly above and to the north; they were a comforting reminder of home, and Napoleon wondered if he would ever see home again.

"Makes a body think of home, doesn't it?" Reuben stood beside Napoleon, his eyes on the sky.

"Yeah," Napoleon said as he scanned the horizon. "I'm just trying to keep my mind off tomorrow." His thoughts drifted to the day ahead; the images of today's fighting fresh in his mind.

"Napoleon?"

Napoleon's heart jumped as Reuben spoke.

Just Reuben, he assured himself.

"Yeah?"

"Do you think we'll ever see home again?"

Napoleon gazed at the Big Dipper and didn't answer.

At 11:00 the next morning, the 80th troops were relieved from sentry duty. They fell out on a piece of broken ground covered with rocks, underbrush, and a few trees. With the rest of his regiment, Napoleon ate a few hard crackers, stretched out on the ground in search of sleep, and prepared for whatever the day would bring.

Would he still be alive this time tomorrow? Napoleon dreaded the battle to come, but he dreaded the brand of "coward" even more. Napoleon was no coward; he would die before he turned tail and ran. He looked at Reuben as he slept beside him and prayed they would survive.

CHAPTER 37

July 2, 1863
Gettysburg, PA

Later that afternoon, the order came for the 80th to fall in. Napoleon groaned and stretched, working out the stiff joints and aching muscles from sleeping on open ground. He wolfed down some hot coffee and hard crackers, grabbed his rifle, and presented for roll call. Their orders were to lie ready on the slopes and to be prepared to support the Second Corps, and the Third Corps that fought ahead of the Second.

Napoleon and Reuben watched as Rebel troops sporadically darted from behind cover, fired at the Union line, and retreated back into hiding. The Union artillery line held the rebels at bay with shell and canister fire. Napoleon and his regiment supported the artillery line.

By mid-afternoon the intermittent shelling erupted into heavy fire. The Confederate line moved closer—bold or crazy, Napoleon didn't know which.

Nostalgia

The order came for the regiment to fall in. The chaplain said a prayer for their safety. Napoleon touched his left breast pocket, where he'd attached the blue, circular badge that identified him as a part of the 3rd Division, 1st Corps.

He watched the battle in front of him as men on both sides fell, heard the explosions that sent body parts flying above him, stepped over broken bodies and into pools of blood and brains. The whole time he kept his eyes focused ahead, passing death without acknowledgment. He couldn't call it courage; it was his duty; sorrow and horror and regret would have to wait for later.

New orders passed down the line: double quick to the front. Napoleon and his comrades scrambled across an open field, staying down to avoid enemy fire. They lay down behind the artillery and waited for orders from Colonel Gates, the commander of the 80th. The only thing between them and the enemy was a wide but shallow ditch thick with bushes, old tree stumps, and large rocks.

The sun began to set behind the Confederate troops, and they continued to advance. The regiment waited behind the three brigades in front of them.

As the Rebel troops pushed ahead, Napoleon saw Colonel Gates wave his sword, pointing to a gap that had formed between the Union brigades. Dusk had fallen, and in the fading light, Napoleon saw lines of Confederates surge through the ditch, hooting their eerie battle cries, muskets firing, charging to break through the middle of the Union line.

The colonel shouted the order. "Fix bayonets! Shoulder arms!"

The men jumped to their feet, prepared to battle. Heavy enemy fire fell as the colonel ordered them forward from their position. Shell and canister fire rained down; bullets flew as the victory-hungry rebels forced their way into the Union lines.

Napoleon and Reuben stood side by side, ducking and dodging the hail of artillery.

"C'mon, Reuben," shouted Napoleon. He could barely hear himself over the cannon fire. "Let's go shoot us some Rebs." He ducked as an incoming shell exploded nearby.

"Whoa, that was a close one!" Napoleon wiped blood and flesh from his uniform and turned toward Reuben just in time to see his friend's headless body fall to the ground.

The Union regiments cheered as they made their charge against Lee's army. There was no time for Napoleon to absorb what he'd just witnessed. He reacted to his orders without thinking, shouldered his rifle, and pushed toward the enemy. Soldiers fell, but the line moved forward, past the bodies and into the ditch.

"Close ranks!" came the order. The line came together, filling the spaces left by the fallen. The Confederates kept coming.

"Stand firm!" shouted a lieutenant. "Do not yield!"

The rebel line weakened and began to give way. A shot from Union artillery hit and killed one of the Confederate generals. Rebel drums sounded the retreat. Union forces continued across the ditch and up the other side, taking prisoners as they advanced. At last, the order came to withdraw.

As they crossed Plum Run, the rebel artillery fire continued. Pieces of iron and trees flew in every direction. Disorganization marked their retreat to safety, but the regiment returned to its original position.

Cheers came up from the men who had helplessly faced the advancing enemy just hours earlier. Weak and exhausted from the long fight, the men sank to their knees; Napoleon wasn't the only one who kissed the earth beneath him and thanked the Lord for His grace.

The night wasn't over for Napoleon and his fellow soldiers. They were ordered to the skirmish line to protect the front of the brigade. Cries of fallen men came from both sides of the battle, some begging for help, others begging for death.

The order to return to Ziegler's Grove finally arrived. The men fell to the ground, overtaken by exhaustion. Although Napoleon had been up for nearly twenty hours, he knew he couldn't sleep just yet. His body ached; his muscles, stretched and strained beyond their capacity, begged for rest. But his mind raced with images of soldiers advancing and bodies falling. His ears rang with the sound of cannons and muskets.

He walked through the grove in a daze. It was raining hard now, and he let the downpour soak through his uniform, hoping it might cleanse him of the odors of blood and gun smoke that stubbornly clung to him.

From the field hospitals in the distance, the sound of patriotic music drifted as surgeons worked throughout the night, tending to thousands of injured soldiers. At roll call that night, only 170 men of the Ulster Guard remained, and the battle at Gettysburg wasn't over yet.

CHAPTER 38

Gettysburg, PA

The past days have seen a battle like never before. Dr. Larssen and I have performed more amputations than seem humanly possible, the necessity for haste cutting the procedure to mere minutes. By the end of the day, I am up to my knees in severed limbs. Every amputation feels like a violation. Slicing through thick tissue, listening to the saw rasp through bone, discarding pieces of a person without his permission. The act of amputation has even overtaken my dreams.

It is unfathomable the things that men and armies will do to one another in the name of what they perceive as justice.

Jim woke to the pre-dawn call of a rooster. For a moment, he thought he was home, but the stony ground poking his backside reminded him he was in a tent. In the middle of a war.

Nostalgia

He rose, tightening his belt. His uniform hung loose on his now-thin frame. Twenty-hour workdays with little food weren't helping. His uncombed hair covered his ears, and his once-trimmed goatee faded into his growing beard. He eyed his tired hands and wondered how much longer he could keep performing surgeries.

As he stepped out of his tent, the sun crested the pine trees to the east; another hot day awaited. Another day of too much work and too little sleep. Shaking the cobwebs from his head, he realized that today was his twenty-fifth birthday. He'd spend it dodging bullets to retrieve the wounded, amputating limbs, and desperately trying to keep men from dying.

He cringed; a barrage of artillery fire rumbled less than a mile away. Maybe closer. He caught the smell of the acid residue of gunpowder drifting through the brush. A few seconds later, another volley of cannon fire echoed. The stubborn Confederates returned fire. It would be a long day. The first wagon of wounded soldiers would show up at any moment.

Long after the shooting subsided last night, Jim worked feverishly to treat the casualties. The stream of injured soldiers was constant, some walking, some leaning on a comrade, some carried on a stretcher. The ambulances—wagons that could carry several wounded at a time—raced in from the front line, hastily delivered their human cargo, and hurried back for more. It was usually the medical team who scoured the battlefield for the living, but tonight they clustered in the field hospital, desperately trying to save whoever they could.

The army commandeered barns belonging to several local families and set them up as field hospitals. Some were very near the battle lines where the boom of cannons mixed with the screams of the wounded, and the whooping battle-cry of the war-crazed Rebels echoed in the rain-drenched air.

Jim's medical unit, the II Corps, had just recently settled into a barn on Miss Catherine Guinn's property. The barn was large and spacious, as were most of the barns around Gettysburg. The medical team had spent their first days preparing for the battle—and wounded—to come. They opened the medical chests, laying out surgical supplies, opiates, and bottles of whiskey. As an assistant surgeon, Jim prepared a knapsack filled with first aid supplies. He and an orderly would set up just beyond artillery range and treat the wounded before sending them to the hospital barn.

All that and more should have prepared them for the upcoming battle. But none of them expected the carnage that happened that second day in Gettysburg.

The patriotic music and the military band that played it had retired around midnight, and Jim was glad for it. There was nothing patriotic about blood and bodies and severed limbs, nor the diseases that seemed to follow the Army wherever they went. The music might help the soldier's morale, but to Jim it might as well be a death knell.

Medical personnel assessed the injuries of the arriving casualties. Medics bandaged the less seriously injured and sent them outside to wait for the surgeons. They moved the gravely wounded to an outside tent. Most who went there died within hours. They set aside another tent for the bodies, but retrieving them from the battlefield would take days.

At the end of the first day, patients filled every open space in the barn: the haymows, the granary, the horse stable, the cattle stalls. They sent anyone not destined for the tents of the dead or dying outside, leaving them exposed to the elements and the potential for heatstroke. It was just another way to die.

But Jim had no time to take in any of his surroundings except the patient at hand. Those treated first were the ones who had injuries serious enough to be life-threatening, but not fatal if treated immediately.

Before now, Jim's title of Assistant Surgeon kept him from performing the actual surgery except in an extreme emergency. But now, they set aside all rules and customs because of the sheer volume of casualties, and Jim, soaked in blood and bits of flesh, stood by a rapidly growing pile of amputated limbs. The area more resembled a butcher shop than an operating theater.

His work with the scalpel and saw was quick and efficient. He removed the useless flesh and flattened bullets, dropping them in a bucket under the broad board serving as an operating table. The surgical team sewed up the wound, bandaged it, moved the patient to a recovery tent, and brought in another patient. It was endless work that he could probably do in his sleep, and he struggled to stay awake despite the chaos that surrounded him.

He'd lost track of when his day had started, unsure if there'd been any respite between yesterday and today and if there'd be any respite before tomorrow.

He knew what to do with the wounded, but it was the soldiers who seemed out of their wits that most worried him. It was their eyes—the wide, wild look of terror, the look of men who desperately wished they could un-see the things they'd witnessed, wandering, mumbling to themselves. Some sat rigidly, as if in a daze, their empty stares reliving the carnage. He wondered how many of them would end up locked away like Nichols—or dead.

As the afternoon waned, Jim took a few moments to stretch his legs and clear his thoughts. Passing the cluster of unloading ambulances, he saw a familiar face.

Was that Napoleon holding one end of a stretcher? Jim shook his head—could it be? The man's beard was speckled with gray. Spidery lines stretched from his eyes. He looked to be at least forty.

Jim stepped closer. "Napoleon?"

The man's eyes flew open as he recognized his name and Jim's voice.

"Jim?" Napoleon signaled to another soldier to take over his end of the stretcher. With his hands free now, Napoleon grabbed Jim by the shoulders and held him at arm's length. "You look like hell, mister."

Jim cracked a smile. "There's the cousin I know and love!" he shook Napoleon's hand. "How are you doing?"

"I've been better," Napoleon snorted out a half-laugh.

"How long has it been?" Jim asked. "Two years?"

"Just about." Napoleon hesitated, staring into the distance. "Feels like a lifetime ago."

The two men stood silently, appraising one another as if trying to find the boy they once knew. A cannon fired in the distance, and Napoleon's attention shifted.

"Napoleon, are you alright?" The blank expression on Napoleon's face worried him.

"You haven't seen my friend, have you? His name's Reuben Davenport."

"Can't say." Jim shrugged. "What does he look like?"

Napoleon put his arm out straight and lowered

it a few inches. "About this tall. Skinny. Light brown hair and a scrabbly beard. Stinks to high heaven."

Jim laughed. "I've treated a lot of men with that description, but I don't recall a Reuben."

"Can't find him anywhere." Napoleon shook his head. "One minute he's right beside me, the next minute he isn't."

"Drown! Get a move on!" The plea came from an overwhelmed ambulance driver.

"Gotta go." Napoleon shook Jim's hand once more. "Keep a lookout for Reuben, will ya?"

Jim waved at Napoleon's back as he rushed to the waiting ambulance. He offered a brief prayer of thanks that his cousin was all right, and, remembering the empty stare he'd seen earlier, worried that maybe he wasn't.

CHAPTER 39

July 3, 1863
Gettysburg, PA

Napoleon and the few remaining men of the 80th spent much of the night scouring the battlefield for the living and burying the dead. When he finally had time to sleep, he lay down behind the rocks, covered his ears against the cries of the trapped and wounded still on the battlefield, and restlessly waited for dawn. Every once in a while, he turned to say something to Reuben only to spark an image of his friend's broken body lying on the battleground.

He gave up trying to sleep as the early light filtered through the overcast sky. Already several companies were skirmishing near Culp's Hill to the east. To the west, Rebel sharpshooters banged away at the Union troop lines along Seminary Ridge.

Finally, they gave the order to fall in. They gave each man sixty rounds of ammunition and sent them out to search for survivors. It wasn't hard to identify the dead; by morning their bodies had started to decay, quickly swelling to twice their normal size and stinking of death. From there, the bodies turned black and putrid, like something straight out of an Edgar Allan Poe story. Napoleon and the others retrieved the bodies as best they could and loaded them onto carts that would carry them off for burial.

Another detail tended to the dead and wounded animals, shooting those injured but still alive. They piled the bodies in a heap and ignited them. The pyres only half-burned and left a putrid stench in the air. Scavengers and flies consumed what remained.

The sun still hung low in the eastern sky when they settled behind a low stone wall near the Brien farm. Occasionally, the shriek of an artillery round pierced the air. They cringed at the sound, but by then the bullet had already passed, and men were dead. A horse, its reins draped loosely in a nearby tree, was struck by a piece of shell and hurled into the stream.

The sky blazed with shells and the missiles they carried. Bullets and shrapnel rained down like tornado-spawned hail. Red-hot projectiles set the helpless wounded on fire where they lay; the roasting men screamed like banshees in the night.

The air whistled, shells exploded, bodies flew into the air and fell in pieces. A shell struck the stone wall, sending a blanket of flames and smoke that choked their lungs and singed their eyebrows.

The regiment, in disarray from the hail of fire, reorganized and formed a line of battle. Napoleon joined the line, armed and ready to fire.

But what they saw across the ridge caused many of the Union soldiers to cringe. The Confederates had formed three lines of battle and were marching straight for them.

"Hold fire!" Colonel Gates directed his men to lie tight to the rolling ground as the Rebels advanced.

Napoleon looked at the soldier beside him. "What on earth is he doing?" Napoleon said. "He's going to get us all killed."

The enemy surged closer, scaling the fences and whooping like poltergeists. When they reached the road, Gates gave the command. "Fire at will!"

Cheers rose; chaos reigned. The smoke of gunfire grew denser until the charging troops were no more than ghostly shadows. But the men of the 111th kept firing, and the rebel soldiers began to fall like ten-pins.

When the Confederate line fell back behind the ridge, Napoleon and his regiment pushed toward them, taking as many prisoners as they could.

Amid the charging men, into the smoke and the carnage, rode General Hays, grabbing a Confederate flag. "So we wipe out Harper's Ferry!" he shouted as he dragged the flag through the bloody field.

All around him, Union soldiers cheered, and a chant rose from the men. "Harper's Ferry Cowards! Harper's Ferry Cowards!" What was once a badge of shame was now worn with honor.

By early afternoon, the clouds were clearing; the heat from the sun further cooked the battlefield remains, and the stench grew unbearable. The fires ravaged the former farmland, which was now littered with the dead and injured. Wild hogs scoured the fields, scavenging for edible bits of flesh. Napoleon surveyed the carnage and once again thought of Reuben. His head reeled, tears ran down his face, and he retched at the sight of blood and brain, at the smell of ruined bodies and drifting gun smoke.

Across the battlefield, the bodies were untouched by the fire. Union soldiers wandered among the corpses, looting everything of value they could find. As Napoleon wandered through the bodies, he came across a deceased Confederate soldier clutching a torn envelope. Kneeling next to the body, Napoleon put the envelope in his pocket, intending to give it to his commanding officer later on. He pulled out the knife he kept in his boot and sliced a button marked with the seal of Virginia from the soldier's coat, and picked up the kepi with its "E" company insignia that lay beside him.

Around six p.m. thunder rumbled in the distance, but few of the soldiers paid any attention. Compared to the artillery fire of the afternoon, the distant booming seemed tame. That changed quickly as a massive thundercloud descended and poured heavy rain across Gettysburg. Napoleon, taking cover in a small shed, remembered the letter as it crinkled beneath him. He pulled out the envelope, postmarked at Bristol Springs, Virginia, and addressed to "Mr. Samuel Parrish. Co. E, 28 regt va. Vol, Garnett's Brigade. Picket Division." On the back was the return address: "Fanney Richardson, clifton, va"

Inside, the letter was wrinkled and splattered with smudges. The handwriting was primitive, scattered across the page like chicken scratches and difficult to read. The text was one long sentence with no punctuation and poor grammar. Clearly, the writer was barely literate. Napoleon squinted at the page and began to read.

Fryday morning May 29, 1863

My dear Sir, I take my pen in hand this morning to drop you a few lines in anser to your most kind and affectate letter which I received last satterday evening it found me well an doing well it is the first letter that I have received from you for about three months ... well sam I hardly no what to write to you that would interreste you there is not much interresting news going at this time thare is plenty of news flying but non of the write sort thar is non that you would cear about hearing most all of the news that is going now is lys and such news as that no boddy doant want to hear... sam I have

got aheap to tell you if I ever see you again… I wish that I was setting hear talking with you instead of writing to you it would be more satesfacting to me than it is sam you must give my respecks to pollard and to all the boys and tell them that tha must not let the yanks get them if tha can help it …you must give my love to all inquiring friends if eney thare be you must anser this letter as soon as you get it…I still remain your affectate Cosen until death
Fanney Richardson to Samuel Parrish
write soon goodby

Napoleon re-folded the letter, returned it to its envelope, and tucked it in his haversack. Maybe someday he would find a way to return it to Fanney. He lay back against a bale of straw and listened to the heavy rain as it pounded on the roof. He'd seen so many bodies that day and, hard as he tried, he couldn't conjure an image of the soldier who was Samuel Parrish. But did it really matter? Other than his politics, he wasn't so different from Napoleon: He had a family, loved ones, a home. Napoleon guessed he was a farmer from a small town like his. Was he married? Did he have a wife? A sweetheart? Children? If they'd met under different circumstances, would they have been friends?

Napoleon would likely never know. But if it was within his power, he'd see the letter would find its way home even if Samuel Parrish couldn't.

The heavy rain that started on the third continued for days. The old-timers claimed the weather always went bad after a momentous battle. Some claimed it was God's way of cleansing the earth of the death and destruction caused by man's folly.

On Saturday, July fourth, the regiment recovered the dead and wounded from both sides. They buried the dead in a mass grave; prayers given for Union and Confederate soldiers alike. In the grave, it didn't matter what side they fought on. What mattered was that each fought with valor and died in defense of their beliefs.

By Sunday, July 5th, there was no sign of the Rebels. The remaining men of the Union Army cleaned their rifles, formed up, and plodded through the rain down the Taneytown Road in pursuit of Lee's Army.

CHAPTER 40

Hospital, 3d Division, 2d Corps
Near Gettysburg, PA.

July 27, 1863
Dear Parents,

I have wished many times to write to you, but my time and facilities for writing have been very limited since the battle. It is impossible for me to give any adequate description by writing of the terrible engagement through which we have passed, and I would rather reserve the tales of horror until I can describe it in person.

It is not the patriotism that has made me take this course. If it had been patriotism, I should have been sick of it long since.

Of course, the Surgeons were all busy and have been until now. When the "Army of the Potomac" moved in pursuit of Lee, I was detailed to remain as an assistant of Dr. McAfee with one other of our Division forming an operating board. Dr. McAfee is the Chief Surgeon of our Division and for over a week I had the opportunity of assisting in hundreds of very important operations and in consequence my mind is impressed with many items relating to Surgery that I should not have gained had I gone on with the Regiment. I should judge that we have now about 600 wounded in our corps including many rebels, perhaps 200 in number, who receive the same attention as our own men. This is only one Corps and considering the fact that there are seven Corps and that every day or two a train containing from 4 to 500 wounded [are] sent away to different Hospitals you can form but a slight conception of the number injured in the engagement. The fact is, no idea of the Army of the Potomac can be formed until one has seen it.

We have been very uncertain how long we were to stay at Gettysburg but I am inclined to think we may stay a week or two longer. I shall probably join the regiment by the overland route on horseback.

Give my love to all my friends in Cato and Ira. Write me as soon as possible and tell me the news. Kiss my little girl for me and Believe me.

Ever your Affectionate Son,

James D. Banyon

1st asst. surgeon, 111th regt.

The 111th had long since left Gettysburg. But for Jim and the medical team, the battle at Gettysburg was far from over. The flow of wounded was constant. On foot or on stretchers, the men came into the hospital barn to be treated. They sent the more seriously injured to general hospitals in the nearest cities.

When he'd graduated from medical college, Jim thought he knew all there was to know about medicine and healing, but now he knew better. The wounds he'd seen were injuries he never could have imagined; the procedures he'd learned were inconceivable before now. He'd learned to improvise treatments and use medicines in new ways. He witnessed men dying in ways he'd never imagined, and images of his mangled friends' and comrades' bodies seared themselves into his mind. When he got the chance to sleep, his dreams were of hurried amputations and discarded limbs, of soldiers screaming for the mercy of death. The foul stench of blood and flesh invaded his sleep, and he often woke to find himself desperately trying to scrub himself clean.

There had been no time for the shell-shocked. Surgeons quickly examined them; finding no physical wounds, they pronounced the soldiers fit for battle and sent them back to their regiment.

A week after the last troops had left for Virginia, a familiar voice came from just outside the barn door.

"Jim?"

Jim startled as the shaky voice broke his concentration. Was that Napoleon? He held up his free hand to signal the person to wait.

"Jim, is that you?"

Dr. McAfee nodded to Jim, who stepped aside for another assistant to take his place. Jim wiped his bloody hands on his shirttail, doing his best to clear the waste from between his fingers. Was that really Napoleon leaning against the door? The soldier resembled him, and he bore the insignia of the 80th NY Volunteers, Napoleon's regiment, but the man he saw was only a relic of his friend and cousin. Pale and emaciated, he had the wild and tortured look of the men who had gathered by the barn the last night of the battle. His eyes were bloodshot, his arms covered with half-healed cuts and scratches. He looked exhausted and frail, as if he might fall if the door frame hadn't supported him.

"Napoleon, are you okay?" Jim wanted to slap himself—of course Napoleon wasn't okay. He put his arm around Napoleon's shoulder, led him to a nearby ambulance wagon, and sat him at the back. He quickly scanned Napoleon from head to toe, making sure he wasn't seriously injured, then he took Napoleon's hand.

"Napoleon." Napoleon stared into the distance as if he hadn't heard.

"Napoleon!"

Napoleon jumped. His eyes widened, and he began to tremble.

"Napoleon, it's me. Jim." Jim gently took Napoleon's chin and turned his head. "Why aren't you with your regiment?"

"I left the regiment." Napoleon's chin dropped to his chest; his eyes filled with tears. "By the time we got to Harper's Ferry, I knew I had to come back."

"What do you mean? You deserted?" This was not the devil-may-care, swaggering man Jim knew.

"I-I guess you could say so." Napoleon raised his head and looked at Jim. "Jim, I think I might be dying."

Jim took Napoleon's wrist, and what he felt alarmed him. Napoleon's heart raced at a dangerously high and irregular pace. His skin felt cold and clammy.

"What makes you think you're dying?" he asked. He kept his voice measured and calm.

"I can't eat. I can hardly sleep, and when I do, I have nightmares." Napoleon placed a hand on his abdomen. "My belly ails me something terrible, and I feel like there's a big stone sitting on my chest. My head is pounding, and sometimes I feel like I can't even catch my breath." Napoleon's arm shook violently in Jim's hand.

"I'm dying, aren't I?" His tears fell freely now. "I came to see you because I know you'll tell me the truth."

Jim's stomach clenched. He'd heard those symptoms far too many times in the past couple of years. *But this is my cousin!* Could the mental stress of war be affecting him? Jim didn't want to believe it.

Jim put his ear to Napoleon's chest. The man's

heartbeat was strong enough. *Maybe if I can calm him down, his heartbeat might get slower.* He cautiously felt Napoleon's torso, front and back, then ran his hands down Napoleon's arms and legs, feeling for any injuries.

Satisfied that Napoleon wasn't physically injured, he said, "Napoleon, you aren't dying." Jim put his hand on Napoleon's shoulder and gently squeezed it. "You're away from home, and you've been away for two years now. You're just homesick."

"Homesick?" Napoleon's eyes were wide with disbelief. "You think I'm just homesick? Why do I feel like I'm going to die?"

"What you've been through—what every Union soldier has been through—would give any man nightmares. You and I have seen things we can't ever erase. It's no wonder you can't eat or sleep. It'd make the strongest of us want to pack up and go home.

"But, Napoleon, you have to go back to your regiment. You can't stay here even if we had room for you."

"Please don't make me go back." Napoleon's voice was a whisper now. "I can't go back."

Jim sat next to Napoleon and reconsidered.

Could Napoleon be going down the same road as his study subjects? Could he end up like Private Nichols? Despite his assurances to his cousin, Napoleon's symptoms still unsettled him.

No, Napoleon is stronger than that.

"I can see that you're exhausted, and weak from hunger," Jim said. "Maybe I can put you on sick leave for a few days. I'm sure that with a little rest and some decent food, you'll feel better. You can sleep in my room while you're here."

Napoleon grasped Jim's hand. "Thank you, cousin," he said. "Let me stay awhile, and I promise I'll go back to my regiment."

Although the armies have moved on, I remain at Gettysburg, treating the sick and wounded who are not well enough to travel. Today I had a surprise visitor in the person of my cousin, Napoleon Drown. The news is not good. He has abandoned his regiment with no intention of returning. More concerning, he shows the signs of stress that I see in my study patients. In addition, the trauma of battle, including seeing his comrade's head blown off by enemy cannonade, seems to have addled his mind. He has pleaded for my protection and begged me not to return him to his regiment. At this time, I agree he is not fit for duty, and I will write a letter to his commanding officer expressing my diagnosis. I hope that with a temporary respite, he will recover his wits and his courage, as I cannot keep him from duty indefinitely.

Major Anthony stormed into the medical tent. "Who the hell do you think you are putting Corporal Drown on sick leave? His colonel is about fit to be tied. The only thing sick about him is he's a lazy bastard."

Jim set down his pen and looked up at Anthony. "I have that authority, Major Anthony," he said, keeping his voice low and even. "When it comes to the health of my patients, I have full authority. And that means nobody—not even General Meade—can interfere with my decisions."

Ten days later, Napoleon reached down from his saddle and shook Jim's hand. "Thanks again, cousin. I knew you could help."

"Anytime," Jim said. "Do you know where your regiment is now?"

"Down in Centreville," Napoleon said. "It won't take me but a couple of days to get there."

Jim nodded. "You take care of yourself, cousin." He watched as Napoleon trotted south, sitting confidently in the saddle.

Now that man is a lot closer to the Napoleon I know, thought Jim. He dusted his hands off and turned toward the hospital barn, only to find his way blocked by Anthony.

"This isn't the end of it." Anthony shoved Jim's shoulder. "It has nothing to do with illness. You let Drown off because he's your cousin, and neither I nor the Colonel will tolerate favoritism."

CHAPTER 41

September, 1863
Culpeper, VA

Despite the rain, well-wishers leaned from the windows, cheering and waving miniature flags as the Union soldiers marched through the streets of Culpeper in pursuit of Lee's troops. The Culpeper town band played, protected by a hastily erected canopy. The men of the 111th stood tall, their faces obscured by the hooded rain jackets they wore; they were no longer the cowards that were taunted in Baltimore just months ago.

Fewer than two hundred of the original one thousand men of the regiment remained, their numbers decimated by battle and disease. The men who remained marched, day after day, chasing Confederates.

By all appearances, they were a proud cadre of men, their backs held straight, their eyes focused on victory. But under the façade, many of the Union soldiers struggled, some from the incessant rain, some from lingering illnesses, some from images that would never leave their heads.

Napoleon lifted his free hand and wiped the snot dripping from his nose. He ached from the pressure in his neck and head. The stuffiness in his nose made it difficult to breathe, but the cold, damp air he inhaled when he breathed through his mouth made his lungs burn. He was relieved it was just a head cold. When the coughing came from deep in his chest, he'd start worrying.

Beyond the city, the roads were swamps, muddy and churned up from the constant movement of men, mules, and wagons. Horses sank up to their bellies, and wagons sank up to the tops of their wheels, making the mud deeper and more treacherous. The heavy artillery sank so deeply in the mud it was nearly impossible to extricate.

Shivering under their rain jackets, the men stumbled against the wind, rain, and shin-deep mud. Boots stuck in the thick clay, abandoned where they lay by men who didn't care much about anything anymore. They hadn't slept well in weeks, hadn't had dry clothes for nearly as long. Their food was waterlogged, their black powder wet and useless. Morale was at rock bottom. To a man, they were irritable as hell and spoiling for a fight.

"Lord knows where we're going," one soldier grumbled, "but I wish like hell we'd get there."

"If you wasn't so slow," snarled the man next to him, "we'd have been there hours ago."

The fuse was lit. The first soldier tackled the second, nearly burying his face in the mud. The second fought back. A third man joined the fight, and then another until the mud bog looked like a pigsty full of hogs fighting over slops.

The officers, too, had had enough. They ignored the mud-covered pile of men, urging their horses forward and out of the mire. When the fighting was over, the soldiers resumed their places and continued to slog ahead, covered in thick mud and no happier than before.

After Gettysburg, confrontations with the Confederates ranged from brief skirmishes to full-on battles. The Army of the Potomac maneuvered through Centreville, Warrenton, and Brandy Station during the Bristoe Campaign. For ten days in mid-October, they chased Lee's army all over Virginia. The rain continued relentlessly, and a cold snap made the weather nearly as dangerous as the enemy.

The 80th New York Volunteers might not have been heavily engaged in combat, but their presence was crucial for maintaining order and security during the Union Army's movements.

As the regiment settled for the night, the only thing more miserable than the weather was Napoleon himself. Wrapped in his rubber blanket, his head covered by his raincoat, he huddled under a clump of trees whose remaining leaves barely clung to their branches. On a dry day, the fallen leaves provided warm cover from the cold. But today, the soaking rain and deep mud made them useless. More than once, Napoleon wondered if perhaps a bullet to the head was an easier way to die.

Ignoring the rhythmic drip of rain as it fell on his raincoat, Napoleon concentrated as he wrote a letter to Jim.

Dear Cousin,

I fear I am on the brink of collapse.

No, that was a terrible way to start a letter. He scribbled out the line and started over.

Dear Cousin,

We have made a temporary camp under a hedge of oaks, but it is poor protection from the constant rain. Johnny Reb is on the run, and we will continue to chase him until he surrenders for good. We have been well-received by the townsfolk, who are grateful for our courageous victory at Gettysburg.

Jim, the memories of Reuben's death still haunt me nightly. I thought your help at Gettysburg would have buried them long ago, but it was to no avail.

Napoleon hesitated. He needed to tell Jim about the nightmares, about the sense of doom that lingered like the rain clouds. Some nights he dreamed of Reuben's headless body lying motionless on the blood-soaked battlefield; other nights that body reared up as if under its own power, pointing an accusing finger at Napoleon.

"How could you let me die?" There was no head—no mouth to utter the words, yet they were as sharp as a sword's edge.

"I'm sorry." Napoleon's tears mixed with the chilly rain as he spoke. The words felt as empty as his food-deprived belly, and there was no one to hear them but himself.

Napoleon wasn't the only one haunted by the things he'd seen this past year. He watched his fellow soldiers struggle; many of them wandered the empty fields at night as if unaware of their surroundings. Some called out for their mothers; some stared vacantly at the starless sky.

Would he end up like his comrades, mumbling at shadows? Could he manage to keep his wits about him? Was he going insane? He'd heard stories of the conditions at insane asylums, and he shivered at the thought of being sent there.

He put down his pencil and reread what he'd written.

No, thought Napoleon, *I can't bother Jim with my troubles.*

Before now, his goal was to stay alive long enough to see home again. But how was he going to protect his body *and* his mind until then?

Napoleon tore up the rain-soaked letter and buried it in the mud. Sobs rose from deep inside. Covering his mouth, he wrapped the blanket tighter and buried his head against his knees.

CHAPTER 42

October 1863

Culpeper, VA

Napoleon wasn't sure what was worse—watching his comrades die in battle or sitting around babysitting prisoners while his country was at war. In how many battles had he seen actual combat? He wondered.

One too many. Reuben's sarcasm echoed in his head. Napoleon waved his hand in the air, swatting at the pest that was Reuben's ghost. Finally surrounded by order, provost duty might have eased the chaos of combat, but his mind was still at war—and there was nowhere to run.

The 80th Regiment left Gettysburg in early July. They marched south, through Emmitsburg, Turner's and Crampton's Gaps, to Brooks Station, and most recently to Culpeper, where their job was to guard the Rebel prisoners, maintain order among the Union troops, and provide security at both headquarters and supply depots. Occasionally, their superiors tasked them with rounding up Union stragglers and deserters and returning them to their units.

The sun rose high in the early fall sky. Napoleon rummaged through his haversack in search of stray coffee beans he could roast. He pulled out weevil-infested hardtack, rancid hunks of pork, a tin plate, cup and utensils—all of its contents, until he reached the bottom of the bag where he discovered a lumpy envelope.

Retrieving the envelope, he saw it contained the "souvenirs" he'd taken from the body of the Confederate soldier back in Gettysburg: a coat button with the Virginia seal, a brass "E" from the soldier's kepi, and a smudged and bloodied letter.

He remembered now, recalling the aftermath of Pickett's Charge, combing the battlefield for survivors, and the body of a boy who had no business fighting a man's war. He might have been wearing gray instead of blue, but he was still a child, and far too young to die.

Napoleon envisioned the gray uniform, tattered, ragged, too big for the boy's skinny frame. Blood covered the boy, and his wide eyes stared at the heavens.

Had he seen God when he died?

I have no business keeping these things. On the back of the envelope was a return address: Miss Fanney Richardson, Clifton, Campbell County, Virginia. Should he return the items to Miss Richardson? Surely she deserved them as well as a letter of explanation.

Napoleon quickly reread the letter, found a blank sheet of paper and took up his pen.

Miss Fanney Richardson
Clifton, Campbell County, Virginia
Miss Richardson,

My name is Napoleon Drown. I am a corporal in the Union army. I am returning to you these items from the body of your cousin, Samuel Parrish, who died at Gettysburg on July third of this year.

After General Pickett's fateful charge, the army ordered my company and me to retrieve injured soldiers from the field. During that assignment, I encountered the body of your cousin, Samuel Parrish, and discovered these items in his haversack.

I am ashamed to admit that I intended to

keep the enclosed items as souvenirs of war, but I now realize that was not the moral choice. I am returning them to you, the author of the letter.

Anyone who has seen combat, regardless of the side they fight on, knows the ugliness of death and the horrors of war. Not one of us remains the man he once was.

I will never understand why God-fearing men from both North and South must be pried from their families to fight in a war none of us started. That "honor" should go to the men in power who seem not to know what they want except to destroy one another.

You may wonder why I felt obliged to enlist. I will tell you, it was for patriotism and duty, and I wish now that I never had. My closest friend died at Gettysburg. The image of his blood-soaked body will remain with me for the rest of my days.

I trust you will treasure these small mementos as I never could, in memory of your cousin, Samuel.

Please accept my condolences on the loss of Private Parrish. I pray he did not suffer overly much.

May God rest his soul.

Yours sincerely,
Corporal Napoleon B. Drown,
80th New York Volunteers Regiment, Army of the
Potomac.

In early November, Major General Sedgwick's forces attacked the Confederates at Rappahannock Station, leading to the capture of over 1,600 soldiers. Now large tents filled the field behind the railroad depot, each crammed with Confederate prisoners waiting to be transported by wagon convoy to the Old Prison Camp building in Washington, D.C.

But today, Napoleon's regiment had a more important task.

The Army of the Pacific—nearly 120,000 troops—was crossing the Rappahannock River between Brooks Station and Brandy Station, where they would spend the winter near Stevensburg, preparing for the spring campaign against the Confederates. The 80th regiment's job was to maintain order and discipline within the long line of troops as they progressed along the trail.

The train of wagons stretched for nearly fifty miles, fading into the dust and haze to the north. Mules and horses pulled wagons loaded with food, ammunition, medical supplies, tents, and personal gear. Companies of soldiers accompanied their wagons, some on horseback, and others on foot. The clump of their boots as they marched created an ominous rhythm.

Injured and ill soldiers, along with their caretakers, rode in ambulance wagons; other wagons carried blacksmith tools, printing presses, and other gear necessary to sustain over one-hundred thousand men for six months. The wagons rocked violently, their wheels creaking as they maneuvered over the deeply rutted road.

At the river's edge, the wagons pushed their way through the shallows, the sound of splashing water mixing with the bray of mules and the neighs of the horses. Whips snapped across their rumps as their handlers shouted orders. From time to time, a wagon became stuck in the mucky river bottom until someone pushed it out, dripping with water and mud as it climbed the bank on the other side.

Napoleon watched the spectacle. Never had he seen so many wagons and soldiers in one place. Every few minutes he scanned the surrounding woods for signs of enemy movement. The Rebs were supposedly to the south, but small groups of skirmishers were a constant possibility.

A lone voice from the line of soldiers captured his attention.

"Reuben?" he whispered. It couldn't be him. But that voice—that same mix of innocence and attitude...

Napoleon scanned the group of men that passed directly in front of him in search of the voice's source. His eyes landed on a short man, so skinny his clothes hung from his body. The soldier's beard and hair, long and scrawny, were the color of day-old straw.

Reuben!

Napoleon's heart galloped; his throat felt constricted, like he couldn't breathe. Reuben's ghost appeared where the soldier had been, staring at him with the empty eyes of the dead.

Napoleon trembled. He scrambled to a nearby tree for support. Gasping for air, he struggled to regain control, but the ghost hadn't finished with him.

Why did you let me die?

Napoleon turned his face away, squeezed his eyes shut and prayed for Reuben's ghost to leave. When he at last turned back to the line of troops, Reuben's ghost was gone, replaced by the young man with corn silk hair.

It was just a crazy coincidence, nothing more. Napoleon consoled himself. *It couldn't have been Reuben. Reuben is dead.* He repeated the words to himself, hoping that if he said them enough, he would believe it.

And he would tell no one.

CHAPTER 43

November 1863

Seminary Hospital
Georgetown, D.C.
Nov. 16, 1863
Dear Father,

... since I came into the hospital here, my health has greatly improved. The change from the ground to a good bed and comfortable room did me much good. My disease was the same as I have been troubled with most of the fall viz intermittent fever with diarrhea which latter I had about two months and I was very fearful that it would become chronic, but I am glad to say that I am better in this respect. My fever has stopped, but I am very weak, and slight exertion starts the sweat.

There does not appear to be any army news at present. I am told that army headquarters are at Brandy Station, doubtless waiting for the completion of the Rail Road which is nearly done. I am inclined to think that there will be another fight before a great while in Virginia.

Wrapped in a thin blanket and shivering from the cold, Jim stumbled across the hospital room where he was a patient. His dysentery at last seemed under control, but he was still weak, unable to take more than a few steps before exhaustion urged him back to his bed.

The past few days had given him a new perspective on hospital life: that of being a patient. He hated being bedridden, so helpless that even his bowel movements depended on the help of a nurse. He'd written letters, read medical journals, and most of the well-worn novels that circulated through the ward. Even those minor acts felt draining until recently. Never again would he shake his head at a patient who complained of boredom, nor would he wave away a bedridden man who merely wanted a drink of water.

"Doctor." Jim recognized the slight accent that even his name elicited.

"Doctor Larssen!" Jim pushed himself to a sitting position and extended his hand. "How are you?"

"The question is, how are *you?*" Larssen shook Jim's hand and instinctively felt his forehead. "Good," he said. "No fever."

Larssen sat at the foot of Jim's bed. "Have you run into Doctor Fisher during your stay?"

"Dr. Fisher? No, I haven't seen him. What ward is he working in?"

"He's not a doctor here," Larssen said, shaking his head. "He's a patient. Admitted for 'rest', but really his problem is drinking."

"A patient?" Jim hesitated. "I guess that shouldn't surprise me. It's not like most of us haven't relied on a touch of liquor, given what we've seen. Some rely on it a little too much." *And who can blame them?* Jim thought. *How else can one numb the images of amputated limbs and shattered bodies, the smell of blood and ether, and the absolute stench of death?* He thought about his last encounter with Dr. Fischer.

It didn't occur to me then, thought Jim as he recalled their conversation, *but even then Fisher always had a flask of whiskey nearby. His breath often stank with the sweet, sharp tang of alcohol, and now that I think about it, more than once I noticed him stumbling on his way back to his office.*

It was a sultry August morning in Gettysburg, and Dr. Fischer was reviewing the patients still hospitalized. He gestured to a boy not more than twenty years old, who didn't seem to notice their presence. "What's this soldier's problem?"

"Private Mitchell," Jim said, nodding toward the patient. "He seems to be addled. He doesn't remember the battle, nor even where he is. I've been seeing a lot of men with this problem." It reminded him of Private Nichols, and he briefly wondered whether Nichols was still under Dr. Earle's care.

"It's as if these men believe they're still on the battlefield. They flinch at loud noises, complain of gunpowder and blood on their skin that won't wash off. Some seem to lapse into what I can only describe as a waking nightmare, fighting unseen Rebels and ducking from phantom gunfire."

Fischer listened solemnly, occasionally nodding his head as Jim described the symptoms of the affected soldiers.

"I'm not sure if his symptoms are legitimate or not, but I'd like to keep Private Mitchell for observation for the time being." Jim looked at the head surgeon for his approval.

"Let's go into my office." Fischer gestured

toward the open door.

Sitting behind his desk, he motioned for Jim to take a seat, picked up the open whiskey decanter on his desk, and poured himself a drink. After putting the stopper back, he placed the decanter on the floor, hidden from view, as if he didn't want to share.

Fischer, as he quietly sipped his drink, appeared to be considering Jim's words.

"Jim," he finally said, with a concerned look on his face, "I know you have compassion for your patients. As a doctor, that's your job. But there's something you have to understand. Some of these boys will do just about anything to get sent home. They get such a yearning for their mothers they can barely stand it, and the only way they can think of to get out of the army is to get a medical discharge. They've seen their friends get away with it, so they come up with the most cockamamie plan, acting crazy to get out of the military. The thing is, you call them on it and most of them will straighten up and fly right, and that's the end of it. Those that don't are just more desperate.

"But the truth is," Fischer leaned forward as if revealing a closely kept secret, "they're all a bunch of lazy cowards in my book. What they need is a little sense slapped into them."

Jim shook his head. "I'm not sure that's true of all of them. Even the rest at winter camp isn't helping. Isn't there something else we can do?"

Fischer shrugged, shaking his head. "My remedy is to give them a swift kick in the pants and tell them to get back to work."

CHAPTER 44

January 1864

Winter Camp, Stevensburg, VA

Jim winced as he stepped out of his cabin and into the crisp winter air. He'd been back from the hospital at Georgetown for a few weeks and was grateful to wake every morning feeling stronger than the day before. Stretching his long-idle muscles, he briskly climbed Cole's Hill, one of a prominent ridge of hills northeast of Stevensburg. Not much more than a small gathering of homesteads, the little hamlet of Stevensburg was like most of the Virginia towns Jim had traveled through: larger on the map than it was in reality. To the west of the town were the larger village of Culpeper and the towering Slaughter Mountain, where, in August of 1862, the Confederate Army of Virginia routed the Union forces at the Battle of Cedar Run. The deep blue of the Blue Ridge Mountains dominated the western horizon, a smoky slate hue that earned them their name.

Although it had no proper name, the 111th's current winter encampment was more like a temporary city, and dubbed the "Camp in the Mud" by its inhabitants.

They arranged the encampment into company streets with proper sanitation. The enlisted men's quarters were log-wall cabins with tent roofs, luxurious compared to their usual ragged tents used when they were on the march. Officers' quarters were log houses.

The 111th's lodgings were a small neighborhood in that city, along with the rest of the II Corps. The relative quiet brought with it a camaraderie that was often lacking during the stress of battle, providing a sanctuary of sanity and a small feeling of home.

Across the Rapidan River to the south, Confederate General Ewing's II Corps stood guard. Barring any unplanned movement from the Rebs, the Union would remain near Stevensburg until spring.

It would be a respite for the battered Union soldiers, but for some the dreary quiet of camp was harder than the pressure of imminent battle. Every day was the same: mind-numbing guard duty, endless drills, fatigue drills that were mostly busy work. They cut wood, carried water, and built roads. They spent their evenings playing cards, drinking, or writing letters home.

The weather was bitterly cold and, unlike the other soldiers, the medical staff stayed busy with the typical illnesses that rampaged through the military camp like a rogue nor'easter. Dysentery was the prime culprit, but the cold brought on bouts of respiratory illnesses that often led to pneumonia and almost certain death.

Invigorated by his short hike, Jim returned to his hut and drew out his journal.

I am witness to the increasing debilitation of these men's emotional trauma, he wrote. I recognize the common look in my patients: the stare to nowhere, the eyes that have seen everything and recognize nothing. Many are subject to sudden angry and destructive outbursts. The men jump at the slightest sound, and often act as if they are in battle rather than in a hospital bed. They rub their skin vigorously as if desperate to rid themselves of the odors of gunpowder and blood. Their minds seem increasingly addled to the point where some seem to recognize neither themselves nor their surroundings. Desertions are common, and I can't say that I blame those soldiers. The battlefield is not a fit place for any man.

Jim laid his pen on the table, remembering the altercation at the hospital a few days ago.

From the outside, the makeshift hospital looked like the rest of the wooden huts with one exception: it was much larger. Inside, it was one large room, made to accommodate about a hundred patients. Cots lined both sides, inhabited by men who were mostly well enough to sit up. A few windows let in what little light filtered through the heavy overcast sky. At night, oil lanterns flickered weakly, as if the ghosts of death awaited.

Most patients stayed only a few days, just long enough for their fevers to ease and their strength to return. A handful of them had been there longer, and Jim intended to keep them there as long as possible. They struggled to sleep, roaming the hospital at night when not tethered to their beds. They needed time. Time to recover from the sights and sounds of death.

It had been a routine day of examining patients, determining who was ready to be released and who needed more recovery time. At the cot next to him, a nurse changed the soiled sheets. A fresh bedpan lay at the foot of the mattress.

"Nurse!" A panicked call startled the nurse; he jerked at the sound, knocking the bedpan to the floor with a loud clang.

Across the room, a long-term patient flew out of his bed. "Attack!" he shouted. "To arms!" The man, his eyes focused on an unseen enemy, rushed to the door where a soldier stood sentry and grabbed the sentry's pistol.

"Secesh!" He aimed his pistol at a patient who lay prone on his cot, reading a recent letter from home, and shot him in the head.

"Anderson!" Jim started toward the armed man, who whirled around and pointed the pistol at Jim.

The sentry pulled out his saber, a useless weapon against a firearm, but the only weapon he had. Anderson reacted, turned the pistol on the sentry, and fired.

"Take cover!" Anderson shouted over his shoulder to his comrades.

In a fraction of a second, Erskine rushed at Anderson, tackling him to the floor, and wrestling the gun from his hands. Jim flew to Anderson's flailing legs, pinning them down. The nurse rushed out the door for help.

By the time help arrived, they'd subdued Anderson, who sat on the floor next to Jim. He appeared to have no understanding of where he was or what had happened. Erskine tended to the injured sentry. The bullet had pierced his shoulder, but he would recover. The other victim had died instantly.

"We've got him," one of the arriving sentries said. He grabbed Anderson roughly and forced him to his feet.

Anderson, now docile and quiet, looked at the sentry like a child who didn't understand why he was in trouble.

"Be easy on him," Jim pleaded with the sentries. "He's not in his right mind."

"There's nothing wrong with this man that a little solitary confinement can't fix," the sentry snarls, pushing him out the door.

"He's lost his mental faculties; he doesn't know what he's doing." Jim stood before Major Anthony. Of course, he'd be the one to hear Anderson's case, Jim mused. "Let me send him to the sanitarium for treatment."

"What for?" snapped Anthony. "So he can kill a few more friendlies?"

A knock at the door interrupted their conversation.

"Beg pardon, sir." The young private saluted nervously, his eyes filled with fear.

"What is it?" Anthony glared at the soldier, which only made the young man even more fidgety.

"Uh," the private wrestled with the words. "Corporal Anderson is gone."

"*Gone?*" Anthony jumped up from the desk, pushing past Jim. "To hell with the sanitarium," he growled at Jim. "He's going to get the firing squad!"

CHAPTER 45

January 1864
Culpeper, VA

Napoleon was no stranger to the cold. Lord knew he'd suffered snow measured by the foot and blizzard conditions in Central New York. But the winter at Stevensburg was a different kind of bone-chilling cold. No campfire was ever enough to warm him; even indoors he was eternally cold. In a few months he'd wish for cooler weather, but for now it was nearly unbearable.

When they were on duty at Kelly's Ford, the conditions were no better. The rickety building they used for provost guard duty barely kept out the wind. Below-freezing temperatures made for icy and hazardous conditions from dusk to dawn; the days warmed just enough to make roads into a mucky mess, sinking men up to their knees and wagons up to their axles.

The sheer number of makeshift shelters and huts, and the wood needed for heat, had all but stripped the landscape of trees. The frigid January air intensified the scents of wood smoke, boiled coffee, and mildewed canvas.

As a member of V Corps, the 80th regiment's quarters were near Rappahannock Station, a few miles from the river crossing at Kelly's Ford, a shallow, rocky crossing often used by the Union that was one of the few reliable crossings on the Rappahannock. The regiment's current headquarters was at Kellysville, the settlement that inspired the name Kelly's Ford. Surrounded by heavy woods and swamps, it offered concealment for the troops but also complicated movement.

All the discomfort intensified Napoleon's isolation. He flinched at every loud noise; he began skipping meals.

Napoleon heard the whispers as they drifted from the street.

"Drown's losing his sanity."

"I heard him talking to himself the other day, like there was someone right next to him you couldn't see."

Heads nodded in agreement; men glanced furtively in his direction and then quickly turned away when he noticed.

He began avoiding his comrades, spending most of his time wrapped in his greatcoat and rubber blanket, huddled as close to the fire as he could manage without singeing his eyebrows.

And Reuben was always there.

Corporal Anderson stumbled through the woods, running as if the devil himself was close behind. He didn't know where he was. He didn't know why he was running or where he was running to. And he desperately wanted to go home, even if he wasn't sure where that was.

He remembered being confined in a small tent. Daylight faded into darkness. Through a small opening in the flap, he saw a young soldier who guarded the tent. A light breeze lifted the tent flap— someone had left it untied.

The guard chatted with another soldier, complaining about the weather, or this shitty assignment they gave him. All Anderson could make out was the whine in his voice.

He didn't know what made him do it—charging out of the tent and running into the woods beyond Hansbrough's Ridge. The icy cold bit into his bare feet. Small rocks and roots poked at the soles until they bled. Behind him, the young guard shouted for Anderson to halt, but Anderson didn't hear him above the word that echoed in his head.

Run!

The early winter darkness shrouded the riverbank at Kelly's Ford. The air was heavy with moisture and wood smoke. Heavily laden wagons clattered in the distance; the drivers' voices urged the horses ahead.

A loud splash at the river crossing grabbed Napoleon's attention. He peered into the night, scanning for movement. Was it a wild animal? Not likely—the vast encampment had scared away most of them. Blinded by the bright light of the campfire,

Napoleon couldn't see anything between it and the river.

The splashing stopped. Someone gasped for air. A minute later, a silhouette appeared in front of the fire, dripping wet, shivering violently.

Napoleon pulled off his greatcoat as he raced toward the soldier, who stood in a daze, as if he didn't know where he was.

"Are you alright?" Napoleon wrapped the coat tightly around the soldier's skinny frame.

"Have to run." The man stared, hollow-eyed.

Napoleon noticed his bare feet, bloodied, and blue from the icy river. "Come inside," he said, nodding toward the rickety shelter. "You'll freeze to death out here." He guided the soldier inside to a wobbly chair and motioned for him to sit.

"Let me tend to your feet," he said.

The soldier stared at him. His eyes showed no recognition, no sign that he knew where he was or that he was wounded.

Napoleon grabbed a dry rag from the table, ripped it in half and bound the man's wounds. He rummaged through his haversack, pulled out a pair of dry, wool stockings and held them out. When the soldier didn't react, Napoleon gently eased the stockings over the man's bound feet.

"What's your name, soldier?" Napoleon asked.

The man blinked; a bit of recognition came into his eyes. "Anderson," he said.

The man who went crazy at Jim's hospital yesterday? The big brass would have a fit when they discovered he was gone. There'd be a bounty on his head for sure. He'd address that problem later, but for now…

"Let's get you out of these wet clothes," he said, lifting the dry greatcoat from his shoulder. Napoleon helped him out of his wet trousers and blouse, then guided his arms into the greatcoat's sleeves.

The coat did little to warm Anderson. His blue lips trembled; his teeth chattered. Nor did he seem any more aware of his surroundings.

"Sir?" Anderson spoke timidly. "Are they coming to get me?"

"Who?" Napoleon played along, hoping to help clear Anderson's muddied brain.

"Soldiers—I—I think." Anderson stared at the door. "But I don't know what I've done."

Napoleon placed a hand on his shoulder. "We'll worry about that after you get warm." He made up a makeshift bed on the floor and urged Anderson to lie down, then took his wet uniform and hung it by the fire outside. Hopefully, it would be dry by morning.

Anderson was sleeping fitfully when Napoleon got back. mumbling in his sleep. *Run...they're coming...run...*

Napoleon stared at the sleeping soldier. This wasn't a case of desertion; that was certain. It was a mental collapse. How could he turn in a man he believed was innocent? Reuben's headless body appeared in his mind. *You're just as crazy as he is.* He shook a finger in Napoleon's face. *You might as well stand in front of a firing squad yourself if crazy is the only requirement.*

Napoleon squeezed his eyes shut, willing Reuben to go away. If he didn't arrest Anderson, one of his comrades might well turn him in for the money.

And they won't be gentle about it.

CHAPTER 46

On a snow-covered plain near Stevensburg, Virginia, all eight thousand men of Hayes' division of the II Corps lined three sides of an imaginary square. Inside the square and facing the open end, the ten-man firing squad awaited orders. The day was just beginning to dawn, the throng of soldiers a thick shadow against the lightening sky.

Jim stood at attention next to Erskine and the medical staff. He wasn't there to support Army orders; he was there to honor his comrade, who would die a hero, as far as Jim was concerned.

It started with the ominous rumble of muted drums. Brass and winds joined, the music plodding, respectful. The band of musicians paced forward, their movement slow and stately, somber and reverential as they played Handel's "Dead March." Commonly played in honor of the already dead, this time the song heralded the death of a traitor.

Jim ignored the music. All he could think of was the boys behind the instruments, so young, many still so naïve, and so obviously uncomfortable. Stretcher bearers when they weren't playing rousing and patriotic tunes, their music was meant to motivate, not mourn.

At the head of the band, Anderson, his hands and feet shackled, shuffled behind the officer of the day, Lieutenant-Colonel Johnston, who escorted Anderson to a marker placed in the center of the square. The chain-gang clink and jangle of his restraints added the condemned man's rhythm to the mournful dirge. He turned to face the firing squad. The officer placed a blindfold over his eyes; Anderson removed it as soon as the officer left his side.

As Johnston returned to stand next to the firing squad, a minister dressed in black robes approached Anderson. He whispered in Anderson's ear and beckoned; Anderson strained against his chains as he struggled to kneel, his knees hitting the ground hard as the minister knelt beside him in prayer. Moments later, the minister lifted his head and took Anderson's arm as if to help him stand. Anderson shook his head—he would stand on his own. Placing his hand on Anderson's shoulder in blessing, the minister turned and returned to the crowd.

"To all assembled here," Johnston read from the order of execution. "Corporal Jasper T. Anderson, Company D, 111th Regiment of New York Volunteers, charged with murder and subsequent desertion on the fifteenth of December, eighteen hundred and sixty-three and judged guilty by the court, is presented here for the purpose of execution—to be shot to death with musketry as ordered by the court's findings."

Anderson stood at attention. He remembered nothing of the incident at the hospital, but he welcomed death, praying it would release the images of war from his head.

The officer of the day stepped back and gave the command.

"Ready!" The rifles' locks clicked, breaking the ominous silence.

"Aim!" Ten soldiers lifted their guns, aiming at Corporal Anderson's heart.

"Fire!" Jim winced at the sound, instinctively covering his ears as he watched Anderson fall to the ground.

Finished with their role, the firing squad lowered their weapons and marched from the field.

The division dispersed, filing past Anderson's dead body and leaving the field to the burial detail.

Jim knelt by the body as the brigade passed. Let the big bugs think he was confirming a death. He whispered a prayer, touched Anderson's bloodied chest, and placed the unused blindfold over Anderson's face.

Amid the assembled division, Napoleon watched, his eyes wide. This. This is what he would face if he let the ghost of Reuben have his soul.

"One down, more to come." Major Anthony, still in formal uniform, leaned back in his chair, and propped his spit-shined boots on his desk. "Let's see what that yokel tries next." He downed his whiskey in one gulp, set down his glass, and poured another. A little liquor was exactly what he needed to ease the stress of command.

If he could just get rid of Banyon, the military world would be his oyster. He was tired of being forced to bend to the will of doctors. There was no place in the army for compassion. *Men are men,* he thought, *heroes are heroes and cowards are cowards and cowards deserve to die.* It was as simple as that, and none of that namby-pamby "mental illness" nonsense would change his mind.

Anthony swigged down the waiting glass of whiskey and poured another.

Military life wasn't much different from his childhood home. He'd spent most of his life clawing his way from bottom to top, starting with his military family, to whom he could never measure up. The youngest in the family, his older brothers were now Lieutenant-Colonels and Generals; he was still a Major and thus the skeleton in the family closet.

But that would end now. Starting today, malingerers would be put on report, jailed if necessary, and executed if all else failed to convince them to fight.

Jim went through the motions of his job, desperate to ignore the images of the morning. But that night, as he wrote in his journal, the scene of Anderson's execution flooded his mind. As he imagined the gunshots, he burst into tears. Anderson was an innocent man, and Jim had failed to save him.

He thought of Napoleon. Six months ago, he'd shown up at Jim's door in Gettysburg, pleading for his help.

And what did I do? Jim thought. *I told him he was imagining it. I told him the nightmares would go away.*

How many men had he returned to duty when he could have kept them safe a few days more? How many men had he let down, sending them back to their terrors? One could easily see the physical effects of war; nightmares, ulcers, and a galloping heart could all be quantified, but Nichols' internment had revealed the psychological effects— the deep mental distress some men suffered. They were as legitimate a wound as the physical ones, but far more difficult to prove. How could he ever convince the big bugs the condition was real?

I am reminded of Hippocrates' axiom, he wrote. Am I doing harm? It seems as if either route I choose causes harm, so I must ask myself which choice causes the greater harm: sending these men back to duty, or keeping them from it? Which course will inflame their souls the least? And which will keep them alive?

He knew one thing: these men needed an advocate. He wanted to be the one to stand up for them when they couldn't. For now, he answered only to Larssen and the Surgeon General, but how long would that last? Soon enough, the spring campaign would begin in earnest. Despite protocols, Jim was certain the time would come when the Army brass would demand his nostalgia patients return to the front lines alongside every other able-bodied soldier, and Jim suspected even the Surgeon General would be powerless to stop it.

CHAPTER 47

January 1864

Winter Camp, Petersburg, Virginia

Disease has taken control at Winter Camp. The extreme cold, the poor and dense living conditions, and the lack and quality of food all contribute. We have all we can do to isolate the sick and treat them while keeping the other soldiers healthy. First, we battled an outbreak of pneumonia. Just when that was under control, there was an outbreak of typhoid fever that spread like wildfire, followed by a measles epidemic that spread even faster.

Treating these men is like fighting a raging barn fire and praying it won't burn down your home as well. There is only so much we as a medical team can do. We use everything at our disposal: opiates, turpentine, whiskey, quinine, capsicum, ammonia—anything that seems like it might help. More times than not, none of it works. Sometimes it seems that doing nothing is the wisest course of action. Perhaps we must learn to accept that some patients are beyond saving and instead concentrate on the men who have a chance of survival.

Jim didn't know how he was still standing. How many hours had it been since he'd had more than a catnap? The entire medical team—in fact, every medical team in winter camp—had pushed their minds and bodies to the limit.

Working through their exhaustion was the only ethical option, but Jim worried. Would his lack of sleep cause him to make mistakes?

What if I choose the wrong treatment, give up on a patient when he might survive, or misdiagnose an illness? Thank God there were no battle wounds to treat as well.

There was one small benefit to the contagion: Pegleg, terrified of catching something, stayed away.

A stray bit of sunshine found its way through the hospital window. It was a welcome sight in a month filled with overcast skies. Jim shook his head—Mother Nature was teasing again. It might look warm and inviting outside, but the frost-covered ground said otherwise.

Jim pulled his pocket watch from his jacket. *Erskine should be back from his nap by now,* he thought, *and I'm desperate for a little sleep.*

"I'm going to rouse Erskine," he said to Larssen, who was tending to a feverish patient. "He's overdue."

"Tell him to get a move on," Larssen said with a wry smile.

The frosty air bit at Jim's cheeks as he walked to the surgeons' quarters, despite his heavy topcoat. Nor was it much warmer inside the quarters. The fire in the woodstove was down to barely glowing ashes; Jim stopped to add a log and fan the flames to get it going.

Across the room, he saw Erskine huddled under a pile of blankets.

"Get up, lazybones," Jim teased. He crossed the room to Erskine's bed and shook his shoulder. Erskine moaned and turned away from Jim.

"Come on, Erskine," Jim was frustrated now, and a little bit angry. "The patients need you, and so do Dr. Larssen and I."

Erskine wrapped his blankets tightly around him and struggled to sit up. "I'm so damned cold," he said. "I just can't get warm."

Jim looked at him closely. "Your face is flushed," he said, instinctively reaching to feel Erskine's forehead. He pulled his hand away. "Good God, you're burning up!" He pulled back the blankets and opened his blouse.

Rose spots.

Jim flinched. Rose spots were a hallmark of typhoid fever.

"What other symptoms are you experiencing?" Jim struggled to keep his voice even. "Tom!" Jim shook Erskine's shoulder when he didn't respond

Erskine shrugged. "I just feel all-over lousy," he said. "I can't get warm, can't get comfortable, can't seem to care about much of anything else."

This is bad, thought Jim. He knew there was no sure treatment for typhoid. He recalled what Dr. Larssen had said about his typhoid patients:

"Once I put a man in the hospital, I might as well dig his grave."

I'll be damned if I let Tommy die, Jim vowed. *If it takes every bit of medical knowledge I have, I won't give up on him.*

He re-buttoned Erskine's blouse and wrapped the blankets around him. "I need to talk to Larssen," he said, patting Erskine's shoulder. "You rest. I'll be right back."

Jim hurried back to the hospital. A small tear trickled down his face, stinging like ice against his cheeks. His heart pounded. *I can't let him die. I can't let him die.* That would be his mantra until Tommy was well again.

He stopped just outside the hospital, took a deep breath, and pushed away the panic that threatened to derail him. Panic would help no one, least of all Erskine.

"Dr. Larssen," Jim said, using his most formal medical voice. "I need a word." He tipped his head towards Larssen's office. It afforded little privacy, but it would have to do.

Jim stood stiffly in front of the desk; Larssen relaxed into his chair. "Is Erskine coming?" he asked, raising an eyebrow.

Jim started to tremble, stumbling to find a chair just as his knees buckled. He felt the muscles in his face contract into a grimace.

Larssen held himself in his chair, letting Jim have whatever time he needed to gather himself.

"Erskine's caught typhoid fever." Jim's voice shook as he forced out the words. "His fever is high, his stomach swollen." He swallowed hard. "He has rose spots."

Larssen stiffened. "Are you sure?"

"As sure as I can be," Jim answered. "All the symptoms are present."

Larssen sat, letting Jim's words sink in.

"We need to isolate him," he said. "A well-heated room, close enough to monitor him, but far enough away from the other patients that he won't infect anyone." He looked around his relatively spacious office. "We could put him in here."

"My office might be better," Jim said. "If you don't mind my sharing your office for a while."

Larssen stood. "I'll have the stretcher bearers move him here." He walked to the door, then paused and turned to look at Jim. "We're going to pull him through, God willing," he said.

Jim nodded weakly. He knew that was unlikely, but for now, he was willing to believe in miracles.

Dear Mr. and Mrs. Erskine,

I know you've received word of your son's death, but the military can be cruelly cold when delivering their news. Please allow me to tell you about the Thomas Erskine I knew and loved...

He had tried every treatment he could think of, even the ones he knew were useless. He put his own life in God's hands, knowing that the typhoid could spread to him.

Jim desperately wanted to live for his girls' sake, but God had seen him through riskier situations, and Jim had to put his trust in Him. As Erskine's fate became apparent, Jim placed him in God's care.

Grief added itself to Jim's list of burdens. Exhaustion, hunger, and thorns in his side like Pegleg suddenly seemed unimportant. He was determined to survive this war, no matter what it took.

At times, his emotions won out; his heart filled with despair and discouragement. *How could I have let Tommy die?* Though he knew the thought was unreasonable, he still felt responsible. He wanted to quit. He wanted to go home. He wanted to wake up from this horrible nightmare.

Something needed to change. Doctors were pushing themselves too hard, and Jim wondered if maybe the health of the surgeons should come before that of the patients. *If the medical team is suffering,* he thought, *how can they give their patients the treatment they deserve? What good is prioritizing patient health if the exhausted surgeons cannot treat them properly?*

The alternative was to ensure the medical teams' fitness by putting their needs first. *But then how many more patients will die?* Jim shook his head. *It's completely unethical and unacceptable.*

He had taken an oath, a promise to put his patients' health above all else and do his best to save them. Whether it was physical wounds, illnesses, or mental affliction, he would stand by his promise to do no harm.

CHAPTER 48

February 1864
Stevensburg, VA

The rumors flew. The camp at Stevensville was bitter and boring. Spring was not far away, but the cold weather would not relent. Men spent their days drilling, writing letters, and desperately trying to get warm.

But in the south, the battles raged on. Sherman's forces marched from Vicksburg to Meridian, destroying railroads, depots, and supply lines to cripple the Confederates in Mississippi. A group of over one hundred Union prisoners escaped from Libby Prison in Richmond. The Union army captured Jacksonville, Florida. But most frightening of all was the report of a submarine that patrolled Charleston Harbor, sinking the USS Housatonic. Although submarines had been in use since the 17th century, the Hunley's attack at Charleston was the first time a submarine had destroyed a ship in combat.

The Union was gaining ground. Would the spring bring a Confederate surrender?

Brandy Station was a hive of military activity. Rail lines, supply depots, and headquarters operations required constant oversight. The 80th NYV guarded prisoners, maintained discipline and order, handled logistics, and provided administrative support.

In his quarters near Rappahannock Station, Napoleon lay curled up on his cot. He wasn't interested in socializing. He didn't care about rumors or card games.

The constant noise in his head, the never-ending nightmares, would not leave him alone. Other voices who argued bitterly about Napoleon's complicity in sending Anderson to his death joined Reuben's voice. Loudest of all was the voice of Anderson: *"You saw me. You knew. You let me down."*

He'd followed orders. He'd done his duty, but the voices would never let him forget. Not because he failed, but because he succeeded. A stern military voice reminded him he'd only upheld the law, and he was not responsible for Anderson's actions. Another voice was soft and maternal, *You could have helped him. You knew he was broken.* It was the part of him that still believed in compassion. The part that wondered if justice without mercy was just another kind of violence. But how? How could he have snubbed his nose at the entire Army of the Potomac? Soldiers who defied their orders were as likely to be executed as deserters.

More blood on your hands. Why are you killing your own people? He was now responsible for two deaths, and neither one was an enemy.

It had been a month since Anderson's execution. Nearly six months since Reuben's death. Anderson haunted his nightmares; Reuben never slept.

Every day he spent at Kelly's Ford started with a search of the riverfront. He scoured the ground, stirred through the campfire ashes, in search of some vestige of Colonel Jasper T. Anderson. Every scrap of cloth, even the faintest footprint, could be his. He clung to the hope he'd discover Anderson was still alive.

"You're fucking falling apart," tsked Reuben.

Napoleon had done his duty. And now he was unraveling because duty wasn't enough.

CHAPTER 49

February 6, 1864
Demonstration on the Rapidan River,
Morton's Ford, VA

Once again, the battlefield calls. Pegleg has mustered the support of the big brass, who have pressured me to relax my stance on retaining emotionally traumatized patients (in their words, an "imaginary illness"), and return what they consider "able-bodied troops" to active service. I have presented my case to Dr. Joseph Barnes, the acting surgeon general of the United States, who commands all of our medical personnel. He alone has the power to enforce the military's demands on me.

The plan called for a demonstration only: a foray toward the Confederate picket line to test the position and strength of the Rebel entrenchments. The goal: remind the Rebs that Lincoln's Army was just across the river and ready to fight if necessary.

General Hays, who led the demonstration, received orders not to press too hard lest he trigger a battle.

Major Anthony was determined to use every able-bodied man he could muster, and that included all but the sickest of Jim's patients.

"For God's sake," Anthony raised his arms in frustration. "It's just a demonstration. Nobody's getting hurt. I'll be damned if I have to fight you every time I need my men."

Jim stiffened. "You'll have to—"

"I know, I know! I'll have to clear it with the Surgeon General." He paced the floor as he ranted. "By all means, call in your all-powerful Surgeon General so we can settle this once and for all."

Dr. Larssen tended to a nearby patient as Anthony stormed out of the room. "And I want you there too!" Anthony growled and pointed at Larssen.

Larssen waited until Anthony was out of sight. "You have to quit baiting him, Jim." He spoke softly. "You two are like a couple of tomcats fighting over a tabby in heat, and it's not going to get you anything but a lot of scratches."

Jim tensed. Determination shone in his eyes. "It's true that Anthony and I disagree, but how can

I send these men to the battle line? Legitimate or not, their erratic behavior makes them more of a danger than an asset."

"Major Anthony is right," Larssen said. "Hays has been ordered to harass the Rebs and not engage. This might be the perfect situation to test their fitness."

"We'll see what Dr. Barnes decides. Until then, I'm standing up for my patients."

That afternoon, Anthony presented his case to Dr. Barnes.

"I must remind you," Anthony concluded, "that I am not bound by your decision."

Dr. Barnes nodded. "That is true," he said, "but Drs. Larssen and Banyon are." He stood, extending his hand to Anthony. "I will consider your request and present my decision by the end of the day. Please send in Drs. Larssen and Banyon on your way out."

Anthony nodded brusquely, turned, and left the room. As he stepped into the anteroom, he eyed Jim and Dr. Larssen and jerked his head towards Barnes' office. "He wants to see you," he sneered. "Good luck."

"Dr. Banyon. Dr. Larssen." Barnes nodded as

Jim and Larssen entered. "Please take a seat."

Jim and Larssen sat, clearly uncomfortable.

"Dr. Banyon," Dr. Barnes started. "I understand that you have refused to return your patients to active duty. Can you explain yourself?"

"I can, Doctor. These patients are exhibiting extreme mental distress combined with dangerously high heart rates and intense intestinal pain." Jim realized he was fidgeting and slipped his fingers under his legs. "I cannot in good conscience return them to duty when they may be a danger to the regiment and themselves."

Dr. Barnes nodded. "I understand your concern, Doctor. I myself have studied mental and emotional diseases of the brain, and I sympathize with your apprehension. But have you considered the legitimacy of their complaints? I attribute the racing heart rate to battle stress, and of course, dysentery is widespread, but a determined man can fake insanity if it suits him."

"I don't think they're pretending, Doctor."

"May I suggest that you have enough to do treating illnesses and injuries? You don't need to conjure up something more to worry about. And you certainly don't want to alienate the military staff. I can back you, but Major Anthony and his superiors can make your life miserable if they want to."

Jim contemplated Dr. Barnes' advice. "What if I were to resign my commission?" He'd signed up for a three-year stint, but after everything he'd sacrificed for his country, surely they would make an exception.

"Certainly you can do that, although it will cost you your enlistment bounty. But are you sure that's what you want? I can't imagine that would sit well with the army or with the folks at home."

Jim hadn't thought about the fallout a resignation could cause. Surely his community would not take kindly to a man who "abandoned" his duty.

"I'll consider your advice," Jim said, still fidgeting the fingers he sat on. He felt like a child being scolded by his father. He wanted nothing more than to run and hide. "Am I free to go?"

"You are." Barnes' stare felt like a knife in Jim's gut. "Release your able-bodied patients to Major Anthony immediately."

Jim stayed far ahead of Dr. Larssen as they rode back to their quarters. Although he knew Larssen was caught in the middle of his fight with Pegleg, the fact that Larssen had not voiced support for him in front of Dr. Barnes felt like a betrayal.

Are they right? Jim wondered. *Should I give in to Pegleg's demands? Do I have a choice?* Jim felt dizzy with frustration. *How can I let down the men who need my help if I don't stand my ground?*

Late that evening, Jim's worst fears proved true. When the army forced him to return to duty, Corporal Nelson, one of Jim's "able-bodied" patients, broke ranks, charged into the Rebel picket line, and died instantly.

Jim was furious when he heard the news. He grabbed his greatcoat from its hook, intent on confronting Anthony.

"Don't do it." Larssen stepped in front of Jim and blocked the door.

"But damn it!" Jim threw up his arms in frustration. "Peleg will think he's won!"

Larssen gently took Jim's arm and pulled him to his side. "Jim," he said. "You're a brilliant doctor. But sometimes you have to choose your battles." He released Jim and stepped aside. "This is a battle you don't want to start."

Later that night, Jim added his thoughts to his

journal:

Perhaps Larssen is right that I should acquiesce. My conclusions regarding these men's fitness for duty may be errant, and I am beginning to question the harm it may do to my reputation and career if I continue to resist.

February 7, 1864
Dear Parents,

Although a few weeks of relative peace remain, the spring campaign will soon be upon us, and in my opinion we have never seen any fighting which will equal what is coming. It will be the climax of desperation. We are all satisfied that however short the campaign may be that its battles will be fought to the bitter end and mercy will be a scarce article.

CHAPTER 50

May 5, 1864

Near Chancellorsville, VA

Napoleon sat listlessly against the temporary breastworks, trying to ignore the sharp end of a stone poking against his back.

"We're in the soup now, Corporal Drown."

He jerked up his head, nearly upsetting the rifle propped next to him.

Who said that? Not a soul glanced in his direction; every face stared at the ground, every body squirmed restlessly against the hastily built wall. They were all too absorbed in their own fears to bother with Napoleon.

"The wood is full of Johnny Rebs hell-bent on taking your head off."

Napoleon recognized the voice: Reuben.

Reuben's dead. He shook his head, slightly at first and then violently. *Reuben's dead!*

"You think you can get rid of me just because my body's not here?"

Napoleon jumped up, grabbed his rifle, and cautiously scanned the area where the stumps of newly hewn trees stuck up from the ground like half-buried bodies.

"Get down, you idiot!" The soldier next to him grabbed Napoleon's pant leg. "You tryin' to get killed or something?"

They'd arrived at their encampment along the Brock Road late last night, just north of the unfinished railroad. Too dark to see in the underbrush-filled woods, fighting had stopped until morning. But before dawn, the sounds of artillery recommenced; their booms and whistles muted by the dense undergrowth.

Known as "The Wilderness," the large wooded area covered over seventy square miles. Years ago, loggers harvested the trees, leaving the area bare and vulnerable. Heavy underbrush grew and made the once lush woods nearly impenetrable. The trees that remained formed a thick canopy. The forest was perpetually dark and dangerous.

The primary force, led by Generals Grant and Meade, was a few miles north, along the Orange Turnpike. The Confederate forces, led by General Ewell, approached them from the west.

Colonel Gates' aide moved down the line of soldiers.

"Form ranks." His whisper might otherwise have been a shout, but no one wanted to draw the attention of the enemy.

"Right behind you, buddy." Reuben's voice whispered in Napoleon's ear.

"Go away." Napoleon waved at the side of his head, as if he were driving off a swarm of gnats.

Quickly and quietly, the regiment formed a long line down the length of the breastworks. A second line formed directly behind them. When the order came to move forward, the first line climbed over the stone barrier and entered the woods.

"Jesus Christ!" A soldier cursed as he tried to penetrate the thick underbrush. "It's all pricker bushes in here." He used the barrel of his rifle to push away the thorn-covered canes; they slapped back into his face as the rifle passed through them, leaving behind deep scratches and broken barbs, tearing holes in his uniform as they pulled away. "Can't see a damned thing but brush and trees."

Napoleon moved in with the second line. Chigger bites from last night covered his body; he subconsciously dug at the itchy scabs. Poison ivy vines peeked out from among the briars and hung from the trees. Napoleon ducked his head to avoid their rash-inducing sap.

He jumped as a large corn snake slithered out of the debris. *Thank God it wasn't a copperhead or a rattler,* he thought, reminding himself to be vigilant against the wood's natural inhabitants.

Not a half-mile ahead, the front line of Hancock's II Corps met Lee's Confederates. Napoleon and his comrades could hear the enemy, but they couldn't see them. A canister burst in the brush ahead. The soldiers ducked and frantically searched for the approaching army.

Suddenly the Rebs were upon them. First one, then two, then an entire regiment surged through the underbrush, firing indiscriminately. The man on Napoleon's left went down, then the one on his right fell. Napoleon tripped, going to his knees, and saw he'd fallen over a Rebel body. He scrambled to get up.

"Well, buddy." Reuben's voice seemed to come from the body in front of him. "Is this a hero's charge or a coward's retreat?"

Napoleon scrambled deep into the brush and struggled to catch his breath.

"Coward it is," Reuben taunted.

The familiar stench of gunpowder suddenly changed: what Napoleon smelled now was smoke. He peeked out from his hiding place to see a dark plume rising from the forest floor. Sparks from fired rifles and artillery had set the woods aflame.

Men scattered. The frantic Union troops mixed with the panicked Confederates until even the color of their uniforms seemed to blend together. The battle scene was now an inferno, burning everything in its path. Wounded soldiers, unable to stop the rapidly advancing blaze, screamed as their clothes caught fire. Their comrades tried to rescue them, but the thick smoke and flames beat them back.

"Run, you idiot!" The soldier who'd entered the woods ahead of Napoleon grabbed his sleeve. "Get the hell out of the woods!"

Napoleon ran, unable to see through the smoke and fire, tripping over tangled bushes and mangled bodies. For all he knew, he could be running *into* the inferno. His foot caught on a decaying tree lying in his path; it grabbed his ankle like a madman and pulled him to the ground, twisting his ankle as he fell.

He continued his retreat, on his hands and

knees now. The woods smelled of roasting flesh; live shells exploded from the heat and fire. The screams of men trapped or fleeing filled his ears from every direction.

At last, he felt the hard-packed road under his feet. Moving cautiously but quickly, he followed the road out of the woods and found what remained of his regiment, most of them covered with soot and burns, and choking for air.

Napoleon collapsed onto an open spot, gagging from inhaled smoke and desperate for breath.

Bad luck. Reuben laughed. *I'm still here.*

CHAPTER 51

May 7, 1864

Near Chancellorsville, Virginia

In the dark dampness of the nearby woods, Napoleon sat against a moss-covered rock. His hands shook as he contemplated his decision. He had to do this. He had to get the demons out of his head.

It was the nightmares that got him, the battles that took place the minute he fell asleep. Decimated bodies. Blood, brains, the moans of barely alive soldiers stuck under bodies and unable to move. He tried to free them, but no matter how many dead soldiers he dragged away, more appeared. The wounded men underneath struggled to breathe, and he could not save them. And Reuben's headless body was always there to admonish him. *How could you let me die?*

Napoleon had kept his promise never to touch a drop of whiskey, but he'd discovered a few drops of ether on an old rag were nearly as good at keeping the demons away. When the army doctor gave him laudanum to dull the pain of a minor injury, Napoleon quickly became addicted. A few drops of the opium/alcohol mixture were all he needed to keep Reuben at bay and raise his spirits. But of course, the effects wore off before long. Reuben came back like an angry bee; not even laudanum could stop the nightmares.

Yesterday's battle loomed fresh in his mind. In so many ways, it was just like all the other battles he'd fought: friends and comrades falling dead on all sides. Panic and confusion as Confederate shells exploded around him. The screams of the dead and dying, beseeching their God for salvation. But yesterday... yesterday was the worst carnage he'd seen, and the reality hit him: he would see much worse before it got better.

That was a prospect he couldn't bear to consider.

He sighed and stared at the revolver in his hand. A Colt Army Model 1860, one .44 caliber round would guarantee success—or was it failure? It wasn't his first attempt to still the voices, but he always chickened out. Not this time.

Reuben was right: This was the only way he

could make it go away.

Napoleon rested his forefinger on the gun's trigger and pulled back the hammer with his thumb. He ordered his hand to raise the revolver, but it wouldn't respond.

He hesitated. *Do I really want to die?*

His mother's voice shouted from his brain. *No! Napoleon, no!* Her horror-stricken face loomed in his mind.

You can't do this to her. He eased his finger off the trigger.

But you must. Reuben's voice overshadowed his mother's. His boyish image appeared before Napoleon, whole and youthful as it had been when they first met, his eyes tearful and unforgiving.

Napoleon nodded.

He put his finger back on the trigger, lifted the revolver until it pressed against his temple.

God forgive me, he whispered, and pulled the trigger.

The odor of death hit as soon as Jim entered the woods. Lord knew he recognized death when he smelled it. He followed the worn path. The brook along the tree line babbled as its water tumbled over stones and branches, but the wildlife was still quiet.

Less than a hundred yards in, he had his answer. Napoleon's body slumped sideways on the ground, his army-issued pistol by his side. Flies buzzed around the body, attracted by the smell of the blood that stained the earth beneath him. There was evidence of scavengers having picked at the remains.

A thick line of dried blood ran from the small hole in Napoleon's temple to his jawline. A black smudge of gunpowder darkened the wound; the heat of the round had singed his hair as it entered his skull.

Jim cautiously approached Napoleon's body, circling around it as if he needed to take it all in. Blood heavily splattered the rock behind his cousin; bits of brain matter blended with the rock's algae—a three-dimensional image of life and death.

He leaned down to retrieve the gun.

Jim woke with a start, disoriented, short of breath, and afraid to open his eyes. He lay still, listening for any familiar sound to confirm where he was. As he regained control of his breathing, he realized he no longer smelled blood or death. There were no sounds of flies or wildlife. Slowly, he brought his face from under his blanket. He looked around him. *It's okay,* he thought. *I'm in my tent, where I should be.*

He took a deep breath and rolled out of bed.

"This arrived for you this morning, Dr. Banyon." Colonel MacDougall's assistant handed Jim a folded and sealed envelope.

Jim stared at the handwriting. He didn't recognize the scrawl. Was that good or bad? He turned the envelope over and broke the seal.

Headquarters, 80th NY Volunteers
Chancellorsville, Maryland
May 8, 1864

Doctor Banyon,

I regret to inform you of the death today of Corporal Napoleon Bonaparte Drown by his own hand. I have known Corporal Drown since I came to the 80th in October of 1862. Dedicated to the Union cause, he performed his duties with honor until his untimely death. I do not judge his actions, but will only say that he seemed to be tormented by some prior incident that would not leave him.

Corporal Drown left orders to contact you in case of his injury or death. Let this be our notice to you of the same. You may claim his body for burial at the regimental hospital within the week; otherwise, he is to be interred in the local cemetery.

Enclosed is a letter addressed to you in Corporal Drown's hand that was found amongst his personal effects.

Please accept my deepest condolences and convey them to Cpl. Drown's family.

Colonel Theodore B. Gates,
Commander, 80th New York Infantry

Smudges and wrinkles marred Napoleon's letter. Jim turned it in his hand, imagining the man who wrote it, and the boy who was his friend and kin. He opened the paper and laid it on the desk in front of him.

Jim, I know you said it would get better. But I can no longer control the voices and the nightmares that haunt me day and night. I understand now why Father drank so. Had I not sworn off liquor long ago, I might have done the same, although I think it would not have helped. Pray for me, dear cousin, and forgive me. Napoleon

Napoleon was dead, and it was Jim's fault.

The world has gone upside down. I have received notice of Napoleon's death at his own hand. Why did I not heed him last summer when he came to me for help? I could have—would have—found some way to send him home to safety or at least to

a sanitarium for treatment. I have failed him and every other man I willingly returned to duty.

Jim guided the wagon to Chancellorsville to recover Napoleon's body under overcast skies. The hexagonal-shaped coffin he'd built from scavenged pine boards rattled on the wagon-bed as it traveled the rutted roads. Lined with lead and zinc to make it waterproof, he didn't have to worry about it falling off.

At the field hospital in Chancellorsville, the hospital stewards stood by, ready to load Napoleon's body in the wagon, but Jim silently shook his head and shooed them away. His dream had shown him the details of Napoleon's death, but he needed to see the remains. He carefully loosened the shroud and recoiled when he saw Napoleon's mangled head.

Re-wrapping the shroud, he bent down, slid his arms underneath Napoleon, and lifted him into his arms. Silent tears trickled down Jim's cheeks. His body trembled with grief as he carried his cousin's body to the wagon and gently laid it in the coffin. He covered the body with charcoal to help control the odor as it decomposed, filled the coffin with sawdust and tamped it down as tightly as he could, then screwed on the solid lid. There would be no glass-covered opening for the mourners to view Napoleon's body. Jim vowed he would be the only one to have the image of Napoleon's mangled body etched in his brain.

CHAPTER 52

May 10, 1864

Spotsylvania Court House, VA

"Surely you can do without me for a few days." Jim pleaded. He and Dr. Larssen stood just outside the barn they'd commandeered for a field hospital. A normally fastidious man, Jim's hair was uncombed, his clothes rumpled and stained, his shoulders slumped. Dark circles ringed his eyes—he wasn't sure when he had last slept.

"How am I to manage this?" Larssen swept his hand across the wide barn door. "We haven't had a decent steward since Erskine died, the other medical teams are up to their necks in casualties, and now you want to leave too?"

Jim fidgeted with his shirt sleeves, shifting his eyes away from Larssen to stare at a distant mountain. He knew Larssen was right. Worse than that, disobeying a direct order could ruin his career once and for all.

Jim bit his lower lip. *I have somehow failed my*

cousin at every turn. I dismissed his worries, sent him back to battle, and now he's dead. He forced back tears. *I can't fail him this time.*

"Doc!" A wounded patient called from inside the barn.

"Let's go inside." Larssen laid his hand on Jim's shoulder.

Barely controlled chaos reigned on the barn floor. Lit only by dim lanterns and what little light filtered through the dirt-covered windows, Jim and Larssen waited for their eyes to adjust to the darkness.

Makeshift cots—rough-hewn wood planks hastily nailed together—dominated the room, each one occupied by a soldier wrapped in a tattered, blood-stained blanket. Some still wore their threadbare uniforms; others wore only undershorts or less.

In one corner, two operating tables—each cobbled from a door and set on hay bales—stood ready. Heaps of gore-covered and bloodied rags waited to be washed in one of the nearby water barrels. Across the floor, the wounded moaned. Others cried out in agony.

The worst part was the smell, a mixture of

sweat, blood, and body parts mixed with the sharp scent of the whiskey they used as an anesthetic. The sour stench of vomit mingled with the faint aroma of hay. Jim and Larssen covered their noses as they entered the room.

"I know you're not one to shirk your duty, Jim," Larssen said as he bent to check on a patient. "But we've got our hands full here, and surely you've heard the rumor that General Grant is getting ready to attack Petersburg. Are you certain you can't send the body alone?"

Jim raised his grief-stricken eyes to Larssen. "I—I have to go. I have to take my cousin home. It's my duty." He shuffled his feet and stared at the floor. "Please let me take him home."

Larssen studied Jim for a moment, his eyes filled with worry. "You've cleared this with Colonel MacDougall?"

"Not yet." Jim didn't elaborate: he had no intention of requesting a leave he knew they would not grant.

"Alright," Larssen said at last. "You have one week. That's all I can authorize, and more than the big bugs will be pleased with."

"Thank you, Dr. Larssen." Jim bowed his head.

"I am in your debt."

Jim hurried to his quarters to collect the bags that were already packed. At the station, he supervised the men who loaded Napoleon's body onto the train that would take him home. The coffin would have to ride in the baggage compartment along with the rest of the freight, but Jim would stay by Napoleon's side until they reached home.

"What the hell do you think you're doing?"

Jim stopped dead in his tracks. *Pegleg*. The voice was unmistakable.

"I'm taking my cousin's body home for burial." Jim's body tensed as he turned to answer, his senses on alert. He was stunned at how ridiculous Pegleg looked in his formal uniform with its black-feathered hat. The man might as well have been a peacock for all his strutting. "I have Dr. Larssen's permission."

"Well, you don't have mine," Pegleg thrust out his chest. "While that might not mean a thing to you, I'm sure Col. MacDougall feels the same."

Jim clenched his fists at his side as he approached Anthony until they were nose to nose. He struggled to control his expression. "The man was my cousin—my blood kin. I owe him far more loyalty than I owe the United States Army." He spat at Anthony's brightly polished shoes. "You can go to hell."

Anthony jabbed a finger in Jim's face. "You don't want to disobey a direct order, soldier," he sneered. "I can bring you down before this train leaves the station."

"You do that." Jim turned his back on Anthony and boarded the train as it started to move. "I'm taking my cousin's body home."

With no one beside him to enforce his order, Jim knew Anthony was powerless. He stood at the back of the rail car and watched as Pegleg the peacock, waving an angry fist in the air, grew smaller and smaller. When he was no longer visible, Jim returned to Napoleon's coffin, moved a crate next to it, and sat down. He looked around the railcar to be sure no one else was there. His shoulders fell, his body shook, as he laid his head on the coffin and burst into tears.

It was nearly dark when Jim took his journal from his medical bag. He'd spent his grief for now, but he wasn't yet ready to write it down. He thought of the look on Major Anthony's face when he spat on his shoes.

Pegleg is livid, he wrote, *and I suppose I can't* blame him. *There comes a time when one must set aside the demands of others to stand by their convictions. I must believe God is at my side in this case and will stand with me whatever the cost of my actions.*

CHAPTER 53

May 14, 1864
Ira, New York

Jim kept one hand on Napoleon's casket as two railroad attendants unloaded it from the train. The trip from Virginia was no more than a blur, the rhythmic clackety-clack of wheels against steel lulling him into a restless existence. His mind wandered, not thinking of where he was, but about how he'd gotten there.

How many times was he tempted to open the lid of Napoleon's casket—just to be certain he wasn't dreaming? But the heavily wrapped shroud held little meaning for him. The Napoleon he remembered was the carefree boy he spent his childhood with, the Napoleon who was determined to defend his country despite the cost and was determined that Jim fight alongside him. The Napoleon who had begged him to make the nightmares go away.

The casket jostled as the attendants carried it down the railcar steps. For just a moment, Jim was not with Napoleon. The casket he caressed was not that of his cousin, but his young son. *Has it been only two years?* He imagined what Jacob might look like now, a healthy two-year-old just finding his sea legs and into every sort of mischief he could discover. It seemed like a lifetime ago, and Jim was no longer the man he was when he buried his only son.

He rehearsed the story he would give the family: Corporal Napoleon Drown died in battle. A hero's death. No one but Jim would ever know anything different.

Stepping off the train, Jim noticed the difference in the northern climate. The light green of new leaves filled the trees. Spring flowers—daffodils, hyacinths, and lilacs—were in full bloom, filling the air with a scent unique to that time of year. Lilacs had always been Jim's favorite, their scent so strong you could smell them even when you couldn't see them. He wondered now if he would always associate that sweet aroma with death.

"Jim!" His father's voice pierced the sea of voices. He was not normally a demonstrative person, but he wrapped his son in a bear hug. "How are you, son?"

Jim stared ahead for a moment, then blinked, as if just recognizing his father. "I suppose I'm still in a daze," he said. "I've seen so much death. But—Napoleon…"

Jim's father squeezed his shoulder. "Come on, son. Let's get Napoleon home."

The sights and sounds of spring were everywhere as the wagon made its way north. Spring was a time of renewal. New plants, new offspring, freshly turned soil. Along the way, bright yellow dogwood and red and white trilliums dotted the forest. Cowslips grew in the swampy parts of the wood; Jim could almost taste the tangy greens mixed with the rich flavor of salt pork. It was the homecoming he'd dreamed of—for all the wrong reasons.

His mind teemed with conflict—the decisions he'd need to make in the next few days. Could he really lie to the family about Napoleon's death? Would the harsh truth serve any purpose? He thought back to his patient, Ezra, and how he'd bluntly told Ezra he was going to die. Could he justify this one small lie, at least for now? Could he keep the lie from showing on his face?

What if someone who knew the truth came

forward? How many in his regiment knew Napoleon's death was a suicide?

And then there was Pegleg. Would he really bring charges against Jim?

Probably.

What would Jim do then? A guilty verdict could be the end of him.

"Here we are." Jim's father tugged on the reins as they pulled up to the family homestead.

His mother was the first to greet him, rushing down the steps the moment the carriage came to a halt. She pulled him into her arms, holding him tight. He could feel the warmth and the emotion as they rushed from her body to his. "Welcome home," she said, taking a step back.

Two small arms wrapped around his legs. "Daddy!" Jim couldn't help smiling as he looked down at the mass of blonde curls that was Jessie. He bent down and scooped her up; she wrapped her arms around his neck and covered him with kisses.

At least someone still wants me, he thought.

Then, the best feeling of all: Maggie. She gently kissed his cheek and took his arm, escorting him toward the house. "Let the rest of them get the casket," she said.

They walked through the ripening wheat. In another two or three months its tassels would turn from their current green to golden yellow. Beyond the wheatfield was the family cemetery.

Jim's heart pounded as they approached their son's grave. He could feel Maggie's arm tremble, her breath caught in her throat. Together they knelt and prayed for the boy they deeply loved and barely knew.

Maggie tucked her skirt around her legs and sat on the ground. Jim looked at her, his face ashen.

"Remember when I first met Napoleon?" She put a hand on his shoulder and spoke softly. "He didn't like me very much." She smiled, remembering. "He was a lost boy."

"He thought I was abandoning him." Jim wiped away his tears, a wry smile on his face. "He was just getting over my being away at medical school for two years, and then I married you.

"But I loved him, too," he said. "Before you, he

was my life." Jim stared toward the horizon, his eyes glassy with tears.

"There's something else," Maggie said.

Jim startled. "What do you mean?"

"There's something you aren't telling me. What is it?" She put her hand on his leg and looked into his eyes.

He couldn't talk. Grief and guilt sat like a rock wedged in his throat; the truth was on the other side, unable to get out.

Maggie silently wrapped her arms around him. A soft keening escaped from his mouth and built into a wail. Tears fell, his breath hitched as he tried to speak. He laid his head on her shoulder and let the grief overtake him.

"H—h—he killed himself." Jim's words came in whispers and hiccups. "He put a gun to his head and pulled the trigger, and it's my fault."

"That's not true," Maggie whispered.

"It is." Jim sat back and wiped his face. "He came to me for help, but I minimized his pain. He wrote me letters, and I should have seen him slipping into despair. But I refused to see what was right in front of me. I was so consumed with fighting for my patients that I neglected to fight for my own flesh and blood."

"Does anyone else know?"

"Only his commanding officer, I think, and I hope he has the good sense to keep it to himself."

"Will you tell Leta?"

Jim shook his head. "Aunt Leta needs to believe her son died a hero—that's the least I can do for her."

The body lay in the front parlor for three days. Friends and neighbors stopped by to pay their respects, approaching the coffin for a moment, offering a prayer for the deceased. The women took Aunt Leta in their arms to give her strength, to give their sympathy. They brought support and empathy to the family, as well as casseroles and baked goods so meals would be one less worry. They shared memories of Napoleon, talked of his being one of the first to volunteer for the Union Army. They called him a hero.

Jim insisted the coffin remained closed. He

surreptitiously nailed down one corner of the coffin's lid to deter the curious. No one, Jim thought, should be a witness to what remained of Napoleon Drown.

On the third day, they laid Napoleon's body to rest alongside his father. A small U.S. flag marked his grave to denote his service. His headstone would note that he was a veteran and a hero.

The next day, Jim took the train back to Virginia, ready to face Anthony, MacDougall, and the whole Union Army if necessary. Napoleon's death had given him the one thing he needed: a spine. From now on, he would stand up for his patients regardless of the cost. Let them threaten anything they wanted; it didn't matter anymore. He would never back down again.

CHAPTER 54

May 15, 1864

Ira, NY

Maggie stood tall, smiling and waving at the carriage until it was out of sight and she could let go of the facade. Her smile disappeared; her shoulders slumped. She dropped to the porch step and buried her face in her hands.

What had happened to the man she knew and loved? He'd lost so much weight, and when had his hair gone gray and wrinkles overtaken his face?

But it was more than his physical appearance that worried her.

The man returning to his war duties was not the Jim Banyon she knew. This Jim was vulnerable and insecure. He carried the weight of the things he'd seen and done during the past two years. His careworn face showed his feelings of defeat, but his eyes shone with the determination to defend and protect his patients no matter the cost.

Maggie wasn't sure it was worth the price. She

almost longed for his sometimes arrogant manner, for the man who had a tendency to look down on others, but believed in himself and his ability to conquer anything.

How much longer would this "new" Jim be able to cling to his own sanity?

During the time he'd been away, Maggie had dismissed her worries about his well-being. She kept busy caring for Jessie and managing household tasks. Although he sent most of his salary to her, she'd still had to manage their money carefully and keep their home in good condition while he was away.

When she'd visited him last year, she'd worried about how exhausted he looked and the toll it might take on his health. But those things were temporary—or so she thought. Now she worried it might be more, and her husband might not recover.

A gentle hand touched Maggie's shoulder. Deborah sat down next to her.

"You're worried," she said.

Maggie nodded. "The war has changed him." She looked at Deborah, her eyes red from crying. "I worry he won't recover," she whispered.

Deborah laid her hand on Maggie's lap. "It's the

price we women pay for the folly of war that takes our men and sucks the life from them."

"I think of the women whose sons and husbands will never come back," Maggie said, wiping her face. "Those women would gladly welcome home their man no matter his condition. I should be grateful to have him back in one piece, even if he has changed inside."

Deborah looked off into the distance as if searching for the words to say. "I'm worried too. Jim will never be the same man he was. But we must love him all the same, and trust in God to do the rest. And when the war is over, we will have him back."

"Do you really believe that?"

"I have to."

CHAPTER 55

May 17, 1864
Fredericksburg, VA

Jim grasped the pen in his left hand, curled it to meet the left-leaning angle of the ledger he wrote in, and cursed his grade school teacher. Why she had insisted on such a backward way of putting pen to paper was beyond him. It would make so much more sense if he could have turned the ledger to the right instead of forcing his wrist that way.

Seated at a small desk in an upper room of the Farmer's Bank, a federal-style brick building that stood across Princess Anne Street from the church where he and Dr. Larssen had set up a temporary hospital, Jim paused his writing and took in his surroundings. Used as a headquarters by the Union command, the Bank had several rooms for lodging on the second level. The room he'd taken three days ago was small, containing only a narrow bed, washstand and basin, and a writing desk that sat against a window overlooking Princess Anne Street.

Rain pelted against the windows; occasional gusts of wind rattled the glass. Outside, men shouted from their sliding wagons, and horses whinnied as they splashed through the puddles, fighting the thick mud all the way up the hill.

At least there are fewer ambulance wagons today, he thought. The rain had slowed the fighting; after five days of almost continuous rain, General Grant notified Washington that the army could not resume offensive operations until the weather improved.

The pause in action gave Jim time to reflect on the past week.

Had it been only a week since he'd taken Napoleon's body home?

Jim's failure to recognize Napoleon's distress until it was too late nagged him all the way from Virginia to New York, and all the way back. Ever since Harper's Ferry, he'd seen the increasing mental distress in his patients. But for too long he'd brushed them off, explaining away their complaints in any number of ways.

He'd dismissed Private Nichols' confused state as an anomaly. When Corporal Anderson broke down, he understood the risk that mental instability posed to others. Then Napoleon came to him for help. Jim didn't want to acknowledge what he still saw as a moral weakness in a family member and told him to get over it.

He thought of the focus of his original study: the physical symptoms were important, but now he understood the toll on a man's mental health—and no one was immune. Nichols, Anderson, Napoleon—what had driven them to their insanity? How did some men seem to manage while others could not? Perhaps writing out the details of these three men's declines might give him some insight.

I'll start with Napoleon, Jim decided. *I knew him best.* He rested the pen against his cheek. *When did I first notice his distress?*

A picture of Napoleon carrying a stretcher at Gettysburg came to mind. The empty look in his cousin's eyes was what jumped out at him. It was a stare he would see often, and not just in Napoleon's eyes. They met for the first time since Jim enlisted, less than two years, but the change in Napoleon shocked Jim because he looked much older. His hair was going gray; his face was lined and haggard. He'd lost at least twenty pounds, and his uniform hung loosely on his body.

Later that same day, Napoleon came to Jim, asking after a friend. *Reuben*, Jim recalled. Had Napoleon lost track of Reuben after the battle? *Yes, that was it.*

Jim was still tending to recovering patients at Gettysburg in late July when Napoleon showed up again—AWOL from his regiment. *And there were the physical symptoms: the dangerously high heart rate, complaints of nightmares and insomnia, intestinal distress.* Jim put him on sick leave, hoping a little rest was all he needed.

From then on, their only communication was through letters, the last one written on the day Napoleon committed suicide.

He hadn't known Nichols nearly as well; Anderson barely at all. But as he wrote his summary of each man, the similarities in their physical symptoms and their mental stress were clear. Presumably, Nichols was still in the hospital at Georgetown. But Anderson... he had failed Anderson as surely as he'd failed Napoleon.

It wouldn't happen again.

Jim set down his pen and looked up from his writing. He picked up his cup of coffee, noticed the rain had slowed to a drizzle, and went to the window to open it. He filled his lungs with fresh, rain-washed air and sipped his coffee, grimacing at its stale flavor. He took a hard roll from the plate on his desk, took a bite, and chewed thoughtfully.

What sort of trouble would his decision lead to? Standing up for his patients was the ethical path and might result in the medical community accepting his findings. The more likely result would be the ruin of both his army and medical careers.

Jim returned to his desk, re-read his notes, and added these thoughts:

How can I prove this condition of nostalgia is just as legitimate as a severed limb or a debilitating illness? How can I convince the big bugs to show compassion? Surely they must see that these emotionally scarred soldiers will be of no good to them in battle.

Shall I follow the rules and report patients who show signs of "cowardice" or continue to protect my patients at the risk of losing my commission and perhaps even my medical license? I realize I could simply resign my commission and rid myself of the entire process, but I would still face humiliation at home, and I must stand for my men.

It all came down to a single question: How far was he willing to go to defend these men? Jim returned to the window, poured out his coffee, and stared at the street below.

It was a question he was not ready to answer.

CHAPTER 56

"All the public buildings—the Court-House, churches, hotels, warehouses, factories, the paper mill, theater, school-buildings, stores, stables, many private residences—and, in fact, everything that could give shelter was converted into receptacles for the wounded, until Fredericksburg was one vast hospital."

~May 1864: Julia Wheelock, Union Relief Worker

May 18

Fredericksburg, VA

Twenty-four hours after the last of the rain, General Grant resumed military operations. That morning, Jim rode out to the 111th's field hospital at Spotsylvania Court House with a load of fresh medical supplies and offered to help.

They fought the battle mostly with artillery rather than musketry. Wounds were likely to be mortal, amputations almost guaranteed. At the end of the day, the field hospital held few casualties. Most of them were dead.

Jim returned to Fredericksburg the next day. The streets bustled with horse-drawn ambulance wagons filled with broken and bloodied bodies. Minor chaos reigned in the streets. Church bells from around the city—Methodist, Baptist, Presbyterian, and Episcopal—chimed the hour as if conducted by an ethereal maestro, their differing pitches creating a harmony in time.

Although the rain had ended, the air was still humid. Steam rose from the sodden streets as the sun bore down. Jim's blouse clung to his torso. He was desperately in need of sleep.

As he approached the church-turned-hospital that housed the medical units of II Corps, the sound of picks and spades rang from the churchyard that would be the ultimate resting place of many a soldier, both Union and Confederate. Under a tree between the church and cemetery, teams of surgeons amputated limbs and tossed them into a pile.

The smell of whiskey and rotting flesh was overwhelming as Jim entered the church-hospital. A few pews, crowded with wounded soldiers, lined the outer walls of the sanctuary. They had broken up the rest of the pews to use them for coffins and bedsteads. Ripped-up carpeting served as bedding. The feeble light from a dozen lanterns gave a ghostly pallor to the large room.

They threw open the windows to let in the fresh air. Local women moved along the line of soldiers, distributing crackers and soup to those who could eat. Along the aisles, a single soldier sang.

"Mid pleasures and palaces though we may roam."

More voices joined in, a high tenor harmonized. "Be it ever so humble, there's no place like home."

Jim hurried across the sanctuary to the sacristy, where he knew he'd find Dr. Larssen. As he entered, he recognized the voices: Dr. Larssen, always calming and in control, and one other—a voice that made Jim wince.

"I demand you return these men to my command!" Major Anthony had his back turned to Jim as he sullenly addressed Dr. Larssen.

"I won't release them." Jim answered before Larssen could speak. Hot, tired, and in no mood for an argument, he clenched his fists and stretched his spine to its full height.

"You have no choice!" Anthony whirled around to face Jim, his face purple with rage. "I've spoken with Dr. Hammond, your so-called authority, and he agrees with me."

Jim glared at Anthony. *To hell with what Pegleg wants! To hell with what Hammond ordered!*

"Listen, *sir*," he said. "I will not change my mind. You can argue and rant and spew your demands all you want, but I *will not* release my patients. Their ailments are just as real as a gunshot wound or a contagious illness. Returning them to duty is not only a disservice to them, but to the army as well."

Anthony strode across the room, not stopping until he stood nose to nose with Jim. "There's nothing wrong with any of them." He poked a manicured finger in Jim's face. "They're nothing but cowardly, lazy bastards, and I want them back by morning."

Jim growled and paced, his anger rising. *What an arrogant imbecile!* He struggled to calm himself. If anger wouldn't get him anywhere, he'd try reason.

He took a deep breath and adopted his most professional voice. "Major Anthony," he started. "With all due respect, what these men have experienced in battle has affected their minds in such a way that they are incapable of adequately performing their duties. You saw what happened with Anderson's breakdown. Do you want another rampage like that?"

Major Anthony took a step back, his face menacing. "Anderson got his due," he growled. "He was a fake and a coward. The firing squad was what he deserved."

Jim's fists clenched. He forced them open, relaxing his shoulders. He would *not* let Anthony goad him into another fight.

"You know, Major," he shrugged, "I might have agreed with you at one time. I might even have had second thoughts about Anderson. But since then, I've seen too many soldiers with the same symptoms. Don't you wonder where they go when they get that look in their eyes?" he reasoned. "Are you sure it's fear that you see?"

"What would you call it?" Anthony snorted.

"I call it defeat," Jim said. "Look, Major, they're not making conscious decisions. Their brains have taken them back into battle, and they're fighting for their lives."

Anthony's stare wavered. Was there hesitation

in his mind? Jim wondered. Was there a moment of doubt?

Anthony's stare turned to an ugly grimace. "Prove it."

Jim's shoulders slumped. "I can't yet," he shrugged. "But I will."

Anthony turned to leave, a smug look of victory on his face.

"In the meantime, you can take your orders and burn them." Jim couldn't help but take one last shot.

"In the meantime," Anthony snorted, keeping his back to Jim, "you can kiss your career goodbye. You'll never work as a doctor again." He stormed out the door, slammed it shut behind him, and stomped noisily down the steps.

"That was not your smartest move." Larssen cautiously touched Jim's shoulder. "You were right to try to reason with him, and it might have worked if you hadn't let your temper take over."

"He's such an ass," Jim shrugged.

"Regardless," said Larssen. "I think you've poked that hornet's nest once too often."

CHAPTER 57

Late May, 1864
Near the North Anna River, Virginia

"You must do something about Doctor Banyon." Anthony paced the length of Colonel MacDougall's tent. Unlike the enlisted men's shelter tents, MacDougall's wall tent was large and comfortable. A narrow cot along the tent's short wall allowed him respite from the rain-soaked ground; a small rug helped keep his feet dry. Next to the cot was his camp desk, littered with maps, battle plans, and correspondence. The dim, flickering lantern light made the rain-soaked day even drearier. In one corner, a wooden pail gathered the rainwater that seeped in and traveled down the tent's peak. The tent stank of wet wool, ink, and tobacco.

Grant's overland war was intensifying by the day. His troops had chased Lee's army south to the North Anna River, and the two sides were currently at a standoff at Hanover Junction. Skirmishing was light. To occupy their time, Union troops tore up five miles of the Virginia Central Railway. Both sides were restless: demoralized by the endless rain and mud, frustrated by the lack of progress.

MacDougall, commander of the 111th, wearily looked up from his desk. "What is it you want me to do, Major?"

"He's come up with the cockamamie idea that malingerers are suffering from some sort of medical problem, and he's refusing to release them back to combat. There's nothing wrong with any of them that a good turn in the brig won't stifle."

"And you want me to—?" MacDougall impatiently raised his eyebrow. His voice was flat and irritated.

Anthony lifted his arms as if the solution should be obvious. "Sanction him! Force him to hand over my men!"

MacDougall set down his pen and took a gulp of whiskey. "How many of your men does he have?"

"At present, three or four." He'd been certain MacDougall would issue an order with no questions. Now he wondered if he'd gone too far.

The colonel leaned back in his chair, crossing his arms. "And you're bothering me about three or four soldiers who may or may not be fit for duty?"

"No, sir," Anthony's stomach clenched. "I'm asking you to force Banyon to back down. He's willfully obstructing military operations and has been doing so for months now."

MacDougall rubbed a hand across his face, pushing his scraggly, unwashed hair back over his forehead. "The Union is facing down Lee's army, and you want me to go argue with some country doctor over a handful of soldiers?"

"Yes, sir. It's a breach of protocol if not—"

MacDougall raised his hand and interrupted. "I haven't the time for your nonsense, and neither do you. Bringing charges against a surgeon when the army desperately needs their help is ludicrous, and I won't condone it. You would be wise to settle your differences with Dr. Banyon and leave me out of it." He waved a hand in dismissal and returned his attention to his paperwork.

The windows rattled as Anthony slammed the heavy front door and stormed into the church, where Jim and Larssen tended to their men. He pointed toward the sacristy, strutting across the room like a triumphant bull. Jim and Larssen shared a cynical look and followed him inside.

Anthony sat at Dr. Larssen's desk as if he owned it. "I've taken my complaint to Colonel MacDougall," he said. "I have his authority to bring charges against Dr. Banyon." *Screw MacDougall,* he thought. *He wants me to handle it, so I will—my way.*

"You can—" Jim fumed, but Dr. Larssen held up a hand for silence.

"I speak for myself and my team," he said. "Whatever complaint you have, you bring to me."

"Fine." Anthony turned slightly to face Larssen. "Tell your *assistant,*"—the word slithered from his mouth like a snake's venom—"that the army will no longer tolerate his refusal to return my soldiers to duty." He shot a sneer at Jim, then returned his eyes to Larssen. "Tell your *assistant* that if he insists on continuing, the military will bring charges against him."

"Understood, Major Anthony." Larssen laid

a steadying hand on Jim's shoulder. "And you tell your commander to send his accusations directly to me."

"Oh, no," Anthony waggled his finger at them. "The order will go directly to the Surgeon General. There will be no chance for either of you to quash it."

Dr. Larssen nodded. "Don't say a word," he whispered to Jim as they turned to leave.

With the sacristy to himself, Anthony rubbed his hands with the glee of a man who'd just won at poker. Nobody needed to know that, without the support of Colonel MacDougall, Anthony's charges would go nowhere. *Let Banyon stew about that,* he thought.

The momentary panic on Jim's face made every bit of the deception worthwhile. He'd crush the bastard so hard he'd never get up. A dishonorable discharge was a career-killer, and he'd make sure Jim never worked as a doctor again.

As Anthony returned to the encampment, he considered Colonel MacDougall's words. "You handle it." Well, he had handled it. Jim's likely action would be to resign if he believed charges were imminent, which would rid Anthony of him for good.

Let that be a message to those upstart surgeons. If they thought that going to their esteemed Surgeon General would make him back down, they were sorely mistaken. The Union was at war, the U.S. Army made the rules, and he was damned well going to enforce them. The medical teams worked *for* the army, and as far as he was concerned, that meant he could give them orders and expect immediate compliance.

CHAPTER 58

Late May, 1864
Office of the Surgeon General
Washington, D.C.

Jim stepped out of the pounding sun and into the anteroom of the Surgeon General's office. Assistants and clerks bustled about, delivering reports and whispering orders from Dr. Barnes. Even here, a medicinal smell filled the room; the dense, humid air intensified its distinct aroma. An aide looked up from his desk.

"Dr Barnes wanted to see me," Jim said. His stomach was in knots—what could the Surgeon General of the United States want? Had Pegleg taken his complaints that far?

The aide nodded and gestured toward Barnes' office, "He's expecting you."

Jim knocked softly on the door and entered. Dr. Barnes, seated behind his large, paperwork-filled desk, motioned for Jim to be seated. Behind him, detailed maps showed hospitals, troop movements, and supply depots. Bookshelves filled with medical texts and ledgers lined one wall; wooden cabinets filled with orders and correspondence lined another.

At forty-six years of age, Major General Joseph K. Barnes was a veteran of the Seminole and Mexican Wars. He was no novice when it came to battlefield medicine. Jim hoped that fact would earn him some sympathy.

After Jim had settled into his chair, Dr. Barnes set aside his pen and paper. He sat ramrod-straight behind his desk. His red hair curled at his ears from the humidity; his blue eyes seemed to bore into Jim's soul.

"Major Anthony has lodged a complaint." His tone showed no emotion. "He is charging you with obstructing military operations."

Jim scowled. "Yes, sir, he informed me of his intentions last week." Hearing of Anthony's accusation didn't surprise him, but having to leave his patients to explain himself to Dr. Barnes annoyed him more than anything. "He's been out for me since we mustered in."

"Did you leave camp without permission?" Barnes stroked his meticulously trimmed beard.

Here we go, thought Jim. He swatted at a mosquito that had just settled on his arm and begun to drill. It reminded him of Pegleg.

"I did not." Jim could feel the anger as it built in his stomach, threatening to climb up his throat. "Dr. Larssen gave me leave to accompany my cousin's body home to his family."

"And you didn't see fit to clear it with Major Anthony?"

"If I had cleared it with the military, it wouldn't have been Anthony's permission I'd seek." Jim gritted his teeth. "He would have denied me leave out of spite." Clenched in his lap, his hands trembled. He had to get the words out right; it could mean his career.

"Look, Major Anthony wants to ruin my reputation. I've known all along that he'd do whatever he could to get me to back down. I tried going along with him. At first, I thought maybe he was right, so I released my patients to duty although it was against my better judgment." His eyes were steely. "But not anymore."

Barnes looked skeptical. "Why is that?"

Jim took a deep breath. "My cousin Napoleon's death was the last straw. He came to me nearly a year ago complaining of nightmares and physical complaints. I kept him under observation as long as I could, then returned him to his unit. I told him it would get better, and I believed that." Tears formed in Jim's eyes, and he struggled to ignore them.

"Last week he killed himself." Jim's voice trembled. "He told me he couldn't take the nightmares anymore, that the voices in his head wouldn't leave him alone."

Jim clenched his fists and fought back his emotions. "I let him down. I let down Private Anderson, and all the other war-scarred men who never should have gone back to duty." He hardened his face and looked Dr. Barnes in the eye. "But I won't do that anymore.

"You can say what they see in battle would and should scar anyone. But for some soldiers, it's more than that. There is something about battle that warps these men's minds so that they can't think clearly, that dogs them until they can no longer separate the imagined from the reality."

Dr. Barnes steepled his hands, absorbing Jim's contention. "Can you prove any of your suspicions?"

Jim paused, searching for the words that would make Dr. Barnes believe him. Clattering carriages and the voices of pedestrians on the busy street outside made it difficult to hear, and strained their conversation even further.

"I've documented both physical and mental symptoms," he said. "It is easy to see the physical symptoms—even an army officer recognizes dysentery and elevated heart rates when he sees them. But the mental effects aren't that easy to prove. What I call nostalgia, Major Anthony calls cowardice. It's his word against mine, and you are the only person who can back me."

Barnes nodded. "If you would please return to the anteroom for a few moments, I will consider Anthony's accusations and your rebuttal."

Jim stood, turned, and retreated to the anteroom, where the assistants still bustled and the clerks still delivered. He forced his pounding heart to slow, pushed the bile back to his churning stomach. The clock ticked off the seconds, minutes passed, and while Jim waited, he considered his options. He could resign, likely angering the folks at home. His career would likely be ruined. Or he could take his chances, risk a court martial and prison time ... and that would ruin his career as well. It seemed it wasn't a matter of *whether* he should leave the army, but a matter of *how*.

Moments later, an assistant motioned him to return to Barnes' office. This time Jim stood at attention in front of Barnes' desk, took one look at the Surgeon General's face, and knew his fate.

"I'm not sure I can protect you this time, Dr. Banyon," Barnes said. "Without proof of your assertion, you look like a man who won't follow orders, and I can't allow that. If I were you, I'd strongly consider resigning my commission."

"Understood, sir." The moment was almost freeing: at last Jim could make his final stand. "With all due respect, Dr. Barnes, please understand *me*. I'm well aware of the consequences. But losing my commission and maybe even my medical license is the least I can do to honor these soldiers. Protecting these men is the hill I'm willing to die on. Too many of them have needlessly died already."

Barnes nodded. "As you wish, doctor." He waved dismissively toward the door.

Have I made a horrible mistake? Has my lifelong quest for success and recognition come to naught? When I joined the army, I believed it would make my reputation, being the first to recognize this disorder. Now I stand to lose what reputation I have, and people will brand me as incompetent.

CHAPTER 59

June 5, 1864
Fredericksburg, VA

All is lost.

Dr. Barnes has stated his intention to side with the big bugs. Although I could have faced a court-martial and sentence, or at least a dishonorable discharge, he has offered me the option to resign my commission, which I have done effective immediately.

No one wants to hear me. All they care about is putting bodies into battle. They don't care that those bodies are already broken.

My reputation as a war surgeon and a general physician is in tatters. I do not know where I will go from here; I only pray that Maggie will accept me as I am.

Jim lay awake as dawn broke over the city of Fredericksburg, his night spent considering the choices ahead.

But even Jim knew there were no choices. Anthony had made that clear. Dr. Briggs had made it even clearer. Jim's only option was deciding how he would leave: on his terms or theirs.

If he resigned, he would be admitting defeat, accepting that he had failed in his duty. If he refused, the jury would decide. He had no illusions about winning. A public trial would be more damaging than a quiet resignation; it would bring humiliation on his entire family.

After his meeting with Dr. Barnes, Larssen had taken him aside.

"Look, Jim. I know you believe in what you're doing, but the odds are stacked against you, and you cannot win." Larssen scuffed his feet on the worn carpet. His eyes were careworn and near tears. "The best thing you can do is resign and save what little dignity you have left."

No matter what, Jim realized, he would lose at trial. Found guilty and forced to resign, he would lose his license. Even if they acquitted him, likely no one at home would trust him again. Either way, the events shattered his credibility and reputation.

A letter to his parents was long since overdue— it had been months since he'd had time to write. But he would reveal nothing about his situation. They would know the truth soon enough.

June 5th 1864
Dear Parents,

... You wish to have me give you some of the incidents of the battles but I must say that it is almost impossible for me to do so for my time has been so much occupied with the care of the wounded that very little of my attention could be given to the details of military movements. All we know is that Grant is master of the situation and that he proposes to fight it out on this line if it takes all summer. We have men enough, and we have 15 or 20 acres of artillery that have not yet fired a shot.

Jim continued, asking after the family, the weather, and any other mundane questions he could think of, ending his letter as usual:
Your son,
J.D. Banyon

Dr. Larssen approached Colonel MacDougall's tent and took a deep breath. He'd lain awake last night, unable to sleep at the thought of Anthony's claims and Jim's resignation. Before Jim left, Larssen wanted to be sure MacDougall knew the complete story.

He lifted the tent flap and poked his head inside. MacDougall was at his desk, pen in hand.

"A word, please, sir?" Larssen asked.

MacDougall impatiently set down his pen. "What is it, Doctor?"

"I don't mean to be impertinent, but did you tell Major Anthony you would file a complaint against Dr. Banyon?"

"Anthony said that?" McDougall's face reddened. He stood abruptly, knocking the bottle of ink to the floor.

"This morning, he informed me you agreed to bring charges against Dr. Banyon for refusing to follow Major Anthony's orders. In the wake of that accusation, Dr. Banyon has tendered his resignation.

"With all due respect, Colonel, I don't trust Major Anthony as far as I can throw him. He and Dr. Banyon have an ongoing dispute, and Major

Anthony has repeatedly threatened to ruin Dr. Banyon's reputation if he doesn't back down."

Larssen hesitated, gathering his thoughts. "I hope you understand the army is losing a talented surgeon based on the accusations of a man whose motives are questionable."

"Thank you for that information," Colonel MacDougall said as he bent down and picked up the ink bottle. "I'll take care of Colonel Anthony," he said.

"Please tell Dr. Banyon he is in no danger of facing charges."

CHAPTER 60

June 5, 1864
Encampment of the 111th NYV,
Near the North Anna River, VA

"Did you tell Doctors Larssen and Banyon that I authorized you to bring charges against Dr. Banyon?" Colonel MacDougall paced in front of his desk, his chin jutted out, his fists clenched.

Anthony stood at rigid attention, struggling to keep his face from showing his discomfort. "He left his post without permission, sir." He summoned his anger, the indignity he felt by being ignored but a subordinate. "Took a train to goddamn nowhere, New York, to bury his crazy cousin when we were already short on doctors."

"Did I not tell you to let it go?"

"You told me to handle it—and I did."

MacDougall stopped, scowling at Anthony. "What I told you was that I had no time to worry about such a trivial matter, and neither did you." He sat at his desk, his anger simmering. "Do you believe the doctors aren't busy enough treating wounds and contagious illnesses? Do you think our doctors don't have enough on their hands without having to deal with some arrogant ass like you who is determined to get his way?"

"But Dr. Banyon displayed blatant insubordination, sir! He—"

MacDougall's face grew red, beads of sweat lined his brow, and he slammed his fist on his desk. "As the son of a rich businessman, Major Anthony, you may be used to getting your way, but this is the army, I am your commanding officer, and you blatantly disobeyed *my* order!"

MacDougall sat quietly, took a deep breath, and lowered his voice. "I am reducing you to the rank of captain effective immediately. You're lucky I don't court-martial you."

Anthony remained at attention. Neither man spoke.

"You can leave now, Captain." MacDougall said at last.

Anthony turned, ducking under the tent flap held back by MacDougall's assistant, mortified that the assistant had heard every word.

"One more thing, Captain."

Anthony stopped.

"If I hear of you harassing the medical staff again, I will bring charges so fast you'll be sitting in prison before you know what's happened."

CHAPTER 61

June 6, 1864
Fredericksburg, VA

Jim and Larssen carried the final trunk of supplies to the wagons headed for the next line of battle, and what they hoped would be a siege resulting in the end of the Confederacy. They would send the remaining patients at the church-hospital to Washington, D.C. until they fully recovered.

In his cramped room off the church sanctuary, Jim filled a small wooden trunk with his belongings. He picked up his leather-bound journal, leafed through it, and set it in the trunk. Next were the notes from his study, followed by patient notes, and what few medical journals he still had. The letters from home, tied up with twine, would go in his saddlebag.

He picked up the picture of Maggie and Jessie and tucked it into his coat. Worn from the heat and the rain and the battle, it had followed him religiously these two years.

They're all I have left. Jim thought. He raised his eyes to heaven. *Please, God, don't take them too.*

As the ranks formed for the march south, Jim and Larssen stood on the dusty street to say their goodbyes. In his civilian clothing, Jim felt even more of an outcast, but a lone man wearing a Union uniform made him a sure target. He clapped Larssen on the shoulder and hugged him like an old friend.

"MacDougall promised there'd be no charges," he said. "And I heard Anthony got busted down to captain for lying about it.

"Won't you reconsider?"

"No," Jim shook his head. "I know I've made the right choice," he said, "but I hate to leave you and all the men I've stood for."

"We'll make do," Larssen said. "Godspeed on your journey home."

Larssen mounted his horse next to the medical wagons. Jim strapped his trunk behind his horse's saddle, mounted, and flicked the reins.

"Aren't you taking the train home?" Larssen asked, motioning to Jim's horse. "It'd be a lot faster."

Jim shook his head. "With both sides eager to

either take or destroy the railroad, I don't want to be anywhere near it."

I could take the train, he thought. *The horse will travel well enough.* He patted the horse's neck—they'd grown fond of one another over time.

Truth is, as much as I long for my girls, I'm in no hurry to face the backlash from my resignation. The ride on horseback might take weeks, but he was glad to have the time to himself.

As he left Fredericksburg, taking Princess Anne Street north, a small bonfire caught his attention—perhaps someone burning their trash. Hardly knowing what he was doing, he stopped his horse, dismounted, and retrieved the small trunk. It seemed heavier than it had just minutes before. He carried the trunk to the bonfire, took a deep breath, and threw it into the flames.

There, he thought. *Now I can go home.*

ACKNOWLEDGEMENTS

I was blessed with ancestors who were hoarders. I grew up in a two hundred-year-old nineteenth-century house built by a Revolutionary War veteran, its attic filled with generations' worth of treasure. I spent many of my younger days exploring that space, and as an adult, I took care of the wealth and history in its many trunks and boxes.

I have tried to maintain historical accuracy as far as dates and important battles by consulting a number of print, video, and online resources (see below). Note that Jim Banyon and Napoleon Drown are only *loosely* based on the real-life soldiers, Dr. James Dana Benton and Cpl. Napoleon Bonaparte Drown; Dr. Benton mustered out of the Union Army at the end of the Civil War in August 1865, and Napoleon died in 1875.

Thanks to my wonderful editor, Jeni Chappelle and to my beta readers: Pat Kirell, Brenda Marie Smith, Janice Matthews, Brian Porter, Kenn Allen, Lisa Thomspon, Mandi Schmitt, as well as Civil

War and 111th New York Volunteers expert, Chris
Loperfido. Thanks also to K. J. Harrowick for her
cover and interior design talents and advice.

About the Author

Susannah Willey is the award-winning author of *War Sonnets* (JUL 2023, Utter Loonacy Press). Given a five-star "award of excellence" by the Historical Fiction Company, *War Sonnets* was also awarded third place in the General Fiction Category of its 2022 Book of the Year awards.

Susannah was born in 1952 in the small town of Ira, New York, where her family settled over 200 years ago. She received her undergraduate degree in Instructional Computing from SUNY Empire State College in 1998 and a master's degree in Instructional Design from Boise State in 2002. She and her partner make their home in Central New York in the foothills of the Adirondacks. A baby-boomer and a first-generation computer geek, nature photography and hiking are among her passions and, like all good grannies, she knits.

Susannah loves to tackle the less explored emotional experiences of war. Her rich family history often serves as the foundation for her historical novels. Poetry written by her uncle about his experiences in the Pacific War during WWII inspired her first novel, *War Sonnets*. Her upcoming novel follows a Civil War surgeon and is loosely based on the military service of two ancestors.

About the Surgeon

Dr. James Dana Benton was born on July 22, 1837 Dr. Allen and Deborah Willey Benton. He was the youngest of five children, the other four being Heman, Allen Richardson, Charles Darwin, and Matilda Willey.

Jim attended Albany Medical College in Albany, New York, graduating in 1857. He returned home, opened a medical practice in nearby Cato, NY, and married his wife Maggie (Margaret A. Rich) in 1858. Their only child, Jessie, was born in 1859.

He enlisted in the 111th New York Volunteer Infantry in August 1862 and served until February 1865, at which time he was appointed surgeon of the 98th New York Infantry Regiment. On August 31, 1865, he was mustered out with the regiment at Richmond, Virginia.

Dr. Benton returned to his practice in Ira, NY, moving to Syracuse, NY to continue his medical practice in 1874. His business card shows that his practice was located at the corner of Elbridge and Barrett Streets, a short distance west of the current location of Syracuse University. His card also noted, "diseases of females made a specialty."

Given that he witnessed so much violence and death, did Dr. Benton suffer from PTSD? It's possible. Jim died on May 16, 1892, at the age of 54. This is notable since his father, his brothers, and generations since, all lived into their late eighties and early nineties.

ABOUT THE CORPORAL

Napoleon Bonaparte Drown was shot in action and sustained a wound at Todd's Tavern (Battle of the Wilderness) on 8 May 1864, by a "bullet through his right ankle, breaking it badly." The wound never fully healed, plaguing him until his death in 1875 at the age of 38 years, 3 months, 11 days.

Military Record of Cpl. Napoleon B. Drown
<u>Co. E, 10th New York Cavalry Volunteers</u>
(formed Dec. 12, 1861, in Rochester, left Rochester Dec. 24, 1861, for Washington. D.C.)

Enlisted 10/11/1861

    Rochester, NY, at 24 years of age

Promoted to Corporal

    4/11/1863

Discharged

    12/17/1863 Warrenton, VA

Reenlisted

    12/18/1863 Warrenton, VA

Wounded

    5/8/1864 Todd's Tavern, VA

Discharged for disability

    5/31/1865 U.S. Genl. Hosp. Rochester, NY

According to the Genealogy of the Drown Family, read at a Drown Family Reunion, held in 1908, "He was a Corporal of Captain William A. Snyder..."

In response to a letter requesting additional information for pension benefits, from G.W. Ellinwood (as requested by R.J. Collier), Napoleon's widow, Martha, states: Dr. [unreadable] who attended my husband answers this question: "[he] was wounded by a bullet through his right ankle breaking it badly. He died with Billeous [sic] Erysipelas attacking said wound."

CIVIL WAR RESOURCES

Websites:

The 111th New York Volunteer Infantry: A Civil War History
https://www.facebook.com/profile.php?id=100064859401312
Warfare History Network. Civil War https://warfarehistorynetwork.com/category/warfare/civil-war/. Sovereign Media. 2025
Timeline of the Civil War: Day-by-Day, Battle-by-Battle.
https://www.civilwartimeline.net/.2023.
National Park Service: The Civil War https://www.nps.gov/civilwar/index.htm
The History Network: American Battlefield Trust https://www.battlefields.org/. 2025.
Civil War Talk. https://civilwartalk.com/.1999
History of the Civil War https://www.civilwar.com/. 2019
Civil War https://www.history.com/articles/

american-civil-war-history. A&E Television Networks. 2009

Books:

Adams, George Worthington. *Doctors in Blue: The Medical History of the Union Army in the Civil War*. Louisiana State Historical Press, 1952.

Adams, Michael C. C. *Living Hell: The Dark Side of the Civil War*. Johns Hopkins University Press. 2014.

Billings, John D. *Hardtack & Coffee: The Unwritten Story of Army Life*. University of Nebraska Press,1993.

Catton, Bruce. *Bruce Catton's Civil War*. The Fairfax Press. 1984

Freemon, Frank R. *Gangrene and Glory: Medical Care during the American Civil War*. University of Illinois Press. 2001.

Husk, Martin W. *The 111th New York Volunteer Infantry: A Civil War History*. McFarland & Company, Inc. 2009.

Loperfido, Christopher E. *Death, Disease, and Life at War: The Civil War Letters of Surgeon James D. Benton, 111th and 98th New York Infantry Regiments, 1862-1865*. Savas Beatie.

2018.

Russell, Duncan. *Blue-Eyed Child of Fortune: The Civil War Letters of Col. Robert Gould Shaw* Avon Books. 1994

Varhola, Michael O. *Life in Civil War America.* Family Tree Books. 1999.

Woodworth, Steven E. and Winkle, Kenneth J. *Atlas of the Civil War*. Oxford University Press. 2004.

Movies:

Zwick, E. (Director). (1989). *Glory* [Film]. Tri Star Pictures, Freddie Fields Productions.

First Person Accounts:

Benton, James Dana, Captain. Assistant Surgeon 111th New York Volunteer Infantry. Correspondence 1862-1864.

"Genealogy of the Drown Family", read at a Drown Family Reunion, held in 1908

Other family historical documents in the possession of the author.

WAR SONNETS

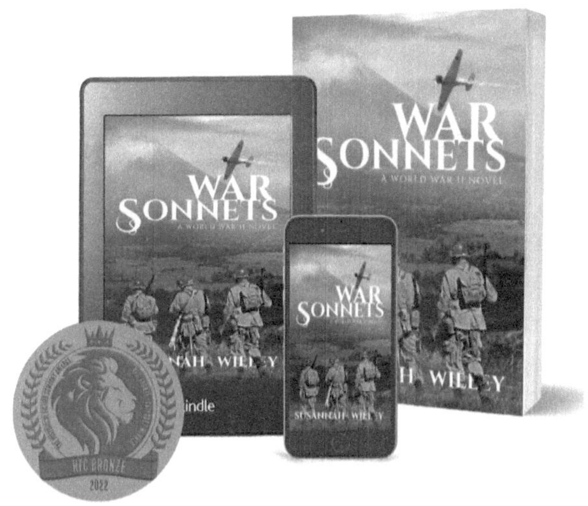

1942: In the war-torn jungles of Luzon, two soldiers scout the landscape. Under ordinary circumstances they might be friends, but in the hostile environment of World War II, they are mortal enemies.

Leal Baldwin, a US Army sergeant, writes sonnets. His sights are set on serving his country honorably and returning home in one piece. But the enemy is not always Japanese...Dooley wants Leo's job, and he'll do whatever it takes to get it...

Leo finds himself fighting for his reputation and freedom.

Lieutenant Tadashi Abukara prefers haiku. He has vowed to serve his emperor honorably, but finds himself fighting a losing battle. Through combat, starvation, and the threat of cannibalism, Tadashi's only thought is of survival and return to his beloved wife and son. As Leo and Tadashi discover the humanity of the other side and the questionable moral acts committed by their own, they begin to ask themselves why they are here at all. When they at last meet in the jungles of Luzon, only one will survive, but their poetry will live forever.

Grab your copy: https://utterloonacy.com/books-2/

PRAISE FOR WAR SONNETS

"[Ms. Willey] does an amazing job capturing the emotions and interactions of the people involved as well as the historical facts about the war... "War Sonnets" receives five stars from The Historical Fiction Company and the "Highly Recommended" award of excellence."

- The Historical Fiction Company

"Compelling depiction of the Pacific theater of WWII through the perspective of an American soldier and a Japanese soldier. Inspired by the poems written by Allen H. Benton, this is a moving tale of Tadashi and Leo, two young men who share similar backgrounds and a passion for writing, but are separated by war, fighting on opposing sides. The story builds gradually toward a horrifying climax and is hard to forget. It brings home the horrors of this war and indeed that of all wars."

- Malve von Hassell, author of The Amber Crane

"Susannah Wiley has written a lovely book of grand scope and has done a standout job of bringing the Pacific Theater of World War II to life and showing us its sheer heartbreak. The poignantly drawn American and Japanese characters continue to stick with me. I'm particularly fond of the poetry pieces that open each chapter, which were written by the author's own uncle during his stint in the very same war. War Sonnets will deepen your understanding of this very important chapter of our collective history. I highly recommend it."

- Brenda Marie Smith, author of *If Darkness Takes Us* & *If the Light Escapes*

"A powerful, dual-narrative novel, War Sonnets probes an underlying truth of war: those on either side of the line are more alike than not; their fears and hopes, the same. Extensive historical detail places readers on those lines, building a sense of sympathy for both sides."

- Janis Robinson Daly, author of *The Unlocked Path*